Mary Y. Oszar

D0734848

A PLACE CALLED SATURDAY

A Place Called Saturday

by

Mary Astor

DELACORTE PRESS / NEW YORK

A PLACE CALLED SATURDAY

MAXIE slumbered in the heat, twitching, whimpering, dreaming old dog dreams. One eye was open, staring sightlessly. Cora reached down and touched the eyelid, saying, "You look like you're dead, silly." At her touch he came awake, stared at her a moment, banged his feathery tail twice on the tile floor, and dropped his head back with a comfortable groan.

Cora picked up an orange stick, twisted a wisp of cotton around it, and poked at the base of her nails. In the corner a fan hummed, whipping the hot air into turbulence but offering no relief of coolness. Pale green venetian blinds clattered softly as it turned, paused, and turned back. Cora watched it and saw it as a kind of living creature, looking curiously out into the hall, sweeping slowly toward the bed, staring a moment, looking haughty, then turning back to the hall.

They had both been watching that day. Both Maxie and the fan.
The fan looking haughty, and Maxie friendly and indifferent. Two
months ago. Ten weeks ago. Friday, June twenty-fourth. Four in the
afternoon. Like about now, with the sun in tiger stripes on the bed.
You couldn't forget because the mind would push a button, and it
would be like an instant replay. Maybe when the weather changed,
maybe when the desert winds came and howled around the small
house and she and Rafe worried about the rattle of loose tiles on the
roof, and they covered the car at night with a tarp so the sand
wouldn't take the paint off, and there was a fire in the fireplace, and
the world seemed cozy and closed-in and safe—maybe then the tape
would grow fuzzy and vague, the details no longer sharp.

Beside the bed the radio was muttering. Dean Martin started to
sing "Amore," and Cora sang along with him, "Bells will ring, ding-
a-ling-a-ling—" and then, annoyed because it made her sing, she
switched it off.

Sitting cross-legged on the bed, she stretched her arms and yawned,
and grimacing, ran her fingers around the elastic band of her shorts,
loosening it, wiping off perspiration with her palm. She looked at
the small alarm clock—nearly five. She'd better begin thinking about
what to have for supper. Rafe was off his shift at the airport at five.
Usually he wouldn't get home until about six because he'd stop and
have a beer with one of the fellows from Operations. But ever since
June twenty-fourth he had been coming directly home. Out of anxiety to a certain extent, but she wondered if also, for some strange
reason, he just didn't want to get into social conversation with the
boys after working hours. Maybe it was shame. Guilt. Frustrated
fury. She didn't know.

Macaroni and cheese. Cold meats. Iced tea, maybe. Some salad.
Cora sighed with the very effort of planning. She pushed her long
hair up onto the top of her head and twisted it into a knot. It wasn't
long enough to hold and came down again, slithering around her
neck. There were hairpins and bobby pins and ribbons in the
drawer of the dressing table, but inertia held her from getting up;
instead she sat staring into the fan, which stared back at her and
then turned, staring into the hall. The hall where Maxie had stood
wagging his tail, watching in friendly curiosity . . .

There was nothing to arouse Maxie because Cora's mouth was taped securely, and she couldn't scream—all the sounds she made stopped at her front teeth. Her hands were tied together to the frame of the headboard. A cord around each ankle, secured to the bed posts, spread her legs wide apart.

Finally the suffocating weight lifted, and the man—sweating, exhausted—heaved himself free and stood up, looking down at the wild-eyed face wet with tears. He glanced out of the window through a crack in the drawn blinds, and then he asked, "Will somebody be here pretty soon?" There was no response except the low, monotonous moaning and the staring of the drowned blue eyes. "Well, you can nod your head, can't you?" he shouted. "I can't let you loose. You understand that, don't you?" He looked at the bruises that were coloring up angrily on her arms and at the one just under her ribs, where he knocked the wind out of her when he had first walked in the door. He went into the bathroom and wrung out a towel placed under the cold-water tap, and coming back, wiped the sweat and tears from her face. Anxiously he looked out of the window again, but on this hot day there wasn't a car in sight; the house itself was a good hundred feet from the road and sheltered within a windbreak of cottonwoods, and the nearest house was a quarter of a mile away.

He picked up a duffel bag, ran a hand over short-cropped white-blond hair, and then in a kind of agony spoke to the girl again. "Christ, I'm sorry!" he groaned, staring at her as though she were part of a nightmare.

Fishing in his pants pockets, he drew out a small penknife, and as the girl's eyes widened he shook his head sharply. "No, no, no, nothing like that. Here." Opening it, he put it into her fingers, with the blade down, touching the cord. "You work on that awhile; it'll come loose."

He walked over to the hall door where Maxie sat thumping his tail. "Move, dog!" Obligingly Maxie rose and stepped aside to let him pass.

The sun lowered and slanted through the slats of the blinds on the west windows, painting hot stripes on Cora's body, drying the sweat and blood and fluid still seeping from her loins. Gripping the knife, she tried to work on the cord as the man had told her, but the knife was dull or the ropes were tough, and she felt faint; the knife slipped from her fingers and fell behind the bed to the floor.

The phone rang, and as always Maxie set up his barking, cheerfully running back and forth from the bed to the living room. Cora roused at the commotion in a start of fear, and then closed her eyes again, thinking, "You're a hell of a watchdog, Maxie!" The phone rang and rang, which she felt was a good indication that it was Rafe. Others would hang up after four or five rings. He was probably calling to see if she wanted anything from the market on his way home. The phone stopped. Then after a moment it began again; Maxie barked some more, and Cora's hopes rose. Rafe would worry at her not answering, because on such a day she would be indoors, out of the heat. Even the water in the small swimming pool in the back yard would be soup warm, and she wouldn't be out there. He would hurry home, anxious and annoyed.

His first words when he came in the door from the carport would be, "Cora, where were you when I phoned?" His wide-set black eyes would be blacker under the shadow of drawn black brows.

Rafe could tolerate no mystery, nothing unpredictable in his wife. He was the kind of a man who hated surprises, secrets, anything hidden. He was possessive, but he gave as much in return and was as scrupulous of keeping her informed of his actions when they were apart as he expected her to be. Early in their marriage she had teased him about this, and he had said, "I want to be sure my other heart is beating." It made her want to laugh, but he was so serious she didn't dare.

Finally, in a stuporous sleep, she heard his voice in the distance.

"Cora? Cora!"

She waited for the familiar sequence of sounds. Door slam. "Maxie boy, you want to go out?" Door slam again. Footsteps on the kitchen tile. "Cora, where were you when I phoned?"

Her relief was drowned in the wave of pity that swept over her, knowing what he would feel when he found her. In spite of her own need, she treasured any moments of delay. The sounds still in the kitchen: rattle of a pan; "God, you haven't even fed Maxie!"; silence; refrigerator door slam; "There you are, fella!"; kitchen door slam;

footsteps; "What are you doing, sleeping?" And he appeared in the hallway door.

The expression on her husband's face became something Cora had never seen before. And never wanted to see again.

He turned gray-chalk, and the day's stubble on his wide, lean jaw blackened the outlines of prominent cheekbones. His mouth opened and closed as though he were trying to scream. Then, reflexively, his control returned, and he spoke. "Take it easy, darling. Have you out of that in a second." Turning, he strode back to the kitchen.

He came back with a small, sharp kitchen knife and slashed at the ropes, hard, quickly. From the bathroom he brought a bottle of alcohol and a cloth and worked at the edges of the adhesive on her face. "Now, take a breath," he said, and he ripped off the remainder as she gasped.

For a long moment he held her close, and she could feel his deep sobs. When he drew back, he said, "Who was it? Did you know the sonofabitch?" She shook her head. Weakness was overcoming her.

"When was it—what time?"

"Around four."

"Did he have a car?"

"Yes."

"What kind?"

"I don't know. A panel truck. Small. Said he'd come to fix the radio."

He pulled the sheet up over her and said, "Lie still. I'll take care of you in a minute. I'm going to call the sheriff. We can't lose any more time. We've got to catch the bastard."

When he came back, he was carrying a water glass half full of brandy and managing what he thought was a smile, for comfort.

"I phoned Doc Titus. He's out on a call, but his girl said she'd get hold of him. And Sheriff Boyd's on his way. Now, down the hatch. It'll fix those shakes."

She was rubbing her wrists and hands. "It's too much. You drink some; you need it, too."

He shook his head. "I had a swig, don't worry."

Neither of them wanted to talk—or think—about what had happened. Not yet.

Rafe filled the tub and helped her into it, bathing her gently, muttering over the bruises, the raw, skinned wrists and ankles, and the yellow swelling over the rib cage.

By the time he helped her out into the living room, dressed in a nightgown and robe, they could hear a siren in the distance, and in a moment the sheriff and his deputy pounded up the front steps.

"Hi, Rafe. Sorry to be so long. Damned weekend drivers hear a siren, and they think they're being pinched and slow up right in front of you. Hi, Cora—oh, fer God's sakes!" He growled angrily as he caught sight of her face. Kneeling beside the couch, he took her hand, turning it to see the rope marks on her wrists. "How do you feel?"

"Okay, Sheriff. How's Mrs. Boyd?"

"Pretty good, pretty good. Arthritis is no fun. But we're all gettin' old. Now—real fast, honey, do the best you can with a description so's we can get busy. We've got the State Highway boys on what Rafe gave me about the truck, but we need a lot more. Coloring, age, you know."

Cora closed her eyes and took a deep breath. The last thing she wanted to do was to bring it all back into focus, to remember, to talk about it to anyone but Rafe, who was perched on the end of the couch at her head. She looked up at him, and he nodded encouragingly at her, understanding her reluctance. "Tell him, honey—all of it."

Forgetting would have to be postponed for a while.

"He was—blond. Crew cut. Hazel eyes."

Sheriff Boyd wrote rapidly in a little book. "Height, weight?"

Cora shook her head. "I don't know how to—taller than Rafe." She looked over at the young deputy standing by the door. "Like him. Very much like him. Athletic. But even younger, maybe twenty-two, -three."

Deputy Wood blushed deeply and came up dutifully with his statistics. "Height, six-three. Weight, one ninety-eight."

"Okay, good. Now then, I want anything you can think of, anything you might have noticed about him. I don't expect much, Cora, but do your best. He won't be carryin' a sign on him, you know."

"I don't know what you mean."

Boyd included Rafe in his glance, saying, "When I ask for an identification, I usually say, 'If you saw this person sitting next to you in a bus, what would you think about him? What would you guess he did for a living?'"

Cora nodded quickly. "I know. Well, let me say this, Sheriff, this boy wasn't a—a bum. You're right, you know, in spite of fear and pain and horror you *do* get an impression. He looked—sort of like a younger Burt Lancaster—not so smiley——"

"Herb Lancaster? He's a little guy!"

"No, Gus, she means the movie actor."

"Oh, him. Okay."

"He didn't have alcohol on his breath. He was under some kind of horrible pressure—I mean outside of sex—like he was angry. He didn't use dirty language or do anything that was obscene, or perverted. You understand what I mean? I mean I think he only tied me up so he wouldn't have to hit me again. He was violent, yes. He exploded, and I happened to be in the way." She was looking at the floor now, concentrating. Sheriff Boyd glanced at his deputy and handed him the notebook, jerking his head toward the car, and the man went quickly outside.

Cora was talking rapidly now, unemotionally, getting rid of her assailant once and for all. She couldn't know that it wasn't going to be that easy.

Sheriff Boyd had asked, "How did he get into the house?"

"I was outside with the hose. I'd turned the sprinklers on, but they don't reach the shrubs on the east side. When I finished, I put some water in that old tank top we keep for the birds, and there was a jack rabbit watching me, and I watched him to see if he was thirsty enough to come closer. What I'm saying is that I didn't notice the truck come into the driveway for a moment. This young man was carrying a canvas bag, and he kind of waved at me, and I said, 'Wait a minute till I turn off the sprinklers,' because he'd get soaked crossing over to the steps. And when I came back, he was already there, holding the screen door open." She frowned a little. "I suppose I thought he was just anxious to get in out of the heat, but anyway I said 'Yes?' a little huffily because he hadn't waited to be asked in. He said, 'I'm the radio man you telephoned for,' and I said, 'I'm sorry, there's been a mistake. My husband's a radio operator, and he does all the fixing around here.' This is all—very quick—you know? It's faster than I can tell about it."

She looked briefly at Boyd, and he nodded, saying, "You were inside the house by now, huh?"

"Yes. And, I don't know, but even as he said he was the radio man I felt something wrong. He looked at me too steadily, and he closed the other door behind his back and set the bag down on the floor. And when he said, 'There's been no mistake,' I kind of froze." She looked up, beyond the sheriff's face. "I know how the little animals out here in the desert feel now—you know—the way they stop cold in their tracks at the sign of danger. I think they pray that a merciful God has made them invisible. They don't make a sound, and then they run. I turned and started to run to the kitchen door, but I hadn't taken three steps before he had me, and then I yelled, and then he must have hit me in the stomach, because I blacked out."

Rafe's shaking hands clinked a glass against the brandy bottle on the drop-leaf table by the wall.

Cora turned toward him and said sharply, "You'll get swacked if you drink any more of that stuff!"

Sheriff Boyd was anxious that this first rush of words not be interrupted. She was on an emotional high, and when the reaction set in, the story would get muddied up. He echoed Cora's tone. "Siddown, Rafe." Then he said to Cora, softly, "Go on. When did you come to?"

"On the bed. The tape was over my mouth." She made a sound that was an imitation giggle. "I felt sick to my stomach and thought, 'What's going to happen if I have to throw up?' I could feel my hands were tied, and I started to roll around and kick. He'd pulled off my bathing trunks and bra while I was still out. I kept kicking, but I ducked like a boxer and went to the end of the bed and got my ankles tied up—so easily." Her breath came faster as she said, "He pulled off his pants and—my God, he was as big as a bull!" She sobbed into her hands.

Rafe slid down beside her, pulling her close. He growled at Boyd, "Christ, Sheriff, give me something to do. I want my hands on this guy!"

Sheriff Boyd got to his feet and looked down at him.

"Yeah. So do I." He waved a freckled hand. "But that isn't the way it's done. And I've got to warn you. Stow it! Stow the revenge stuff. The law will clobber him good, but you got to stay out of our way. Don't let me have to worry about you, now. You stay close to Cora. She's not going to think less of you if you don't fly off in all directions avenging her honor. So don't get any ideas. By the way, where is Doc Titus? He ought to have a look at her."

"I'm right here. I'm right here." And a little man scurried in like one of the creatures from the desert country of his practice. He wore a summer suit of natural tan pongee that rustled drily as he moved. His face was bony, lined deeply, and dark from the sun. His head was barely covered with bleached wisps, and his voice came from a gravelly throat.

"Why, Miz March." He drew out his words in a compassionate sound as he placed his medical kit on the floor beside her. He tipped his head up, reaching for her hand, and peered at her face through the lower section of rimless bifocals. Steadily he said, "My, my, my, what's happened here?" Not waiting for any answer, he quickly and gently touched her face, her throat, her wrist, talking all the while.

"Hm. Well, now. Yes. Uh-huh. Well. That hurt? Uh-huh. Now look right at my finger, please. Uh-huh. Mr. March, will you get me a couple of clean bath towels, please, and let's just go in here, won't take a minute." He steered her toward the bedroom.

Sheriff Boyd touched his shoulder. "Doc, I'm going to want fingerprints from in there. Be careful, huh?"

"Yes, yes, yes, of course," said the little man, and he firmly propelled his patient ahead of him.

The sun had set, the temperature had dropped a few degrees, and over the mountains to the east the thunder rumbled. Rafe and the sheriff stood on the walk in front of the house. From the patrol car came the rasping, indistinct voice of the radio.

Sheriff Boyd felt the tension in Rafe's shoulders as he gave him a heavy-handed pat. "You take it easy now, man. Remember what I told you. And if you can't *be* patient, *act* patient." He sniffed the air. "Smells good this time of evening—the desert. Don't think I could live anywhere else." Lightning flickered, revealing the shapes of clouds crowning the peaks. "We ought to be gettin' some of that down here pretty soon—cool us off."

Rafe glanced back toward the house.

"Sheriff?"

"Yeah, Rafe?"

"You said you wanted fingerprints. Cora said the fellow opened the screen door and also closed the other one——"

"Oh, yeah. Woodie already picked them up, when he first got here. I want a man from the lab to do a more thorough job, in case they're just partials or smeared. We're doin' our job, Rafe. We already got—besides route ten out here—we got eighty-two, six, and nine covered, and the fellows down at Nogales have been alerted. A two-hour jump on us is quite a lot, though. 'Course, if he's dumb enough to try to go through Nogales, we'll have him nailed. If."

"If what?"

"Well, you can't tell. Might have ditched the truck and got a ride. He might pick up a bus in Tucson. Yeah, that's covered. So's your airport."

"Who did you talk to at the airport—MacIntyre?"

"I don't know. They put the call out from town."

Rafe swore softly. "I hadn't thought about all that part of it."

"What do you mean?"

"Oh—everybody's got to know. Poor Cora. Newspapers, I suppose. Our friends. It's surprising nobody's phoned, isn't it?"

Sheriff Boyd said, "Your phone's out of order till six A.M. I figured you'd need some rest. Let's go, Woodie."

He grunted as he heaved himself into the car, which backed out toward the carport, and then turning, headed down the drive.

Rafe watched the red taillights wavering and flickering through the line of cottonwoods, then disappearing as the car turned west onto the highway.

Silence fell around him like a huge, soft cloak, and his shoulders relaxed under its protective weight. He took long, deep breaths of the sharp air, and finally he could exhale without shuddering. His muscles ached from pent-up fury at being unable to either avenge the loss or restore the precious possession of which he had been robbed.

It had all been so right, so good between him and Cora. From the very first, they had been blessed with a mutual satisfaction that was always a source of wonder to him. In the light of his own violently promiscuous youth, which had spun him around in confusion and dissatisfaction and kept him in a web of cynicism, it had been like a rare gift of joy, of contentment.

He had done two hitches in the Army, volunteering at eighteen, mainly, he admitted to himself, to avoid getting hooked into marriage. On maneuvers, carrying a radio pack on his back, he was glad he had no other burden, no other responsibilities. He saw the morale of other boys drop from a "dear John" letter, or from sheer worry or homesickness for "the wife and kids" at home, and he felt stronger with nothing to worry about but the mosquitoes and his aching feet and nothing to encumber him but the pack on his back.

Afterward he went back to Cal Tech, where he worked for and received his B.A., and where he was occasionally caught up in casual affairs, both on and off the campus. He successfully extricated himself from several "good kids" who had matrimony in mind, and from then on, he resolved to stick to a lower stratum of female. And that had been like the taste of sour wine.

An Army buddy by the name of Brian Foley had joined the Air Force and later become a commercial pilot. They kept in touch, and Foley was the one who told Rafe of the opening at the airport. In a short time Rafe became First Radio Operator, and that was about the time his love affair with the desert began.

Like a plant that had been barely existing in the coastal cities, he felt healthier and happier in the dry, thin air. He liked the challenge the desert revealed everywhere. Things grew and lived in constant adversity, ingenious in solving problems of existence. It was tough, and he liked toughness. It was beautiful; it was *there*. He learned to ride, and would take off toward the mountains after work and camp out under the stars. He would go fishing high in the mountains with some of the men he worked with, and looking back over the harsh, austerely beautiful land, he would say to himself, "This is for me."

He met Cora in a men's clothing store in town where he had gone to buy some socks. She was behind him at an opposite counter, and he heard her say, "I'd like twenty of those, but I'm not sure of the size." He laughed, and they both turned around. She smiled, saying, "Twenty little Indian boys who want beanies, but their ages are from five to twelve, so it *is* a problem!"

Then they both laughed, and he showed her that a beanie was a beanie, and if any were too large, you could zig-zag the edges with a razor blade and turn up a cuff.

After the problem of the beanies had been disposed of—eight red, eight blue, and four yellow, then changed to all red so there wouldn't be fights—a chocolate soda seemed to be in order.

They sat at a small table at the soda fountain next door, and he learned that as part of her postgraduate sociology studies she was teaching school at the Yaqui settlement three afternoons a week. To earn her living she worked as a night clerk at the Hi Ten Motel, where she also had a room.

To Rafe she was the most beautiful thing he had ever seen in his life: small ("like a desert flower," he mooned); round ("I'll be dumpy when I'm middle-aged," she said); deeply tanned, with light-brown hair bleached in streaks from exposure to the sun ("I like to go for long horseback rides early in the morning on weekends." "So do I, let's go together sometime"); and blue-eyed ("like a puddle in the desert after a rainstorm"), with one small mole accenting the outer corner of one eye and catching the attention until she smiled, showing a row of fine white teeth framed by mobile lips. The combination destroyed him. He was further delighted to discover that she was space-hungry, horizon-hungry, as he was.

San Francisco was the city of her birth. William Reedy, her father, was a minor accountant in a minor shipping firm. With her mother, a younger sister, and an older brother, they lived in a ground-floor apartment that was comfortable but busy. It was busy with her father's departure for work in the morning; with her mother's constant wrestling with the vacuum cleaner, complaining over its roar that "if you girls would just do your part, that's all I ask, just do your part"; with Millicent's cluttering a shared bedroom and bath, mirror worshiping; with Roy's sullen voice and his slamming of doors.

Cora was never conscious of a feeling of familial love. There was intimacy and habit, and when Roy joined the Navy, his absence was felt like the removal of a tooth. It was a gap that was explored and finally no longer even noticed.

Her mother had a little clot of women intimates with whom she drank endless cups of coffee in the kitchen and with whom she exchanged information on the price of food, female troubles, the way to get around husbands, and gossip about other neighbors and near and distant relatives.

Cora would listen to them from the bedroom across the hall, trying to study. Millicent was seldom in the house for long; she was off to a movie or shopping or visiting a girl friend. When Cora was preparing for her college entrance exams, her mother's arriving friends would each be loudly informed, "She's got her nose stuck in a book; we won't bother *her*." They would talk quietly for a while in self-conscious consideration for Someone Reading, and then her mother would tiptoe across the hall and say, whispering exaggeratedly, "I'll just close this, dear. We don't want to bother you."

"Mama, it just shuts out all the air. It won't bother me."

"Why don't you open a window, then?"

"The trucks—the traffic . . ."

Cora's attention would fade in and out of the material she was reading, and sometimes she would catch herself listening to the conversation with great concentration.

On one such occasion she heard a voice say, "So what do you think I told him?"

"I don't know, what?"

Cora listened intently for the answer.

"Well, I said to him, I said, 'You'd just better not try that again. I know when you're not telling the truth. Women can always tell— *you* know!'"

"Certainly can!"

"I told him, I said, 'You're not going to make a doormat outta me, something just to wipe your feet on, and if you think you are, you'd better think again!'"

"Good for you!"

"That took nerve!"

"Well, what happened, did he fire her?"

"He certainly did—the little slut!"

"Oho, *Bess!*" Shocked, appreciative giggles.

"Well, I mean it. Here, finish up the pie, Agnes."

It was not an uncommon subject, the helpless husband under the spell of the office hussy, but this particular time Cora realized it was her mother speaking. This explained the recent endless muttering that had gone on in the bedroom next to hers, the footsteps back and forth, the sobs and silences and more walking. It explained the closed impersonal face her father presented to his family and his bleak descent into the folds of a newspaper in the evening.

There had been other periods when Cora was aware of this grim hostility, but her parents never quarreled in front of the children. They saved it for the privacy of their bedroom, which nevertheless didn't prevent the two girls and the sullen boy from being aware that the foundation of their lives was very unstable. It sent Roy slamming out of the house, and as soon as he was old enough, into the Navy. It sent Millicent to the movies, to overnight visits at a girl friend's house, and later into the back seats of automobiles. It sent Cora into the depths of books and the search for "Why?"

That particular day, when she realized her mother was spewing out the intimacies of her life with her father, all remaining illusions of family solidarity evaporated.

She was in her stocking feet, and the women didn't hear her come to the kitchen door. She saw them with distaste: overstuffed stretch pants, scarf-bound lumpy heads, bifocals, too much lipstick, heavy jaws masticating or dropped in avid attention. She said quietly, "Mama!" Five faces turned to her quickly, half smiling in silly embarrassment. A coffee cup was spilled in the sudden movement, and there were little cries to get a towel. She went on. "Mama, why are you doing this to Papa?"

Her mother shrilled, "Why am I doing *what* to Papa? You mind your own business, young lady!"

"I wondered why *you* weren't."

"Weren't what? Eavesdropping, of all things!"

Cora didn't realize that she had opened the floodgates of her mother's confidences. Like a good mother, she hadn't "burdened her children with her troubles," but since "you poked your nose into it, you might as well hear the rest." From then on, whenever they were alone together, Cora's ears were assaulted by the sordid stories of her father's infidelities over the years. They were, however, so vague, so unsubstantiated, that in spite of her efforts, Cora's mother was unable to enlist her daughter's sympathies.

One evening a few months later, they were having dinner in the usual tense silence. Millicent had rushed off a half hour before on her date. Mr. Reedy had the evening paper folded to the shipping news and was glancing at it as it lay beside his plate. Mrs. Reedy sucked at her soup and sniffed, and Cora crunched down loudly on a piece of celery and said, "Sorry!" Her father raised his eyes to her, and she held them with her look and with her smile. "Papa," she said, indicating the paper, "how many ships leave San Francisco harbor every day?"

Mr. Reedy frowned. "Oh—ah—well, I don't know. It varies. You mean cruise ships, freighters, what?"

"I mean ships that somebody can get on and go someplace."

"Why? Do you want to take a cruise? You want to go someplace?"

"I was thinking about you."

His eyes bored into hers. He understood, and a gentle, grateful smile appeared. Then the smile disappeared along with his face as he pulled the paper up in front of it. She heard him murmur, "I wish I could, I wish I could."

Cora had considered going to Berkeley, but she felt it was too close to home. She decided upon the University of Arizona not only because of the advantage of distance and its curricular attractions but also because of its location. The very words describing the area— arid, dry, clean, windswept—affected her semantically. The mournful sound of foghorns and the moisture-laden days and nights were too closely associated with a house that had heavy drapes and smelled of floor wax and fried potatoes—a home where laughter was an expression of sarcasm, where eyes and words held suspicion, where every act was questioned, discussed, disapproved.

Her decision began to incubate the afternoon she saw a matinee of Agnes de Mille's ballet "Rodeo" at the Opera House. Something about Aaron Copland's music, the blinding brilliance of the lighting, and the colorful, straight-backed arrogance of the "riders" made a strong impression on her. She walked the whole way home that afternoon, a dark and drizzly winter day that served as a convincing contrast. She thought, "I want to live in that kind of country. I want to feel my feet on the *ground*, not on cement. I want to ride toward a mountain. I want to get air in my lungs that isn't weighted with the smell of buildings and people and gasoline fumes."

About a year after she had left for the university, Cora received a ten-page letter from her mother telling her that her father had deserted the family.

"Probably gone off with some woman . . ." she wrote, but she didn't know who. She had had little warning except that for a couple of weeks he had seemed more cheerful, and there were some papers he had asked her to sign. He had said he was transferring some things to her name "for tax purposes," and then one day he had left for the office and said, "Bess, I won't be home for dinner." This in itself was unusual, but when she had asked, "Why not, for Heaven's sake?" his reply had not been the usual patient explanation of his activities. He had said, "I just won't. I won't be home for dinner." And he had walked out of the door.

Bess said in her letter, "I smelled something fishy right then, but when he didn't come home, I cried all night." The next day she had telephoned the office, "and that female answered, the one I told you about that he never did get rid of." There had been an awkward silence, and then the female said, "I'm sorry, Mrs. Reedy, I hope there's no trouble. I thought you knew. He left the company about a week ago, said he was going to Australia."

"Bully for you, Pop!" Cora cheered. "You really did it!"

Cora shuffled the pages of the letter and folded them up thoughtfully. Her father in Australia; her mother in Reno, getting a divorce; her sister in San Diego, married at seventeen; her brother on a ship somewhere in the Pacific; and herself in Arizona—a family was scattered, reaching outward to satisfy its individual needs and desires, unable to find or create such satisfactions within its unity, a total failure as a family.

Feeling a sharp twinge at the thought of her own omissions, Cora crumpled the pages and tossed them into the Papago Indian basket beside her desk and picked up a textbook.

It was one of those "You're going to marry me, you know" romances, and Cora said "Probably." For a while they were happy in just getting to know each other: driving, riding, and hiking around the countryside, picnicking beside Rose Canyon Lake, spending a day eating indigestible food and buying pottery and tin trinkets in Nogales.

They discovered Aravaipa Canyon on one of their "Let's just take off" drives. It was uncluttered with tourists because the roads were rocky and narrow, and to a tourist, "There was nothing after you got there." Beneath the sheer sandstone wall of the canyon ran a wide, shallow stream dappled with sunlight and shaded with great sycamores. Cattle grazed in a distant meadow; the air was cool from the protection of the wall; mourning doves called softly. In this Arcadian setting they played like children, skipping flat stones on the surface of the stream, laughing, and wading in the sandy, murmuring water. They ate cold fried chicken with a bottle of ale. They lay in the speckled sunshine and talked and kissed and fell asleep.

On the way back to town they stopped to see the progress on the house that Rafe had started building just before he met Cora. The workmen had left, and Rafe and Cora sat on the new steps of the veranda, which ran the width of the house.

"I think this should be enclosed, don't you?" asked Rafe.

Cora said, "Oh, I don't know. The lines of the house are so pleasant, and you wouldn't see the stone facing. I think it would spoil it."

"Whatever you say, darling. It might be cooler and a nice place to put a couple of cots. It's nice to sleep outside, sort of outside, don't you think?"

Cora was so silent that Rafe said softly, appealingly, "Baby?" reaching down to bring her chin up so she would look at him.

"Oh, Rafe," Cora said. "We've only known each other—what?—six weeks. How can anybody be sure?"

"That's right. How can anybody be sure—ever? I know that I've been sure before."

"What?" She wrinkled her forehead.

"Sure that I *didn't* want to take a chance."

"And now you're sure that you do."

"That's right."

"Do you think it's possible that this"—indicating the house—"has something to do with it? I mean, you've decided to settle down in one place, you're building a nice little home, and you want somebody to take care of it for you."

"Oh, sure, that's it. I just want a cook and a housekeeper. You know that's not true! If that's all I wanted, I'd hire a nice, big, strapping Mexican girl who'd wash my shirts and build my fire and call me Senor——"

"And go to bed with you."

"Why not? If she wanted to. But that's not what I'm talking about, and you know it. I love you, Cora. I want you with me. I want a wife. I want a family. I want to build a room over there for a nursery. All that stuff."

To change the subject, Cora said, "Oh, speaking of family, I got another postcard from Papa from someplace called Alice Springs. He says they call it The Alice. He lives with the fellow he works with—with him and a great big, noisy family—and he sounds like a happy man. He says the kids call him Uncle Bill."

Rafe pulled out a pipe, stuffed and lighted it, and for a while they watched the sky as it tucked its spangled blanket of stars over the Rincon Mountains.

"I know, Cora. He's a happy man. And your mother's happy in her bridge clubs and movies and shopping with her girl friends. And your sister is a nice soapsuds and diaper girl in a housing project. And Roy's got the Navy. And it all adds up to your being afraid of getting involved in something that might come apart—the way your family did."

"Of course it does."

"Well, remember me? We're in the same boat."

"But you're an orphan. You never watched people you loved as a child grow to hate each other. It's an ugly sight, Rafe."

"I'm sure it is, I'm sure it is. It's traumatic and all those other things, those terms they kick around so carelessly. I'm sure that one of the reasons I didn't want to get married—till I met you—had something to do with the knowledge that my parents either came apart or never were parents, except biologically. But I'm thirty-five years old now. I don't care about all that. Sure, I may even be a bastard. My name is March because that was the month when I was found on the chilly steps of an orphanage in Portland, Oregon. I know I was named Rafael, because that was what the note said that was pinned to the blanket. One of my parents, or both, was Spanish; I look it, and the note was written in Spanish: 'His name is Rafael. He is baptized. He is two months old. Take care of him. I cannot.' How's that for total rejection?"

"And how many homes did you live in? Three, wasn't it?"

"Yeah, I never stayed for long. I was miserable and hard to handle. I was actually happier—or as the fellows say, more secure—in the impersonal, non-gushy atmosphere of the convent home. They were great, those sisters. Kind, tough, strict. And the brothers on the youth farm. I was well prepared for the Army. But hardly for marriage."

"I should think you'd understand then, Rafe. I'm just leery of all this. It's like being drunk. It's lovely, but I don't trust it."

"You won't unless you put away the textbooks, Cora. Forget all that stuff. Don't believe that because we had unstable childhoods we must necessarily make an unstable marriage. It's such an easy out when the going gets tough. You can overdo it and say your parents were what they were because of the way *their* parents behaved or were—and kick it clear back to Adam. It's ridiculous. All this self-pitying nonsense kids spout about 'What kind of a world you made for us! I didn't ask to be born!' Well, who the hell did? This is passing the buck instead of grasping life firmly and saying, 'I'm going to do better, by God!'"

Cora laughed. "You're very eloquent, Rafe. I didn't know you had such strong ideas."

"I didn't, either, if you want to know the truth." Rafe laughed and tamped out his pipe. "I'm giving you the hard sell. If you want to analyze and talk, talk, talk, I'll go along with you even though I think it's a waste of time. I don't mean that all I want to do is to rush you into bed. That would be easy——"

"*What?*" she squealed, even though she hadn't misunderstood.

"Oh, come on. I mean—I'd have taken another tack, another method. I'd never use up all this"—he waved a hand at the evening —"just in talk. But I want you to believe we could be reasonably happy together. Ever since I met you, I've said, 'This is for me. This is it. This is my wife.' Therefore, certain things are just *out*. No wrestling in the back seat of a car, no getting drunk and going to a motel—not that you would," he said hastily as he saw her shaking her head, and then added, putting his arm around her, "nor going beyond a certain stage beside a lovely stream under a sycamore tree."

She put her head on his shoulder. "I know. I'll admit that was a little rough this afternoon. I just might have, you know."

"I know, Cora, my darling—my other heart." He held her so closely she finally gasped, "Hey, my ribs!" and he let her go.

They both rose from the chilly steps and started down the path to the station wagon.

"You free tomorrow, Rafe?"

"Yep. My Sunday off."

"I'd like to take another look at the kitchen. I like a kitchen with a lot of storage space."

The interval between the lightning and the sound of thunder had shortened noticeably. The stars had disappeared, and the wind rose and began to moan around the house.

Rafe held out his hand and rubbed his fingers with his thumb, feeling the moisture, thinking, "We're going to get it. Only the end of June. It's early. . . ." What would heavy rain or a flash flood do to the search? Would it hinder or help? Probably hinder the police and help the guy to hide, or to get a ride. He could ditch the truck off the road, and a storm would help conceal it.

Rafe turned to go back up the steps into the house. His feet felt heavy, and he tripped on the top step, caught himself, and swore.

The living room stank from the smoldering end of the sheriff's cigar. Rafe emptied the ashtray into the fireplace and pushed open a window. He could hear the rushing sound of the sand; a gust of air billowed the curtains. He closed the window halfway and heard Cora saying "Rafe?"

"Cora! You're not asleep? Doc said he gave you a heavy sedative. You mustn't fight it, honey."

He went to the side of the bed and stroked her hair. She was sitting up, cross-legged, nodding, her head weaving. The muscles of her face crumpled like a child's just before it starts to cry. "I can't sleep in this damn bed. I don't want to stay in here. I don't ever want to be in this damn bed again."

"Okay, okay, sweetheart, now don't cry. Listen to me." The sedative had weakened her defenses, and she whimpered and whined.

He helped her to her feet and walked her gently to a chair in the living room.

"It'll only take me a minute. I'll pull out the couch and make it up. We'll sleep on that tonight."

"There's clean sheets on it, and there are some blankets and pillows in the linen closet. All you have to do is to lift it up and pull it down."

"All right, *okay*, honey. I've done it before. You just sit quiet, now. Just stop babbling." He took the coffee table out of the way and yanked the folding bed out flat as, bleary-eyed and thick-tongued, she continued to instruct him.

He tried to joke. "You know, you sound drunk. You sure it was a sedative the doc gave you?"

She tipped up her head to look at him, and it flopped back further than she intended. She put a hand behind her neck to steady it. "Of course it was a sedative! Two big fat capsules—white, with a blue band around 'em."

Rafe managed a chuckle. "No sense of humor at all! I'm kidding, sweetie! Here now, lie down and I'll get a blanket." He helped her over and sat her down on the edge.

She peered up at him, weak tears running down her cheeks. "I love you so, Rafe. I love you so!"

"I know, darling, I know." Rafe rubbed his nose hard to stop the itching. "Hey, how would you like a warm drink? Maybe it might be a good idea. Some chocolate? Or maybe some of that beef con-sommé?"

She shook her head. "Uh-uh. I'm kinda sick in my stomach. I'm so dizzy—whew!—I'm scared to lie down."

The room turned white for an instant, and the thunder blasted them both into startled silence.

They stared at each other, listening in the dead silence that followed. Then they heard it. With the rush of a waterfall the rain began. It hammered on the roof and blew in through the window, which Rafe hurried to close. He put a door stop under the front door to keep it open, since it was protected by the overhang of the ve-randa, and they would need the air, which had become heavy and sultry and only a little cooler.

"Don't you think you'd better bring Maxie in?"

Rafe shook his head, almost laughing, for it was an old argument, and he answered the way he always had at the beginning of any rainstorm. "Maxie's perfectly dry and comfortable in his house, and he's heard thunder all his life, and he's not scared, and why don't you lie down?"

"Well, I just hate to think of him shivering out there."

"Shivering! He probably opened one eye and turned over."

He tucked a thin blanket around the foot and sides of the couch-become-bed, dropped a pillow behind her, and gently eased her head down. "There, now isn't that better?"

There was no pink in the tanned face, and her eyelids looked like oyster shells when she closed them. With a fingertip he rubbed a minute bit of stickiness left in the hollow under her lip from the adhesive. He watched her as she lay quietly now, backed into a chair, and lighted a cigarette. Then he started to remove his shoes and socks. He had no desire for the usual routine of going-to-bed, of teeth brushing and gargling and donning of clean pajamas. Instead, he pulled off his clothes and dropped them, letting them lie where they fell, and prepared himself for his first ordeal. He was aston-ished that it was going to be an ordeal—the simple act of getting into bed and lying quietly beside his wife. His reason fought with his odd revulsion. He desperately wanted her to awaken and talk to him, or cry; it would keep his sympathies straight: for her, where they belonged.

He switched off the lamp on the end table. The room flickered occasionally with lightning, but the thunder was distant and rumbling itself away into the mountains. The rain had stopped as suddenly as it had begun, and now there was only a busy drip-dripping from the eaves.

Rafe blew out a final heavy column of smoke and ground the cigarette out into the ashtray beside the lamp. Slipping under the sheet, he lay stiffly; his breath was shallow and rapid. Deliberately, he put an arm beneath her head and drew it to its customary resting place on his shoulder. She stirred a little and made a soft sound, a long-drawn-out "Mm-hm," ending in a sigh. This was her familiar affirmation, her "yes" to him, to his arms, to her commitment. He relaxed and thought, "That's something the sonofabitch couldn't steal." It had to be enough, for now.

No matter what accident, physical damage, damage to possessions, fire, flood, or broken bones, people who attempt to console the injured are aggravatingly prone to say, "You were lucky!" You were lucky that it wasn't some other misfortune, as though the one you had wasn't bad enough. If your left arm is broken, you were lucky that it wasn't your right arm. If it *was* the right arm, "You might have broken a leg!" Usually it is followed with an account of a misfortune similar to yours (only worse) that happened to them or to someone they know whom you don't know. But the reminder that there are people who have worse troubles than you is not an effective pain-killer, for some reason.

Constanza knew this when she once said to Cora, "Other people's toot'ache is not your toot'ache. You feel only the pain that is yours." But Connie was an intuitive comforter. The Mexican grapevine had it that her Senora March had trouble at the house, and even though it was not her regular day, her brothers drove her out and dropped her at the gate at seven-thirty the next morning.

His hair still wet from the shower, Rafe unlocked the back door for her.

"Why, hi, Connie, this isn't Tuesday!"

Her earrings jingled, and she smiled her beautiful smile and said, "I know. I hear about the bad man. I come help the Senora." Maxie was sniffing at her hands, the basket she carried, and she said, "Ah-ha, Maxie, I bring you beautiful bone. See, see how Connie love you, the big piece of the cow's leg." Maxie took the joint tenderly from her hands and then bolted away to his secret place of bone-chewing, at the end of the yard.

The phone rang, and Rafe went to answer it as Connie followed. She took a look around the living room, which was still dark from drawn shades, musty with the odor of sleep and cigarettes. Her large eyes rested a moment on the still-sleeping figure of her Senora. Unobtrusively she made a quick sign of the cross and said, "Firs' I make coffee."

Rafe was on the phone with Sheriff Boyd.

"I've already called them, Sheriff. It's okay, I'm going to stay home today. . . . When? . . . About three this morning—that was after the rainstorm. . . . They did, huh? Good. . . . What time did you say? Nine, nine-thirty, okay. . . . Well, I'll tell 'em. I'll just tell Cora not to answer the phone. . . . Okay. See you."

Cora was opening an eye. "Who was that?" Then, seeing a swish of bright skirts, she asked, "Is Connie here? What's she doing here?"

Rafe sat down beside her. "Honey, listen—you awake?"

"Mm. Kind of." And then as consciousness came fully she grimaced. "Oh. Oh boy, I ache—all over."

"They found the truck."

"They did?" Cora was awake.

"Not far from here—about six miles—in the arroyo near the bridge. Apparently he was scared to stay in it. He ditched it, and then either he hid or hitched a ride, they don't know. There were fingerprints inside the cab; the outside was washed clean from the rain. They've traced the truck back to a secondhand dealer in Bisbee who gave them the same description you did, and who told them the guy gave his name as C. H. Robinson, but the dealer said he had the feeling it was a phony. The man gave him cash from a fat wallet of bills and hadn't talked much, been in a hurry. They'll get him, honey, they'll get him!"

Cora said mechanically, "I hope so." If and when they caught him, it meant she would have to see him again, to accuse him in court, to live over the horrors in legal terminology. She could imagine him, dressed in clean clothes, his eyes avoiding hers, and that strange cry, "Christ, I'm sorry!" coming out, loud, in front of everybody. No, he wouldn't be saying that. He would be saying what a lawyer told him to say; maybe he would be saying he had never seen her before in his life, that it was all a lie, a mistake. Cora popped her eyes open again; she had been sinking back to sleep.

Rafe was still talking. She felt the energy in him, and it made her feel tired.

"Boyd says not to talk to anyone on the phone from the press or we'll have no peace at all. There'll be the sob sisters, he says, the ones who want an exclusive. He's told the ones who've called him to come out at ten o'clock. He's going to be here at nine, because he figures they'll come early, and he's going to bring a couple of the fellows to keep them in line. Now, if you don't want to see anybody, it's okay. I'll just tell them. But Boyd said it would be easier, keep them from hanging around if we talked to them briefly and got rid of them. Then he could put a man at the gate so you wouldn't be bothered anymore."

The phone was ringing. Rafe picked it up.

"Yes. Yes. I see. . . . No, Mrs. March cannot come to the phone now. . . . At ten o'clock. . . . I'm sorry. . . . Ten o'clock. Thank you."

"I'm up." Cora had staggered to her feet. " 'The world is too much with us.' I think that's a misquote, but it'll do for my bright saying of the morning."

Connie, beaming and pointing to the dining alcove, said, "Coffee is here. I have the omelet almos' ready for the fire. You come sit?"

"Connie, you're an angel. I don't know about the omelet, but Mr. March——"

"You gotta eat, Cora."

"I know. Where's my robe? We gotta eat, we gotta put one foot in front of the other, we gotta live."

By eight-thirty the house had yielded to Constanza's straightening, emptying, thumping, and shaking, and presented a normal face. In the bedroom, which had now lost its emotional reminders, there was fresh bedding, Cora's lacy blanket cover, and pillowcases with bright yellow and white daisies on the hems; the tile was swept, the curtains half-drawn over the venetian blinds. Constanza had even ("*Permiso?*") brushed some shine into Cora's hair and swept it back beneath a pale-blue elastic bandeau, leaving the brow clean. Cora put on a light-blue linen shift and some white sandals. She soon heard the sounds of cars driving up and voices on the veranda, Sheriff Boyd's, Rafe's. She heard the sheriff growling, "No, no photos in the house. Mrs. March will see you out here on the porch."

"But it's hot out here, Sheriff——"

"Can't we talk to her in the living room?"

The sheriff had been almost correct. Ten o'clock meant quarter to nine, and he had beat them by only a hair.

Rafe came in to get her. He stopped for a second when she appeared in the bedroom doorway. He closed his eyes for a moment and said, "You look so beautiful!" So vulnerable, so untouched, and yet with the innate dignity that only pain brings out. He wanted to take her and hide her away; he loathed having to produce her to the small mob at his doorway. He said, "I'd like to put you in my pocket and run like hell." For the next half hour, while the flashbulbs crackled and the questions were repeated, he never let her free from his side. Behind them the phone rang, and Constanza answered, and Maxie joined in and waved his tail and got photographed, not knowing or caring that he would be captioned in one item as "The Traitor Collie," who "welcomed sex fiend, gave no alarm."

Rafe handed her the phone. "Susie Eldridge," he said.

"Hi, Susie. . . . Oh, pretty good. . . . We just had the press. . . . Yes, they're gone, we hope. . . . No, I think. . . . If you want to come by for a minute, make it after dinner sometime. . . . No, Connie's here, thank you, darling. Not a thing. But I'd love to see you—and Charlie. How is he? Another rejection slip? Tell him to paper the powder room with them; it would make an attractive decor. Yes, I will. See you."

She cradled the phone, and it rang again. Rafe reached for it, but she shook her head. "I'll take it."

"Yes. Yes, it is. . . . Well, I promised the people who were here I wouldn't give anybody an exclusive. . . . Well, now, I don't think that's fair, you see——"

Rafe said, "I'll get rid of 'em," and took the phone from her hand. After a few polite, chilly sentences he hung up. The phone rang immediately. "Jesus!" he yelled. "What are we supposed to do, sit by this damned phone the rest of the day? *Hello!* . . . Oh, hello, Mrs. Rinehart. I'm sorry, the phone's been ringing its head off. . . . Yes, it's very kind of people to be concerned. . . . No, they haven't caught him yet. . . . Yes. . . . Yes. . . . Well—ah"—he glanced at Cora, who nodded. "I'll let you talk to her."

Cora put a smile into her voice and said cheerfully, "Hello, Virginia, and how are you? It's nice of you to call." And that was all she said for at least two minutes. Rafe pulled over an ottoman, and she put her feet up, murmuring, "Yes, uh-huh. That's right." And finally, with a few more *thank you's,* she hung up.

Rafe lifted the phone off the hook, cushioning the handpiece against a small pillow so that its signals of neglect would not be heard. "Let's have a little peace for a while," he said.

"Lucky!" said Cora in an exasperated voice.

"What?" Rafe put an arm over her shoulders and steered her into the bedroom. "Take your stuff off and get back into bed. You look pooped. What do you mean, 'lucky'?"

"That's what I'd like to know. That's what everybody says, 'Weren't you lucky!' I know they mean wasn't I lucky that I wasn't beaten or strangled or killed, but I can't think of any part of it as a 'lucky' happening. That gal out there"—she indicated where the press group had been outside—"when she said to me, 'Don't you feel you were lucky?', I knew exactly what was in her little nasty mind."

Rafe took her gown from the bed post and slipped it over her head. "I know. I heard her. She asked me a couple of cuties too. If she'd been a man I'd have socked her."

"Why, what did she say to you?"

"Oh, she was hinting at the same thing that she was to you. Something about the fact that you looked very well, considering."

"Sure, she'd have relaxed and enjoyed it."

Savagely Rafe pulled her tightly to his body. "Did you?" he rasped.

It was so ugly, so fierce that it startled her, and for a second she searched his face to make sure he wasn't teasing. She was half smiling in preparation for laughter at a joke. But it was no joke, and her smile disappeared. She whispered, shocked, "Oh, Rafe!" and he let her go immediately.

"Oh, honey, I'm sorry," he said, instantly remorseful. "Boy, where did that come from? I didn't mean it."

"I think you did. Why shouldn't you? The secret depths, the secret doubts, we've all got 'em. So have I. Let me assure you, darling——"

"You don't have to, you don't have to," he said miserably.

"I know. But let me 'still the dark beastie.' It just so happens that any form of violence revolts me. Pain and sex just don't go together for me. I know they do, for some. Not me. And believe me, Rafe, behind that damned adhesive I never stopped screaming 'No!'"

Rafe was confused at his own outburst. It was part of the feeling that he was riding a very tricky horse, and that he was not in control. There was a lack of response to the reins, a change of pace that threatened to be headlong. It made him angry to have to haul back, to keep conversation on a cool, reasonable level. It irked him to consult with Sheriff Boyd about various points and possibilities, to nod and agree and accept his decisions for action.

Sheriff Boyd himself was not unaware of Rafe's torment. He kept an eye on him all that day when he was at the house, and phoned frequently from the office. He hung around the kitchen, drinking coffee; he used the phone in the patrol car with Rafe beside him so that Rafe could feel he was a part of the hunt. During the day, chewing on a cigar, complaining about the heat, Gus Boyd kept his watch, noticing the little signs: the fists balling the pockets of the faded khakis, the muscles of the jaw, the eyes that slitted constantly. He was more than professionally concerned, because Rafe and Cora were his friends.

Three years ago, late one night, he was on his way home, off duty as much—and as little—as he ever was. A car passed him, making a wide turn—too wide, and accelerated back into what he figured was the high seventies. He hit the siren and took off after it. As soon as the red spotlight flickered in the rear-view mirror of the speeding car it slowed down obligingly and pulled up on the shoulder of the highway.

At the wheel, in the light of his flash, two grinning faces greeted him. They were not kids, as he had expected, but two very happy, very high people. Responding to his formal statement of the fact that they were driving at illegal speeds, the girl said, "We have to hurry, officer. We're out to catch the stars."

"Izzat so?"

"You see those two shining ones just at the top of the mountain?"

"Uh-huh."

"Well, we're gonna trap 'em and bring 'em back to hang up in our house."

"Uh-huh. Lemme see your license, mister."

There were strands of brightly colored serpentine around their shoulders; there was rice in their hair and all over the seat of the car.

"We just got married," the man said, unnecessarily, sounding embarrassed and silly.

The sheriff looked at the driver's license. " 'Rafe March,' is that right? You got that new house on Senita Way?"

"That's right. That's our new home."

"Well, you're not headin' in that direction. Where were you goin'?"

Rafe said, "No place in particular. We were just going to head up into the mountains and camp out. We've got our gear in the back."

Sheriff Boyd shook his head. "I'm sorry, son. I'm sorry to spoil your honeymoon, but you're not driving up any mountain roads tonight. You've had too much to drink." He rubbed the back of his neck, hating his job. "Tell you what. As a wedding present I won't give you a ticket—it'd be for driving while intoxicated and speeding—if you turn around and go back to your house. Now, I'm gonna follow you. See you don't get any ideas or get into trouble. Okay?" There were loud groans of protest, and he spoke sharply. "Now turn around and proceed at not over forty miles an hour."

A few days later he called by the house to apologize for breaking up their honeymoon, and Rafe generously said, "If it hadn't been for you, there might not have been a honeymoon. I don't think Cora and I ever got drunk on champagne before!" They gave him coffee, proudly showed him over the new house, took him out to see the pool, which was being filled for the first time, and made him promise to come for a swim someday.

The sheriff's office was next door to the barber shop, and Rafe got into a habit of dropping in when he came to town for a haircut.

Cora had met Mrs. Boyd at the dentist's one morning. Mrs. Boyd had had a novocaine injection and was nervous about driving, and Cora had taken her home. They discovered they were both U.A. alumni, and Mrs. Boyd had talked about the school "in my day," and the sheriff heard all about "that fine girl."

Nice people, he thought now. Real nice. Quiet. Never any hoop-de-do around their place. Not like some of the kooks around here. Even some of the so-called nice retired older folks seemed to want to hasten their end by a lot of drinking and partying around, acting younger than their age. Trying to prove something. Idleness. Boredom. That was all it was, really. Funny, the younger group, like the Marches, Terry Ostander, the Eldridges, the Demings, they worked hard, lived in the desert not as an escape from winter but because they liked it, and put up with its vagaries of wind and heat and storms. Their hobbies were indigenous: rock hounding, hiking, riding. They were tanned and healthy, and it wasn't from lying around some fancy motel pool, slathered with oil. Nice people. And now this. It was bound to affect all of them, one way or another. Sheriff Boyd bit off the end of a fresh cigar, spat into the weeds, and walked back to the house.

Rafe, with a pair of long-handled shears, was cutting out the undergrowth in the shrubs, bringing the blades together with a vicious snap of his wrists. The sheriff watched him for a moment and said, "I'm goin' on into town, Rafe. I'll leave Mendoza out here till five, if that's okay. He brought out a padlock from the hardware store so you can lock the gate when he goes."

"Never had a lock on it before," said Rafe, sadly. "We don't even lock our front door when we go out. We only put up the fence on account of the dog."

"Well, this isn't for safety so much as just to keep the curious from buttin' in. Mendoza stopped a couple of nuts from taking snapshots awhile ago—damn fools. I'll let you know the minute we hear anything, Rafe. You know that."

"You've heard nothing new."

"Nope. Oh, we've got a couple of calls we're following up. He's been seen at both Wickenburg and Douglas within the same hour. That's about two hundred miles as the crow flies, and a hell of a lot more the way he's traveling."

"How do you think he's traveling, Gus?"

"Oh, I didn't mean I had any idea of that. I don't know how the sonofabitch is traveling. I know for damn sure he hasn't gone over the border, but that's all I know."

"Why are you so sure he isn't over the border? He's had time."

"From things Cora told me."

"What things?"

"She said, for one thing, his forehead and nose and arms were peeling, from fresh sunburn. Also, she thought he might be an easterner from the few sentences he spoke to her—like an 'r' on the end of the word 'idea,' and the way he said 'house.' "

"I don't see how the hell she noticed things like that."

"She didn't—not to think about them at the time—but if you make a person work at it, little at a time, it's surprising what they'll remember. A fellow I knew, he was standing at the receiving end of a gun in a bank holdup, and he remembered that the guy had on socks that didn't match."

"So . . ." Rafe urged, impatiently.

"So, the fellow, Robinson, or whatever his name is, isn't from around here. He wouldn't know the trails, and the only way he'd go over the border is by car. They're searching every car down there as though it was carryin' gold. But my own opinion is that he's holed up in a barn or a shed on one of the ranches, and that makes it literally like lookin' for a needle in a haystack."

"What about the fingerprints?"

Sheriff Boyd grunted. "From the house—nothin'. Yours and Cora's, of course. Nothin' in the bedroom. He must have wiped his own off the door handles when he left. In the truck there were about six sets—different people—nothing in the criminal files."

Rafe swore and cut into a shrub savagely with the clippers.

"You're cuttin' into new growth with those shears, you know. Oughtta just tip 'em."

"Yeah."

"I'll just speak to Cora a minute and then shove off."

"Why don't you leave her be, Gus? She may be asleep."

"Okay, Rafe. And watch the booze, huh?"

Rafe flung the shears to the ground. "Why don't you mind your own goddamn business!"

The sheriff's jaw jutted out, but he spoke quietly. "That's what I'm doin'. Part of my job is seein' you don't get so loosened up you'll take off with a rifle under your arm. You been nippin' all day, and it just ain't smart. Now I'm tellin' you!"

Rafe took a long breath, held it, and then expelled it as he said, "Sorry, Gus. I'll see you," and strode into the house.

Thoughtfully the sheriff picked up the shears, wiped the blades carefully, and stood them, handles down, against the wall.

Rafe glanced in at Cora in the darkened bedroom. He saw that she was sleeping; she was snoring softly, and the pillow around her face was damp with perspiration. Rafe went over to the fan, touched the adjustment for a higher speed, and once again made a firm resolve to do something about a cooling system. There was a water-cooled fan in the living room and one in the window of the kitchen, but they just weren't adequate once the sun was high enough to beat down on the roof. The swimming pool had cost more than they had expected, and there had been the room addition, so he had started cutting down—in the wrong places—forgetting, during the winter and spring, the merciless quality of the heat during the summer and fall.

Constanza, down on her hands and knees, was polishing the kitchen floor.

Rafe said, "Connie, is there anything I should go and get at the market? I don't know what's in the house."

Connie squatted back onto her heels. "No, Senor, don't go to the market. There are a few t'ings, but I could have Julio bring dem, and you pay him."

"But you should be getting home, Connie. It's after four. When are they going to pick you up?"

"I stay till after supper and clean up. Julio will come for me."

"Well, you have your husband stay for dinner, then. We both appreciate——"

"Okay." She smiled. "I give him beans. Is good enough!"

The extra room had gradually become, instead of a nursery, a place to store things—books, odd bits of furniture, a lamp that didn't "fit." Finally, Rafe had built some bookshelves and cleared out the clutter of odds and ends, and he and Cora had refinished a desk and a captain's chair they picked up in a secondhand store. Later a small TV and a studio couch were added. Their collections of rocks and sun-colored bottles glowed brightly on a stand beneath the windowsill. They kept their bathing things in the bathroom, as it was directly off the pool and saved them from tracking through the kitchen and into the living room.

Rafe walked around the room in an agony of idleness. He switched on the TV set and watched a ball game for a few minutes. He flipped around the channels: a cartoon, a used-car commercial, and a monster film that showed a huge spider and a tiny human batting at it with a normal-sized lead pencil. He watched it awhile, wondering how they got the effect. The spider was real, obviously, taken with a close-up lens, then double-exposed with a long shot of the man . . . he switched it off; the hell with it, he thought. He had been about to read some symbolical nonsense into it. Himself or mankind fighting the forces of evil with futile weapons. Nuts!

He wished Cora would wake up so he could talk. He didn't want to wake her because Dr. Titus had phoned just before noon and told him to give her one of the lighter sedatives he had left. She had been restless, complaining about the stitches the doctor had taken in the perineal wall. "Feels like I'm sitting on a teddy-bear cholla," she had said.

"Sleep's the best thing for her," Titus had told him. "Give her nerves a rest. Don't want her stirred up any more than necessary."

Rafe considered the pool. He could swim a few lengths and work off some energy. He looked out at it and saw that it needed skimming after the wind last night. Leaves, clusters of feathery seed pods, scraps of paper, and a label from a beer can floated on the surface of the water, which glinted brassily in the late sunlight. A drink was a better idea.

He opened the doors of a portable bar in the corner and took out some Dewar's and a bottle of soda. At the same moment, Connie appeared with a large bowl. "Some ice, Senor?"

"Thank you, Connie," he said, surprised. "You got ESP?"

"Senor?"

He shook his head, and she went out. He puzzled over the idea. First the sheriff, saying he should stop "nipping." He hadn't been "nipping" at all. He didn't "nip." He had a drink when he felt like he needed one. He had put a slug of brandy in his coffee when he and the sheriff were in the kitchen right after the ladies and gentlemen of the press had left. What the hell! Now Constanza, appearing so opportunely with the bowl of ice. Did they think he was a drunk around here? He built his drink, going heavily with the scotch, merely squirting the siphon. He defiantly took a big swallow.

"What an ass! What an almighty, ridiculous ass!" he thought. Finding things to get mad at. Sounding off at poor old Gus. What the hell had happened to his head? That nice, cool intellect he was so proud of. That ability to deal with emergency situations. The guy who never got rattled. All day he had been on the edge of blowing his top. He had had some notion that the police would appear at any moment with a bedraggled-looking bully and ask him and Cora, "Is this the man?" Instead, the reports had come in, dull with the repetition of people questioned, strangers seen, cars searched. Nothing. Nothing at all. . . . It was dullness that drove a man crazy. Dullness, not emergencies.

"Rafe, honey?" Cora was leaning against the doorway.

"Hi, there, sleepyhead! Come over here and sit down." He patted the couch. "I've been having an awful time keeping from waking you up. I'm lonesome."

"You are? So'm I. I've been half awake for a long time. I don't think I'm more than half awake yet. I hate feeling so dopey. I've had enough sedatives. What you drinking, scotch?"

"Yeah. Do you want a drink?"

"Would it wake me up, do you think?"

"Well, if it doesn't you can go back to bed," Rafe said, and mixed her a light drink.

Cora said, "That goofy Connie, why didn't she put the ice in the thermos bucket?" She took a container from the bar, dumped the cubes in it, and put the lid on. "She knows I fix up the bar about this time, I guess."

"You do?"

"Do what?"

"Bring in ice and stuff."

"Yes, so I won't forget it while I'm getting dinner—so you won't get in my way, digging into the refrigerator. Why?"

"Oh, I'm just slightly paranoid. Last night you yapped at me, this afternoon Gus accused me of nipping, and just awhile ago I wanted a drink and Connie appeared out of nowhere with the ice. You know, 'everybody's picking on me!'" He made a little-boy sullen face with a stuck-out lip.

Cora didn't smile or respond, just sipped her drink thoughtfully. "Has there been any news? Anything new, I mean."

"No. Not a damn thing."

"Well, I don't think I care too much one way or another. What difference does it make? I just want things to get back to normal. I hate this disaster atmosphere. Press and police and friends calling up. Oh, golly, Sue and Charlie Eldridge are coming over this evening!"

"Would you rather they didn't? I can call them."

"No." She rubbed her forehead with the cool glass. "I'd like to get out of the house awhile. After dinner let's drive around awhile and stop in at their place for a minute. It makes it less like a condolence call. You want to phone them? I'm going to get a shower and pull myself together." She looked out of the window. "*Jeepers!* Look at that pool! Why in the world haven't you cleaned off that guck?"

"Nag, nag, nag! God, it sounds good. You must have the resilience of a—of a——"

"Grasshopper?" she suggested, with a smile. "It isn't that. I'm just not made of the stuff that turns inside and tries to digest its miseries. I could roll myself up in a ball and stuff a pillow in my mouth, and everybody would be sympathetic and give me a lot of attention, and I'd love it, I suppose." She shook her head. "No, I wouldn't either, because I just want to get back to our nice, ordinary, comfortable, wonderful life." Without warning, she burst into tears. "We will, won't we? Oh, Rafe, we've just got to! I don't want everything to be changed!"

"Nice try, sweetheart." He held her close and patted her shoulder.

Angrily, tearfully she cried, "Nice *try?* We've *both* got to try! I can't make it if you don't help."

"What do you want me to do, Cora?"

"Just don't look like that!"

"Like what?"

She pushed him away and stood with her hands on his shoulders, looking into his face.

"You need a shave."

He chuckled. "Which will it be, shave or skim the guck off the pool?"

"You've got time for both before dinner."

"Yes, ma'am."

"And call the Eldridges."

"Yes, ma'am."

"Stinker!"

"Yes ma'am." She left the door open, and soon he heard the noise of the shower and her voice singing, "Clang, clang, clang went the trolley . . ."

He shook his head, counseling himself aloud. "She's right, you know. We've both got to try." And stop wondering when he'd be able to touch her, wondering if, wondering how. He tried to suppress the involuntary shudder, the wave of jealous, angry revulsion. Give it time, he thought, just give it a little goddamn time.

Cora received a wild letter from Millicent, asking if it wasn't a mistake on the part of the papers, and if it was true, did she want her to come, and then saying how difficult it would be with the two kids, the baby was teething and all. Cora tore up the letter and waited so long to answer it that she forgot about it completely. The news apparently never reached San Francisco, because her mother didn't mention it in her letter in which she thanked Cora for her birthday present. She just went on to describe the surprise party that Ethel, with whom she now shared a flat, had given her. They had had champagne, and Ethel had invited a couple of nice gentlemen who had brought flowers. "Nary a word from your father, of course," she wrote.

Their friends were wonderful. Terry Ostander invited Cora to come and spend all the time she wanted in her great rambling ranch house. Her two teen-age boys burned up the roads on their motor bikes, intensely playing detective, feeling proud when Sheriff Boyd assigned them some out-of-the-way ranches at which they were to inquire for strangers.

Joe and Myra Deming, who ran a touristy little shop in Tucson, visited them with their indignation and their love, bringing silly little cheering gifts from their shop.

Charlie Eldridge, in the throes of a novella with a London background, had several long talks with Rafe, listening to him, letting him blow off steam.

One evening he and his wife came over for barbecued ribs, which Rafe liked to fuss with. Sue had bought the meat, and told Charlie, "You call them and tell them to get the charcoal ready—and don't take no for an answer."

After dinner Charlie told the girls to "make like squaws" and do the cleaning-up, and he and Rafe wandered out into the desert night together.

Cora said a little nervously to Sue, "I hope Charlie realizes that Rafe hates advice."

Sue laughed and said, "Don't worry. Charlie wants an audience. He knows I won't listen to that yarn of his once more. I bet he doesn't even *mention* your troubles." Sue was fictionalizing, but she felt it time to de-emphasize the March burdens. She went on. "Writers are funny about people. They think of them as either being bothersome or inattentive. I never dare ask him about what he's writing, or he'll yell at me, 'I don't want to talk about it!' Or else he's dogging my footsteps, saying, 'Sit down and listen a minute.' I don't think I'll ever be a Miss Mary to my Hemingway. When he asks me what I *do* think, I usually say the wrong thing. Maybe I don't have any imagination."

"Well, I wish I had your talent for making something out of nothing. Those curtains you made, for instance, they're stunning. Gray stripes, burnt orange——"

"Dyed mattress ticking."

"Exactly."

"Necessity is the mother of."

Sue Eldridge was a tall, bony, "burnt orange" sort of woman of about thirty. She had dark auburn hair, its curly ends faded from the sun, skin that was red-brown from exposure, and long fingers stained with paints and dyes and roughened from sandpaper and steel wool. Profoundly impatient with her husband's staring out of a window in front of a typewriter, she was always busy with some project involving physical effort and a great deal of noise. She had considerately made his tiny study practically soundproof with acoustical panels and heavy curtains so that the sounds of a saw or her wood lathe in the garage wouldn't penetrate his respected "think room."

She had met Charles Eldridge at a party in Paris, where she was attending a school of design and he was working for U.P.I. He had a book to write, and she wanted to paint, and Arizona seemed to be a place where artistic thought could find room to breathe, and also where it would be a great deal less expensive than their native New York. It happened that it was also a place where neither of them went forward. Eldridge's work was successful mainly in the area of articles on "What So-and-So Was Really Like," compiled from voluminous notes taken during interviews with political figures, writers, and personages in the field of the arts and sciences. The book had a title, an outline, and the first ten pages and gathered dust on the top bookshelf. A few short stories had been accepted, and the inheritance from his Uncle Geoffrey had diminished considerably.

In the dusk beside the pool there was a faint, fragrant memory of charcoal smoke and meat and pungent sauce, but a breeze was substituting the elusive incense of the desert, a potpourri of aromatic plants, mesquite, creosote bush, hot sand, and lichened rocks. The coals of the broiler had turned pale cherry and were covered with their own lichen of gray ash.

Sue was fiddling with the ends of her hair, twirling a finger around a curl until it looked like a small pointed piece of rope.

She yawned a little, saying, "I don't know, maybe I should keep my mouth shut permanently. Charlie didn't speak to me for days. But he asked me, and I told him that the kind of thing he was writing sounded like a bad translation from the Greek. It's all about separated pieces of the body clinging to pale-black light or some other hogwash. I said, 'Why don't you write about things as they are?' and he said, 'I cut across to the elements, the basics, to things that are vital and significant,' and I said, 'Shit!' and he went back into his cave and slammed the door. Of course, I'm not entirely truthful. I do understand in a way; my own painting is pretty subjective. Oh, Cora, stop worrying."

She was peering into the gathering darkness in the direction in which the two men had disappeared.

"I'm not worrying. I just know that Rafe's got a very short fuse these days."

"He's got a right."

"What do you mean? Because they haven't found our friend?"

"Oh, I think he'd like to get his hands on the guy and bash his head in, but since he wouldn't be permitted that pleasure anyway, I don't imagine that's his main trouble."

"I don't think I know what you're talking about."

"I think you do. Maybe you're just saying you don't want me to talk about it."

"I'm saying I don't *know!* You're as vague as Charlie."

"Okay, okay. How's your sex life?"

"Oh."

"Yeah, 'oh.' "

"Well, I'll admit neither of us was very enthusiastic about starting anything again. I *was* injured, you know, and Rafe was very considerate, I figured. Also, I wasn't very amorous-minded for a long time. It had been so ugly, so unbelievably ugly. And the way Rafe and I had been—well, it was always as though there was just no other way to express our love. We were so full of it, it was like spontaneous combustion."

"And now?"

Cora lighted another cigarette, exhaling a long, thin column of smoke underlining a sigh.

"It's more deliberate. Less joy. And sometimes, oddly enough, very violent."

Sue stood up. Peeling off her dress and stepping close to the pool, she said, "Keep your eyes open for the gentlemen. I'm going to get wet." Shedding her shorts and bra, she plunged into the pool, stayed under for a long time, and emerged, gasping and blowing, hanging on to the edge in front of Cora's chair.

"Hey! It's gorgeous. Come on in!"

In a few moments they were both spluttering and laughing, and Sue beat Cora by a length in a race from one end to the other. Cora gasped, "It's not fair, with those monkey arms of yours. I take three strokes to your one."

They floated, lying on the surface, relaxed. The sound of voices cut through the soft plopping of the water in their ears.

"Whoo-eee! Nekkid women! Wow!" Charlie and Rafe had returned, and Charlie whistled as the women dropped their feet and swam to the edge.

"We didn't hear you!"

"Sneaking up on us!"

While they kidded, Rafe went into the house and returned with some towels and Cora's white terry-cloth robe. He spoke sharply.

"Cora, here's your robe. Get out of there, now. Come on, Charlie, let's go into the house. I'll buy you a brandy."

Charlie said lightly, "What's the matter, Rafe? You some kind of a prude?"

Sue quickly said, "No, he's not. Knock it off, Charlie. Go on, we'll be with you in a minute."

Subdued, the girls emerged and rubbed themselves dry. Cora was puzzled. "What was that all about?"

"It's my fault. I should have watched out for them."

"But Sue, it's dark, and we were in the water. Rafe and I often swim without anything on."

"That's different. Don't be thick, girl. Just now, Rafe's a little touchy about any other man seeing his wife in the nude."

"But to make such a thing about it. Rafe's not like that."

"I'm sure he's not. Right now, he is. Takes time, honey."

It took time, but finally the police files contained another unsolved "Wanted: for criminal assault" case.

There was a flurry of excitement when a small plane with one passenger became overdue on a flight to El Paso. According to one of Rafe's friends in Operations who had filed the flight plan, the passenger answered the description of the wanted man. The pilot had flown in from San Diego and had not given the name of the man who met him at the airport. In fact, he had seemed in a hurry, too much of a hurry. A full-scale search was about to be inaugurated when the plane reported in from Las Cruces, safe, but out of fuel. Both pilot and passenger were satisfactorily identified.

Rafe and Sheriff Boyd resumed their small talk about business, politics, baseball, and the weather.

In other cities, other towns, the newspapers reported, with the usual indignation, the usual number of attacks upon women and the usual, earnest efforts of the police. Cora was drawn empathetically to each account, reading each article to the end. Disgusted, she said to herself, "Maybe I should form a kind of club—call it Rapees Anonymous. We could tell each other what we were like, what happened, and how we were changed by this great shocking experience."

Cora and Rafe both felt the acute state of shock disappear like a nightmare in the light of day. True, they didn't laugh as much. The things that used to set them off into childish horseplay and teasing did so no longer. And rarely did they just stop in the middle of some job around the house and put their arms around each other. A single, dreadful afternoon had accomplished the settling and sobering it might have taken years to achieve. . . .

Cora gathered her manicure articles together, blowing on her nails, testing the polish with the tip of one finger. She put the things away in a drawer and straightened the bed where she had been sitting.

"You hungry, Maxie-boy?" Maxie stretched and groaned and wagged his tail. "You're always hungry, aren't you, sweetie? You just wait till I get something on, I'll fix your dinner."

In the bathroom she splashed some summer lotion onto her arms and over her breasts and legs. From the clothes closet she pulled out a short white muu-muu gaily splattered with pink carnations, thinking, as she drew it over her head, that it was a good thing she had several of them—she could wear them even after the shifts became too revealing. And then she grew cold with nervousness again. What would Rafe say? Would he jump to a lot of conclusions? How convincing could she be that there was no doubt in her mind, that this is what they had been waiting for? This afternoon Dr. Titus hadn't even mentioned the event of two months ago. He had probably forgotten all about it. He just told her the test was positive, "as I knew it would be," and gave her a little lecture on dieting, cut down the smoking, eat regular meals and don't nibble, et cetera.

Of course, everybody by now had practically forgotten the episode. She could tell because "the look" had disappeared.

"The look" was a kind of double take that would happen when she went into the market or the drugstore or the gas station. She rarely went into town to the supermarket, letting Rafe purchase the items that Uncle Dan's didn't have. When she met one of her neighbors, they would say as usual, "Hi, Cora, how are you today?" Then their faces would quickly change to an expression that said so plainly, "Oh, I forgot, you were raped, how horrible." And right afterward the expression would change back, and they would proceed to gossip and pleasantries, or if it had been more embarrassing, depending on the person, to a quick concern regarding their purchases.

Now there was a nerve behind Cora's eyes that was jumping and thrilling like an electric wire. Her hands shook as she sliced cold cuts from some leftover roast beef. Rolls in a pan for the oven. Coffee ready to plug in. Salad greens wrapped in a towel and placed in the refrigerator. Dressing mixed. Now the ice cubes for the thermos.

She prepared martinis in a tall crystal mixer, stirred them with the mixer's glass spoon, and then after a moment's thought added an extra amount of gin.

She heard the station wagon, looked out the kitchen window, and saw it nudging in beside her Volkswagen. She thought, "I didn't leave enough room again!" and she called out, "I'm sor-r-ry!"

She heard Rafe cut the motor and laugh and say, "It's okay."

As he came into the house he said, "I'd rather have to squeeze in than have you scraping the paint off your fender again. How are you, sweetie?" He kissed her. "Hot as hell, huh? Did Fred Epperson call?"

"No, why?"

"Oh, I was supposed to leave some reports on his desk, and I've still got them in my case. I guess tomorrow will be okay. Oh, you, Maxie, Maxie!" He scratched the dog's head. "Giddown now, giddown. It's too hot to play."

"Want a swim before dinner?" asked Cora.

"No, I think I'll just have a shower. Something happened to our air-conditioning and, believe me, the radio room was like an oven. Weather says there's a whopping low pressure coming in from the south—might hit us before morning."

Cora heard the water from the shower, the distant sound of porpoise-blowing. She poured some milk into a pan of dry dog food, carried it out, and put it down on the kitchen step. She watched Maxie going at it for a moment, then patted his head and came back into the kitchen. Her breathing was short and the wire was zinging. She put her hands to her eyes. "I won't tell him tonight, I'll wait." Wait—for what? It won't go away, she thought. . . .

After icing the martinis, she poured them out carefully, trying not to tremble.

Rafe came in, dressed in shorts and a sport shirt, looking refreshed. "Wow! Martinis, that's a good idea! Or are we out of scotch?"

"No—just for a change."

"Hey, what's with you? You don't look so good!"

"Well, thanks!" she kidded, sipping her drink.

"No, I mean it. You've got two little red spots on your cheekbones. Heat get you?"

And Cora, being guileless Cora, found nothing else to do but say it. After a moment. After a deep breath. "I'm pregnant."

The light in Rafe's eyes was beautiful.

"After three and a half years—my darling! You're pregnant!" And then the light went out, lingeringly, like a candle flame reluctantly giving up in the wind.

He finished his martini in a gulp, sat down on the couch, and lighted a cigarette. He held up a hand for Cora to come and sit beside him. Avoiding it, she took the chair opposite and placed her drink on the table.

With a slight smile Rafe said, "Have you done your arithmetic?"

"Yes. I went in Wednesday to see Dr. Titus, and then again today, and he says the test is positive."

"How long, do you think?"

"Maybe three months."

"Maybe not."

"Well, there's no way of knowing for sure."

"Exactly. Well. What can I say, Cora?"

She was silent; her hands were clasped to hold their trembling.

Rafe stared out at the pool. "What a hell of a break. After three and a half years. And along comes—and bang! Jesus! Maybe there's something wrong with *me*."

Cora was holding back tears. "But Rafe, we don't know!"

"No. We don't. That's it, we don't know. Well, we'll just have to go on waiting, that's all. It's a damned shame. We can't ask Titus to do the job, of course. I'll look into it. Find somebody good."

Cora got up. "Have to put the rolls in the oven."

Rafe refilled his glass and then went into the kitchen, where Cora was placing napkins and silverware on the table in the alcove.

"Got some olives?" he asked, opening the refrigerator door.

"Oh, I'm sorry. Second shelf—in the back."

"Got 'em." He dunked a pimiento-filled olive into his drink and popped it into his mouth.

"I like the ones with onions in them."

"Uncle Dan's doesn't carry them. You get some next time you're near the market in town."

"Roger."

Opening the screen door, he picked up Maxie's pan, which had been licked clean, and put it into the dishwasher. With his drink in his hand he went out and walked around the pool, Maxie following him like a four-legged yes-man. When Rafe touched the back of a chair, Maxie sniffed at the place he touched and looked at him and wagged his tail. Rafe kicked a pebble, and the dog watched where it went and looked up with another approving wag, as if to say, "Wonderful, Boss!" And when Rafe reached down to scratch his ear, Maxie raised dark-brown eyes liquid with gratitude, "What is Dog that Thou art mindful of him?"

Rafe looked along the southern horizon for a sign of the prophesied storm; the sky was still clean and blue, with only wisps of clouds turning pink. Far above, a pair of jets were leaving contrails that stole a bit of the same shade of pink.

Cora appeared at the kitchen door.

"Hungry, darling?"

"Yeah, I guess."

They went through the motions and words of eating a meal, and afterward they listened to the news on television, making appropriate comments.

Rafe turned it off. "Boy, what a stinkin' world! Greedy, power-hungry, money-crazy; people starving, getting killed."

"Well, I don't think the network could sell a newsreel that showed nothing but contented, hard-working, happy people."

Rafe laughed. "Of course not! Our security must be threatened in order for us to appreciate it."

Cora glanced at him quickly, wondering if he intended another meaning.

He continued. "I looked at the sky tonight, and it was just plain blue, and I wasn't interested. If I'd seen some stuff beginning to tower up, I'd have been at least mildly concerned, wondering if the storm's coming in faster than expected; maybe we'd get some flooding—what do we do about it, all that."

"Maybe it's boring when there's no threat of some kind. The way people forget their differences in times of crisis is so amazing." Cora was thinking, "We've got troubles, my darling, please, please help." She said aloud, "I'm sure that if society lived in a state of complete security, the human race would die of ennui."

Rafe didn't bite. He said, with a chuckle, "Why is that, teacher?"

"Sorry, I didn't mean to sound like a book. Even in books the sociologists don't say much about 'why,' they just observe and report. Leave you to do the figuring about 'why.'"

"You ever found any answers?"

"Of course not. The only thing I did get out of my studies was that other people were also looking for answers, and that they were having just as tough a time as I was." She thought, "Don't look for answers, Rafe, just put your arms around me."

"You know, it's a shame you dropped your studies so completely. You've got a whole shelf of books here." Rafe waved an arm at a formidable collection.

Cora's mind stood at attention. "He wants *me* to understand something. What is it? What is it?"

She said, "I can't study by myself. I'm not really a student. I need to have somebody put a set of questions in front of me (tell me, tell me!), really pin me down, make me work. I'm very lazy, a very fuzzy thinker."

"Well, that's good. I don't like intellectual females any more than other men do."

"Quote. 'Threat to male superiority.' Unquote."

"Nah, that old cliché—I don't believe it. You want some more coffee? I'll get it. You didn't unplug the coffee pot, did you?"

"No, there's lots more."

As he refilled their cups he went on talking, raising his voice from the kitchen. "Women are attractive because they are women, it's as simple as that. When they begin to think the way a man does —logically, the if-I-do-this, this-will-happen kind of thinking—they become *like* a man. Fine, if they want that. A man might feel a threat to his so-called superiority if he wasn't sure of his maleness to begin with."

"Why don't you like the word 'superiority'?" Cora asked as she took her cup from him.

Rafe shook his head. "It's a stupid word for what is merely a *difference*. And the greater that difference, the better; but the more a woman tries to be like a man, the more she loses the very thing that is attractive to him." He smiled at her, emphasizing that he meant "*vive la différence* between us."

The look held while Cora caught her breath, and her hope soared.

He continued, still looking at her. "It's so attractive, so charming —and so bewildering. That funny something, those leaps from premise to conclusion; it captures a man's attention. It brings out the protective thing, because even though her conclusions may have been correct, she just could have made a dangerous one, a bad mistake, from which she must be protected."

Cora's smile faded, and she took a long swallow from her cup, thinking, "Well, now we're getting around to it. He knows. He knows what I'm going to say, and he's going to try to stay cool and logical and superior. Okay, my beloved, here we go!"

Aloud she said, "Rafe, I'm not going to abort this child."

Rafe shook his head and in confusion. "Now, what the hell brought that up!"

Cora shrugged. It would take too long to tell him, to explain the process of those funny leaps that weren't leaps at all. They were something a man just didn't know about. They didn't know about that second pair of ears a woman was endowed with. The other pair of eyes. How they heard and saw all the little signs. The signs she had seen and heard for the last two hours. He knew she had rejected his statement, "We'll just have to go on waiting," and he was going to save her from a dangerous mistake. He was being logical: "It's not my child, therefore it must be destroyed." And she was crying in her heart, "It is a child. It must be born." She was supported; she felt so strong. Her very flesh was on her side, altering all its processes in one huge "Yes."

And then with one sentence, one easy, simple blow, he flattened her.

"You would do this to me?"

Her mind floundered and staggered uncertainly. She was appalled that she hadn't considered he might be hurt. Angry, outraged, yes. She could deal with that. But to hurt him? How stupid she had been to surprise him, for he *was* surprised. It had obviously never occurred to him that she might want to have the baby. Then the thought that he was perhaps merely being clever brought her up short. Stay firm; don't underestimate him. It's only the opening gun.

"I could repeat your question, Rafe. I could say the same thing. You're asking me to blow my chance—maybe my only chance—to have a child."

His face turned an unpleasant shade of red, and his eyes sought a way out of the room. He said, "I'm going out for a walk." At the doorway he turned back with something in his expression that might be called a smile, and said, "One of the least attractive qualities about women is that they don't fight clean. Right to the crotch. Unerringly."

She heard the front screen door close, and she ran after him.

"Rafe, please don't go off and leave me just now. Don't think by yourself. I've been doing that all day. Squirrel-cage stuff. Let me go with you, or come back in and let's try to talk. I need to."

He came back inside. "Cora, what's there to talk about? You've made up your mind."

"You don't understand, Rafe. I didn't think I'd have to make a decision. If I thought that, I would have waited—maybe—waited until it was too late."

"No, you wouldn't have. You're not a cheat."

"To me, it's just a—tragic happening—that I look to you to help me endure. I've been going around and around with this problem for days now."

"Yes, I know you have. I thought you were sore at me about something. Do you remember, a long time ago we decided we'd have nothing to do with the usual exchange: 'What's the matter?' 'Nothing.' We decided that 'I don't know' was better than 'nothing'

—no pun intended. I've asked you at least six times, and each time you said, 'Nothing.' "

"Yes. It wasn't a good idea. It got built up to a point where I hurt you, and I'm sorry."

They sat facing each other in the pair of wing chairs flanking the fireplace. They both stared at its black emptiness. Rafe tossed a cigarette butt onto the grate and lighted another. He held out the box to Cora. "Want one?"

She shook her head. "They make me sick."

"Oh, honey—you sick in the mornings?"

"Sure. I've been running to the other bathroom so you wouldn't hear me—soon as I started to get your breakfast."

He got up suddenly. "Let's go out and walk. I can't sit still."

While Cora changed her shoes and got a scarf, Rafe went out the back, whistled up Maxie, and going out past the pool, opened the rear gate to the fence and waited for Cora to catch up.

Cora handed him a flashlight, and they started at a quick pace. The floor of the desert was dark, although the sky held an afterglow and the mountains still carried a mantle of purple and bronze.

Rafe put out a hand. "Sh! . . . Hold it." There had been a small swishing noise, and Rafe trained the beam of his light on the trunk of a saguaro ahead of them. "Can you see him?"

The bright eyes of an elf owl reflected the light. He could be seen perched in the hole made by a woodpecker. He made a strange little call, a dry, warning chuckle, and then vanished.

Maxie set up a barking and rushed the saguaro, but Rafe stopped him. "Don't be stupid, Maxie. I don't want to have to pull stickers out of your paws."

The darkness became complete; there was a granular hissing as a breeze began to pick up the sand.

"We'd better turn back," said Cora.

"Getting tired?"

"Yes. A little."

Slowly they walked back toward the house. The lights they had left on pricked the darkness, and a thin moon decorated the western sky.

Cora gave a deep sigh. "It's so lovely. I could never leave this place."

Rafe laughed hard. "What do you think, that I'm going to turn you out into the cold world?"

"No," said Cora, without humor, "but I had thought we might want to go someplace else, where no one knew."

"I suppose there *will* be people who'll count on their fingers. My God, I don't know how I'd take it. The first guy that made a crack and I'd get into a fight, sure as hell. I swear I don't know how you can even consider going through this pregnancy. Sick, tired. I'm a sonofabitch if I can understand."

Cora was stubbornly silent.

"Is it because you're afraid of the operation? It's as simple as a tonsillectomy."

"It's against the law."

"Nuts. That law's going to be changed someday. You'll see."

"And that will make it right. And then all our little cheating married women can run to a doctor and say, 'My uncle seduced me.' That makes it a combination of incest and rape, so everything's legal. It'll *never* be right, Rafe."

"Cora, you are wrong. This potential child has no rights whatsoever because it violates *my* rights."

"Tribal nonsense."

"Oh, for Christ's sake, why don't you go to Russia or someplace where they spout that kind of crap!"

They reached the gate, and Cora went ahead, slipping off her sandals and then sitting down on the edge of the pool to swish her feet in the cool water.

Rafe walked around the pool, slowly, his thumb flicking the end of his cigarette, keeping it hot and glowing. Maxie was at his heels, taking short, uncomfortable steps. On the second time around, Rafe turned on him. "*Jesus*, Maxie! Stop following me, you're driving me nuts. Now go into your house, go on now, and *stay* there!" Maxie, pleased at being given a definite order from his hero, trotted off to his house at the end of the carport.

There was a silence. Finally Rafe tossed his cigarette away and cracked his knuckles. Cora stood up; they spoke simultaneously.

"I don't understand why——" "I think I'll go——"

"Sorry."

"No, what were you going to say, Rafe?"

"I was going to say, I just don't understand."

"Don't understand what?"

"I don't understand why you should even think twice about ridding yourself of something—a few bits of cell tissue—that could wreck our whole marriage."

Cora thought for a moment before she spoke and sat down again. She was determined not to be rushed into any more emotional, injurious remarks.

"That's kind of a contradiction, isn't it? *If* those 'few bits of cell tissue' can wreck our marriage, there must be something important about them."

"Well, of course it's important——"

"It used to be a highly moral issue, but today, with the easing of morality, we say, 'Let us use the tools of modernity and get rid of something that will inconvenience us.'"

"It's a little more than 'inconvenient.'"

"I know, I know. I'm trying to keep it in generalities. Give me a chance. Who knows, I may talk myself around to your side yet! What I'm trying to say is that instead of a blind morality, we've developed a kind of hypocrisy; we say we have no responsibility because it's just a bit of cell tissue, that it isn't even a human being yet. So why not do the expedient thing, the me-first thing? The trouble is, science is betraying us, it's catching up with the old superstitious morality. Science now tells us that with the union of the first two cells, everything is settled, decided; it's a boy with brown hair and blue eyes, or it's a girl with red hair and brown eyes; it'll be tall or short; there'll be a small mole under the right eye; it's all been programmed. It is something that will never be a sycamore tree or a bird or a rabbit. To me there is something horrible about the idea that just because we can't see it, because it's formless, we have the right to kill it, like a bug under our heel. It can't talk yet. It can't say, 'Please don't!' even though the apparatus for speech is potentially there. Of course, what does a bit of cell tissue know about killing or protesting being killed? I don't suppose that has been programmed; that takes learning. So let's be humane and kill it before it has feelings or knowledge. Ugh! The whole idea revolts me!"

Rafe had remained silent, with the patience of one who permits an uninformed person to have his say. Now he shifted his weight in the canvas chair beside her. He laughed a little. "Whom were you quoting? That was very impressive."

"Damn it, Rafe, I wasn't quoting. It's something every woman knows instinctively. And I am *not* afraid of an operation. I know women who've had more than one, and they think no more of it than having a slightly painful menstrual period. That's what they say, anyway. I wonder if sometimes, in those dark moments we all have when we face ourselves, if they don't say, 'I killed my baby.' Oh, I suppose they can be conditioned so they never give it a thought."

"'Taught' would be a better word."

"I don't think it's a better word at all. Teaching implies learning and elevating, raising up to a higher plane of existence."

"Okay, okay, teacher. Let's get off it." The silence became very thick, loaded with the desire of each of them to hurt, to bludgeon the other with their opinion.

"How the hell you can want to bear the child of a criminal psychotic bastard is more than I can understand!"

"Rafe, I don't *want* to. But I must!"

"Why? Why!"

"Because it exists."

"Oh, brother, that's no reason. You're so strong on heredity, what about this guy's background? There might be some bad stuff there, you know."

Cora turned toward him, her face only a white blur in the darkness.

"That's kind of funny, Rafe, if you stop to think about it."

"What's funny about it, for God's sakes!"

"Well, I mean—what do we know about *your* background?"

"Nothing, of course, except from what I am. And still sticking with heredity, I don't have an RH-negative blood type, I'm not a hemophiliac or an epileptic, I have a sound heart and lungs. And even if we could find our friend Robinson and ask him whether he can provide the same sound heredity, there is still one thing he can't supply, and that's me—*my* blood, *my* heredity, *my* programmed cell."

"I know. I understand better than you think. You don't want his child and neither do I. But I want *my* child. And I think you could, with me, accept that separate entity, the person that this child will be, the individual that is neither mine nor yours nor his."

"Well, now, that's a little lofty for me."

"I don't think it is. Suppose you and I weren't married, suppose I was a girl in trouble—I think you'd marry me to give my child a name. I think if I were a widow with a baby, you'd marry me."

Rafe laughed. "Of course I would. And I'd also have the great feeling of having done something fine and a little heroic. People would say, 'Isn't he wonderful—what he did for that poor girl.'"

"Well, isn't it the same thing?"

"Not at all. I'm a fool—a—a cuckold, isn't that the word?"

"Since when are you concerned with what people think!"

"I don't want people to feel sorry for me!"

"Well, you don't have to carry a sign on your back, 'This child is not mine.' I think that depends upon us. If we behave as though we had no doubts that it was yours unquestionably, people would go along with it. Of course, you and I are assuming that it isn't yours. There is a chance, if you remember."

"I remember. But I doubt it. Not with our record. I think we'd better accept the fact that it's not mine."

"Well, I haven't accepted it. I don't know quite how I'm going to get through this pregnancy without the joy, without the fun it would have been—" She put her hands over her face and began to cry softly.

After a few moments Rafe said, "Come on, honey. Take it easy. We're both in the same damn trap. Let's both try not to make it worse with self-pity. God, I hate to see you like this. It's too much for you. The only sensible thing to do is to get it over with. But I can't drag you into an operating room. I can't demand that you do what I think is right. I love you. I'm not completely a gimme-person. I want to give you what you want. You seem to believe so strongly that you should have this baby, that it might be a worse tragedy if you didn't have it. All I can say is, okay, I'll take care of you."

Cora went on crying, as though she hadn't heard.

Rafe said, "Let's go to bed. I'm beat, and I'm sure you are."

His yielding was disconcerting to Cora. She had been climbing a mountain, grasping at any handhold or foothold that was available, and now she had reached a plateau where no effort was required, and it was sudden and shocking.

"Rafe," she said softly. "Oh, Rafe, is it going to be too much? If you could just agree with me, not give in to me."

"You can't have everything, honey. I'll do the best I can. I promise you."

Dr. Amory Titus enjoyed good food. He was grateful for the metabolism that allowed him to indulge in his wife's hearty cooking and still remain thin. Lillian Titus was not as lucky. Her beautiful homemade pies and chocolate cakes, the generous use of butter in her cooking, all added to her massive proportions. She took thyroid and used saccharin in her tea, but she grew increasingly short of breath and gained pounds every year. The diets she went on were temporary. She felt obliged to "feed up" her husband, who looked as though he could take off in a light breeze.

The doctor paid little, if any, attention to his wife's increasing obesity. It was doubtful that he had even looked at her for the last ten years. He talked to her off the top of his head—about the daily doings of the office, the people he had seen—and it was like talking to himself.

Their big old-fashioned two-story house would have looked homey and charming in the center of a few acres of farmland. A windmill and a big red barn, a small corral and a wagon load of hay would have been appropriate as a background. But instead it stood cramped and uncomfortable on a busy street, opposite a new modern clinic where the doctor had his offices.

In its obscure past, Sabado had probably been the "Saturday town" where miners and cattlemen had come to spend their pay at the saloon, to fight and raise a little hell. Then came a highway and a gas station and a truckers' rest with its café and black coffee and pinball machines. The few who had remained to settle built their austere eastern houses with windows that stared at the nakedness of the desert. A few streets branched off from the highway, and a cluster of cheap stucco houses hung at their tips like dried seed pods. The main street at right angles from the highway was called Main Street and on it were Uncle Dan's Produce, a Penney's, a drug store, a saloon, now called a cocktail lounge, and various small shops and offices. The clinic had been built with an eye to future growth, and its pleasant low lines, its man-made oasis of green lawns, palms, and shrubs, were clean and modern and efficient and made the rest of Sabado look as though it needed a good broom.

Dr. Titus sat at his dining-room table, where he could keep an eye on the door to his offices across the street in case somebody should drive up who needed him. His thoughts rarely strayed from his cases, from the load of work that he was never quite able to lessen.

He said to his wife, "Mrs. March got a positive test today."

"Well, that's nice," said Lillian Titus automatically.

"Very nice people. Don't know them well. Treated the husband for bronchitis last winter. Then again I saw Mrs. March a couple of months ago, when they had that trouble, you remember."

Lillian opened her mouth still stuffed with cake. "And now she's pregnant!"

"Yes, too bad, too bad. Mrs. March was very nervous. They've been married over three years, and this is her first pregnancy. Of course, I didn't let on what was in my mind, just gave her some pamphlets on prenatal care and told her to come back in a month for a checkup. I have a hunch I'll be getting a call from them in a couple of weeks, 'Please, doctor, can you stop the bleeding!' In a hell of a state of shock. Exsanguinated. Mass of infection. They ought to have a law—so we could take proper care of these cases. Not leave 'em to somebody like that lady butcher up in Phoenix. Simple little job like shelling a pea. Ought to have a law."

"Have another peach, Amory. There's some of the whipped cream left, dearie."

"You have it, Lil. I haven't time."

"Will Hugh be home for dinner?"

"Why?" Amory Titus actually looked at his wife. "Is there anything special about dinner tonight?"

"No. I just have to ask. If he was, I was going to fix something he liked—a chicken pot pie."

"You just don't give up, do you?"

Their son, Hugh, was a dentist at the clinic. Lillian Titus could never quite believe he had really married that Mexican girl. After all, she hadn't *seen* him get married. He just came home one morning with this girl with such awfully dark skin—like the ones who lived in the work shacks at the end of town—and said, "Beatriz and I got married last night." She was his assistant, and to Lillian's thinking she looked like a pleased black cat. The way she had clung to Hugh with her little claws all over him. Practically *pulling* him after her while Lillian screamed names at her, names she deserved. And you could believe Lillian when she told you that that woman never came inside her door again.

Marry such a creature! Hugh wouldn't do a thing like that. Sooner or later he would come home and put his head in her lap and say he was sorry, that he had just been sowing a few wild oats, and it would be so wonderful to forgive him. She had been waiting now for five years.

When she wasn't cooking, she was sitting by the window, working on a frame that held a hooked rug. It had a complicated design that she called Persian Garden, and its fine details hurt her eyes sometimes, so that she had to stop and gaze out of the window. At hand there were convenient jars and bowls containing macaroons, peanut brittle, peppermints, anything to keep up her blood-sugar level. She was increasingly tired these days.

The only thing that got her out of the house were her small shopping trips. Uncle Dan's delivered most of her orders, but she liked to get a look at the meat first, and anyway, Uncle Dan's was near the small dry-goods and notions store where she bought her wool skeins. That nice Miss Gordon was so helpful, and together they brooded over samples of Tiger Lily Gold, Sunrise Pink, Woodland Green. And then Miss Gordon was always so interested in what people had to say.

Like this afternoon, when Lillian went in to replenish her Mountain Dew Gray, and among other things told Miss Gordon about
how nicely Mrs. Kearney was recovering from her appendix operation. Miss Gordon said she would call on her and cheer her up, and
no, of course she wouldn't mention the March baby—after all, that
was their own business, didn't you think? Of course, it was just
terrible and all—that *poor* Mr. March!

Myra Deming was wise enough to complain loudly every time
she had to push her husband's wheel chair. They argued constantly,
but pleasantly and affectionately. It was as though they kept a
Ping-pong ball in the air between them all the time. They insulted
each other lovingly and heartily, and they never had a moment of
self-pity. His arms were strong, and he manipulated the chair skill-
fully enough around the shop. But their car was in an area behind
the shop, and the sidewalk and the entrance to the alley sloped
steeply, and she would wait until he said, "Come on and push,
dammit! I haven't got a low gear on this thing, you know!"

"I've only got two hands, Joe!"

"I will carry your bundles, milady. Put 'em on my lap and let's go."

"They'll slide off."

"Put the blanket over them. I don't understand why you can't
carry stuff out to the car first, and then come back for me."

"Don't like to make two trips."

"You've made three already."

"Here we go. My God! Are you gaining weight?"

Joe pulled and shifted himself into the driver's seat, which was
equipped for paraplegics, with hand throttle and brakes. Myra folded
the chair and slid it into the back along with her "homework." There
was always something that needed attention: a beaded jacket to be
lined with nylon instead of the cotton it came with, dolls to be
painted with dabs of red and black paint for the lips, cheeks, and
eyes—they came in kits, ready carved by the Indians on the reser-
vation, with little cut-out buckskin jackets and pants to dress them.
Myra found that if instead of selling them as kits she dressed and
painted them herself, she could add another dollar to their price.
She restrung ropes of turquoise and crystal beads into a more fash-

ionable length and added a clasp and another fifty cents. It all helped.

"You didn't forget the amber for Cora, now, did you?" Joe asked as he made a U-turn at the intersection.

"No, nor did I forget to set the burglar alarm and lock the show window. Gee, won't she love that amber-thing! Wasn't that a piece of luck?"

"When did you find out she was interested in paleontology?"

"I don't know that she is. She just went slightly out of her mind when she found that piece of shale with a fossilized leaf print." She dug into her straw carryall and drew out a package wrapped in tissue, a small clump of amber that just fit into her palm. "It's a beautiful color," she said, holding it to the sun. "I think I'll let her find the bug, let her think she discovered it. You could miss it, you know, if you didn't look closely. It's got the most delicate wings, and I'll bet under a glass you'd find antennae."

"If it's that kind of a bug. You know, you should really save it for a Christmas present or for some occasion."

"I couldn't wait. Besides, those two people are my special love. They have a way of giving that makes you feel as though you were doing them a favor. They make me feel—oh, I don't know—as if they were my own kids."

"Wait a minute, Myra! We haven't hit fifty yet, and I know Rafe's in his late thirties, and Cora must have made thirty by now."

"I know, I know. But they're young. Really young. They're still interested in Life with a capital L; they're both great talkers and readers and Rafe with those wide-set eyes of his, the way they sort of search into what you *really* mean."

"Yeah, nice kids."

"You see, you think of them in the same way—as 'kids,' I mean."

"Oh, Myra, that's just a term. Like the way you and your old-biddy bridge club call themselves girls."

"'Old biddy!' You louse!"

"I didn't call you that, my angel! You're a young biddy. A real chick. I can hear you over the others when you play at our house. You go 'cheep, cheep, cheep,' while they're going 'cluck, cluck, cluck!' Thank heavens it's only once a month!"

"It's good business. I sell those women a lot of stuff. Mrs. Ostander bought those two gorgeous glazed pots for her front entry garden. Eighty-five dollars apiece. She's going to plant a couple of ginkgo trees in them, look gorgeous. You're going to miss the turn."

"How can I miss it when it's—right—here." He turned left abruptly. The articles in the back seat slid and rattled, and Myra reached around to steady them with her left hand.

"You never saw it until I spoke, now admit it."

"That's right!" Joe laughed. "I was busy thinking what a funny word 'ginkgo' was. And how hard it would be for a ginkgo to be gorgeous."

"Rafe's not home yet, his car isn't there. I'll just check and see if Cora's in—oh, there she is."

Cora, clad in her white terry robe, appeared at the screen door, her hair wrapped in a towel.

"Hi!" she said. "You bring your suits? Water's wonderful."

"Hi, beautiful," said Joe. "We haven't got time. Got to make a couple of deliveries." With the aid of crutches, Joe hoisted himself up the steps as Cora and Myra brought in his chair. "I don't need that, Myra! We're only going to stay a minute."

"Yes, you do. Cora's chairs are too low for you, you know that, so shut up!"

"Just has no pity on a cripple, Cora. Hear the way she talks to me?"

Cora smiled. "How about some beer? Go on into the other room. I've got chips and a spread on the table in there."

As Joe settled himself into the chair in the other room Myra took his crutches and leaned them against the wall, and then they looked at each other, questioningly, worried.

Cora could be heard opening cans of beer and getting out glasses in the kitchen.

Myra said in an undertone, "She looks perfectly awful—ghastly! Should we say anything?"

Joe said, "I don't think so. Let her bring it up if she wants to. Don't butt in."

Cora was smiling as she brought in a tray. "Myra, you do the honors; let me go and get out of this wet suit and run a comb through my hair. I look awful."

She disappeared, and Joe muttered, "It'll take more than that."

Myra poured beer and spread chips with a bit of cream cheese, saying, "I wonder what's the matter. She's been crying, obviously. Of course, a woman's entitled to a good cry occasionally, but her color's bad. She was doing so well—bounced right back after that business last June."

In a few minutes Cora returned, looking neat and fresh, but with slightly too much rouge on her cheeks.

"How's business?" she asked.

"Pretty slow—too hot. It'll pick up in a couple of months with the tourists," Joe replied.

"You must see the wild bird cage we're taking up to the old man," Myra said.

"Professor Liebig—on the hill?"

"Yes," answered Joe. "He's got himself a toucan."

"I didn't know he went in for live birds." Cora laughed. "How will the toucan get along with all the stuffed specimens?"

"You'll have to ask the toucan."

"I must go up and see the old boy. I haven't been near the place in months."

"I don't blame you. The whole layout gives me the willies," said Myra.

"Oh, I don't know. Of course, I admire the man enormously, even though he is kind of a kookie specialist. I guess he's recognized as one of the foremost ornithologists in the country."

Joe said, "Wonder what his water bill is—keeping up all that lush planting."

"Oh, he can afford it. He's got millions, Joe."

"So they say. A millionaire playboy who went serious. That's a switch."

"Hey, where's Rafe?" asked Myra.

"Oh, he'll be here in a minute." Cora glanced at her watch.

"Bet we're keeping you from getting your dinner."

"No, you're not, no, sit still. I've got a casserole going—nothing else to do. Enough for you if you want to stay." Suddenly her voice was pleading. "Why don't you?"

"Oh, no, thanks, honey. We've got these deliveries."

"Well, now what, exactly? Liebig's is ten minutes from here. What else?"

Joe smiled. "That's all, really. And a delivery to you. Myra found something she thought you'd like."

"Well, that's simple. I'll drive up to Liebig's with you after dinner. What did you say about something for me?"

Myra had brought out the crumpled package containing the amber.

"I found this on my last shopping trip up north. Here, take it over to the light."

"Oh, isn't that a lovely thing! What a beautiful shape!"

She turned the piece over in her hand and gave a little gasp of appreciation. "Look at that! That tiny creature!"

She held it for a long time, saying nothing, her eyes serious. Then, shaking her head, bringing her thoughts back, she laughed a little. "Does something funny to me. Can't explain it. Looking back, God knows how many millions of years, at a tiny little insect, so delicate and perfect. Like a soul trapped in limbo."

"Cora?" the kitchen door slammed.

"It's Rafe. In here, dear."

"Well, Myra, Joe, how are you?" Rafe greeted his friends warmly, giving Myra a peck and taking Joe's big hand, saying, "How's the real estate business?"

"Better than Myra gives me credit for. She's scared all the time that we're going to lose everything."

A small voice said, "Hi, darling."

Rafe looked at Cora quickly for the first time since entering the room, then embraced and kissed her.

"How are you, honey? How was your day?" He looked at her sharply, seeing the dark circles, the reddened eyes, the pinched look around the nostrils.

"What are we doing all crowded into this little room? Let's move out into the living room. You staying for dinner, aren't you?"

"Cora twisted our arms, thank you."

Myra went into the kitchen with Cora to help her prepare dinner, and the two men made themselves comfortable in the living room.

Rafe had evidently brought home a good story, and their laughter was noted in the kitchen.

Cora said, "It's good to hear Rafe laugh," and then turned back to getting out napkins.

Myra said, "You look tired, Cora. You feeling okay?"

Cora put on a flashing smile that Myra saw was forced.

"Oh, I feel fine. I've been cleaning out closets, putting down new shelf paper. I've had such an urge to straighten drawers, rearrange things. Things Connie just can't do."

Myra gave a chuckle. "Well, well, well, the old nesting instinct! It's a fairly accurate symptom, and quite common."

Cora faced her, eyes wide. "What do you mean?"

Myra was peering into the oven and didn't see the startled, anxious look. "Joe and I both noticed when we first came in. We haven't seen you for three weeks or so—why what on earth?"

Cora had her hand to her mouth, looking frightened. "Don't tell Rafe, will you? Don't tell him you guessed. Don't tell him I told you."

"Why, Cora, what nonsense, we're your friends. What's this all about?"

Quickly, Cora recovered. "I don't know." She shrugged nervously. "It's just a little—early."

"Of course, I won't peep if you say not to." Myra embraced her warmly. "But I can say I'm so happy for you, can't I? It's wonderful, after all this time. If any two people deserved children, it's you and Rafe." She held Cora by the shoulders, looking at her deeply. "I don't understand this anxiety. Are you afraid, honey? You're only what? Thirty? You won't have any trouble."

Cora drew away and got busy again. "I guess I am a little scared. We'd almost given up hope, you know."

"Well, I think it's wonderful. I've always regretted that Joe and I were so damn selfish—and careful—in our early years. Then it was too late. Joe got sick, but since then I'm grateful just to have him alive. Even so—to have missed having kids is no small loss. So, be happy, Cora!"

Something about the silence, the lack of response, the sight of Cora's back as she arranged the table in the alcove, made Myra's brain suddenly spin a dial, and then she was tuned in. Her face reddened, and she felt horribly embarrassed. She closed her eyes for a moment and wished she could talk to Joe—right now. He had more tact, he would know how to get her out of this. Damn her big mouth!

She hurriedly changed the subject and began to talk about the shop, about the weather, about what Joe said when they asked him to speak to a citizens committee about some new storm drains.

Finally Cora said, "Well, I think we're ready. Ask Joe to open this bottle of wine, will you, Myra?" From the refrigerator she handed her a slim bottle of sauterne. "There's a corkscrew on the bar in the other room."

"You sure you want wine? Don't have it just for us, you know."

Cora's eyes were bright. "I thought maybe somebody would like to offer a toast—to the new baby."

Myra smiled. "You mean the sky isn't going to fall in?"

"I don't know. But if it does, I need somebody to help hold it up for me."

"I'll do that, honey. I'll just do that."

The meal had proceeded to fruit and cheese, and Cora had poured out the last of the wine when Myra took her glass and said, "I want to propose a toast—to the new member of the March household. May he—or she—bring all the joy in the world to this good home."

Cora quietly raised her glass and drank. Then she looked at Rafe steadily.

He responded, "To you, Cora." He smiled, although he felt as though something had come unhinged, and swallowed the wine.

Myra said, "It's all my fault. I guessed it, but I'm glad I did."

Joe said, "Well, I'm glad that's what it is. I said to Myra when we first came that we thought you weren't looking too well—not your usual blooming self, at least. How's she been, Rafe—asking for strawberries and pickles yet?"

"Not yet. But I'm expecting it. She's getting pretty tough to live with."

Cora said, "I'm awful. I've got headaches and a stomach that does nip-ups in the morning, and I'm cranky as hell."

Myra said, "Well, it's early yet. That doesn't last long. Not that I speak from experience, but I went through three pregnancies with my sister before I married Joe. She was married to a traveling salesman. I can never remember whether she lived at home because he traveled around so much, or if it was the other way around."

Joe said, "You people are so lucky, you don't know. No, no, you needn't get quiet; we're all over the emotional side of the fact that we never had any kids. It was rough, and we railed against Fate and all that stuff."

Myra added, "It's become a kind of bond in itself. It's strange how disappointment, deprivations, how they can kind of knit two people together." She cudgeled her mind for words that would help Rafe to accept a condition that she knew was strangling him. She was aware that Joe had not done any arithmetic, and she let him talk on. He was good-naturedly kidding Rafe about his having to get up for two A.M. feedings, about how he was going to be so proud there would be no getting along with him. She hoped from the depths of her affection for Rafe that he would understand that what Joe was saying would in all probability be the attitude of most people— that most people would never question the paternity of the child. From the gossip she was exposed to in the shop she knew that many were under the impression that the Marches had been robbed, and that the thief had merely tied Cora up to keep her from giving an alarm. There were other versions, even some fantastic ones: "Hear the fellow tried to drown her in the swimming pool." "Heard he had a knife." As for herself, she knew that if anyone suggested that it had been a sexual assault and that perhaps this child wasn't Rafe's, she was going to lie like hell. As old friends, she and Joe would claim authority for firsthand information and would say if called upon, and volunteer if necessary, that something near the truth had happened, that the man had beaten her up and tied her to the bed but was scared off before anything else happened. Now she broke into the conversation by saying, "Let's go see the toucan!"

"See the what?" asked Rafe.

Joe explained about Liebig and his recent acquisition from South America, about the cage they had obtained after considerable trouble.

"What does it do?" asked Cora.

"I suppose it just sits there and looks exotic and makes some kind of ridiculous sound. He's going to put it in a greenhouse where he's got all kinds of tropicals."

"Would you like to go, Rafe?" asked Cora.

"I suppose. You've been in the house all day, be good for you to get out for a bit."

"That's the stuff," said Joe. "Nothing like potential fatherhood to bring out the consideration in a man."

"Don't overdo it, Joe," said Myra coolly. She gave Joe a "Tell you later" look and said aloud, "We don't want to get icky about it all, you know."

It took them awhile to get going, but finally they moved off down the dusty ribbon of road that led from the highway to the scientist's dwelling.

From the distance the hill looked like a man-made construction in the middle of the desert, like some giant sandpile, roughly cone-shaped. As the base was approached the hill achieved form and character. Great boulders littered the base, and the road ran around to the north and up an incline to the gate where Frederick Liebig had achieved a miracle of engineering. One whole side of the hill had been graded into different levels and filled with the finest soil, which was irrigated, planted, and cared for by a crew of gardeners. And at the top, blending into its surroundings, almost hidden by lush and cool foliage, was the vine-covered house of local stone.

Professor Liebig welcomed them into his little castle with enthusiasm, trotting around, being helpful with Joe's chair, with the carton containing the precious bird cage, exclaiming over their kindness at coming to see him.

The large, low-ceilinged room was unbelievably cluttered. In one corner there was a huge flat-topped desk, lighted by a drop lamp and a goosenecked desk lamp; the desk was covered with drawing materials, manuscripts, and several small stuffed birds in flight attitudes. Behind the desk could be seen the top of the head of a woman engaged in some minute work with a watercolor brush. She did not look up or otherwise notice the entrance of the visitors.

"I hope we haven't disturbed you, Professor," Joe said.

Dr. Liebig replied heartily, "I was expecting you. I have been anxious to have the cage. My poor Juanito needs to stretch his wings. But first, first let me offer you some cognac. Ellie, *liebschen*, will you help me? I'm afraid my good friend Soames has gone to bed. I had him up early in the field this morning. Oh, excuse me, this is Miss Eleanor Girard. She has come to me from New York to work on the illustrations for my book. Ellie!"

The girl had not moved. She went on delicately licking the point of her brush and applying it to her drawing. "One moment," she mumbled.

There was a part down the middle of her head that gleamed in the lamp light, and the drawing paper reflected up into her face, glinting on the heavy glasses she was wearing. She had on a white sleeveless blouse that showed her slender arms. The neckline was high and rimmed with eyelet embroidery.

Cora said, "Let me help you, Professor—if you'll show me where I can find things."

The little man was so anxious and so inept with his hospitality that they all felt that to refuse anything he offered would confuse him. Myra and Rafe and Joe settled themselves around a huge low table, which was a slice of redwood tree mounted on lava stone. It was laden with papers, periodicals, copies of the British journal *Ibis*, Howard Eliot's *Territory in Bird Life*, the *National Geographic*, and a half-dozen paperbacks by Agatha Christie. Flanking the large fireplace were specimen cabinets of birds, birds, and more birds. There were drawings, sketches, and paintings of birds on the wall, grouped for study rather than for decoration. Wide shelves contained a fortune in camera equipment: boxes of lenses, filters, gun-cameras, movie cameras, tripods.

But with all this clutter of material there could be seen care and order. The whole place was simply a laboratory, and outside of a few huge, comfortable upholstered chairs, the furniture was sparse. The floor of waxed, doweled planks was bare, and here and there were some worn oriental rugs of unquestionably excellent origin.

Dr. Liebig went on talking, turning on lights, and from the dining room opposite the fireplace he brought a bottle of brandy. Cora followed him with a heavy tray of magnificent crystal balloon glasses. She signaled her panic of dropping them, and Rafe relieved her and placed them on the redwood table. Miss Girard had risen to join them, and they were all startled into silence. She was a creature that did not belong in this musty cave of study. The modest white blouse did not extend below her ribs, and for about the width of a man's hand the bare flesh was exposed. Gold-belted black stretch pants revealed smooth hips and long legs, and her small feet were encased in black velvet flats. She had removed her glasses, and the black hair that had been pushed back of her ears now swung forward to frame a face that was devoid of makeup. Her eyebrows were arched in a question mark above the large myopic brown eyes, and her lips were full, a natural pale-pink color, tucked at the corners into firm cheeks.

As she stood nodding to each of Dr. Liebig's guests she had a stillness that seemed lazily exotic. But then she yawned and spoke, and the illusion was vocally dispelled in pure Brooklynese. "I'm pooped, Professor. Can we call it a day, do you think? I think it's the change of climate that's got me. All I want to do is sleep ever since I got here."

"Of course, Ellie. Have a little cognac before you go off to bed." He said to the others, "She has only been here a week, and I have been so selfish as to put her to work immediately. She is doing my figs."

" 'Figs'?" asked Cora.

"Yes. Figs. 'Fig ten shows the—uh—size of the arc made by, et cetera.' Figures. She is an excellent draftsman, magnificent. Right now we are making additional—*valuable*, I think—contributions towards understanding the mechanics of flight in the hummingbird. There are certain aspects that have not even been touched upon. The strobe camera——"

Myra turned to the girl with a smile. "How in the world did the professor ever find you?" she asked, being careful not to stress the "you."

The professor answered for her, since Miss Girard's attention seemed to be elsewhere. On Rafe March.

"Out of all the samples of work which were sent to me by my publishers in New York, the ones signed 'E. Girard' were the most satisfactory—the conditions having been specified that the artist be able to work with me here for six months or so."

"At such a salary—who wouldn't, Professor?" said the girl.

Dr. Liebig shrugged. "I need perfection."

"You got it," said Joe loudly, appreciatively, and everyone laughed except the professor, who seemed startled, and then looking at Miss Girard, burst into his own thin laughter.

"Yes, yes, of course—I understand. You think she is beautiful?"

"And how!" said Joe, smiling broadly.

"Well, perhaps my standards—perhaps my age—" and Professor Liebig shrugged again as though it were all beyond him. "Come, let us see my beautiful toucan."

They all moved out of one of the rear doors toward the greenhouse, and Cora asked, "Is the poor thing going to end up on one of your shelves, Professor?"

"Ah, no, no. He is for aesthetic purposes only. Those magnificent colors of the beak, they will set off my tropicals."

Later, in the car, Myra said, "If you want my opinion, I think Miss Girard is also there to set off the tropicals."

Cora, who was sitting in front, beside Rafe, said, "You've got a filthy mind, Myra. She's an artist who just happens to be pretty."

"She's that, all right. But that old Viennese humbug was putting us on when he said she wasn't his type. Pure propaganda. That guest house at the bottom of the hill has a path right up to his bedroom, I betcha."

Joe snickered. "And what about Soames?"

"What about Soames?" Cora asked. "I think it's just too wonderful to have an English butler named Soames."

"You don't know the story. They say that Soames was a none too dependable butler on one of the old English estates, and they could never find him because he was always out bird-watching. Apparently he corresponded with Professor Liebig and found they had many things in common besides birds. Anyway, he left the English family and moved in bag and baggage with the professor, and they've lived happily together ever since."

"Well, so—" Cora said, "so he works in the field with him. That must be very convenient."

"In my own delicate way," said Joe, "I'm hinting that Dr. Liebig wouldn't find Miss Girard the least bit attractive."

"What do you think, Rafe?" Cora asked.

"Oh, I wouldn't know. I don't see how a gal like that could be interested in Liebig. He's a nice old coot, but he can't talk about anything but birds."

"Who's talking about conversation?" Cora laughed.

Myra said, "You know, she's the kind of woman that makes every other woman in the room go off her diet. They take one look at her and think, 'What's the use!'"

Rafe kept his eyes on the moonlit road ahead of him. He took his left hand off the steering wheel for a second and worked the fingers. There was a lingering sensation in the palm and fingers as though he had cracked his elbow. It was a nerve memory that was reinforced by the feel of the steering wheel. Its small protuberances reminded his fingers of the way Ellie's spine had felt in the gloom of the greenhouse when they stood in the rear of the group listening to Dr. Liebig expound about the oddities of the toucan. It had been so completely accidental. In order to guide her politely ahead of him, he had reached around to her, and his hand had encountered the area between the eyelet-embroidered blouse and the stretch pants. Before he could withdraw it with an apology, he had felt her lean in response and trap his hand with her own against her back. And as she moved ahead in the narrow pathway she had locked against his thigh from buttock to calf.

She had not returned with them from the greenhouse, pleading fatigue, and said good night as she went out a side door.

"Do you need a flashlight, Ellie?"

"No, thank you, Doctor. The moonlight is bright enough. The path is quite clear." She had turned her head toward Rafe for a second, and there was a faint smile on her face, but she did not raise her eyes.

In the car Joe and Myra were saying, no, they wouldn't come in, it was late.

Rafe chuckled to himself, still thinking of Ellie. That lovely old game! It was a hell of a lot of fun, but he wasn't about to play it. It all belonged to the days of becoming a man. The experimental times. The before-Cora times. The times when tensions built up and were sustained for the sheer excitement of sustaining them. And when the game was played properly, it reached an enchanting pinnacle of madness from which one tobogganed back into dullness. And that was the finish. But with Cora, it had never become dull; it was never finished. It was something that had enhanced the other sides of their relationship with tenderness and great security. Thinking about it, he put his arms around Cora as she passed him and held her for a moment. They had been moving around the house doing the evening lights-out, doors-locked, ashtrays-emptied routine.

She clung to him, saying, "Oh, Rafe! I thought you were mad at me."

"Mad at you? For what?"

"Oh, for spilling it about the baby. I didn't, really. Myra guessed, and I just couldn't deny it. I know we could have waited, but I'm sure Myra won't gossip. She's too good a friend."

"What do you mean, 'gossip'? Did you tell her the whole thing?"

"No."

"No—but what? Did she guess that, too?"

"I'm not sure. Maybe she did, Rafe." Cora sounded tired. "I have a job to do, and I'm not going to clutter it up with worry and apology."

"I, I, I, that's all you think of. You haven't given me any chance at all. You slammed the door tonight when you and Myra conspired to toast the new member of the March family——"

"Slammed what door?"

"Well, that's it, isn't it? You didn't even give me an opportunity to discuss the matter further with you."

"But you said yourself last night, you said, 'Okay, I'll take care of you.' Didn't you?"

Rafe pulled up the venetians. The moonlight poured onto his face softly, caressingly. He released the cord, and the blind plunged noisily down again. Swearing, he yanked it back up. It stuck crookedly.

Cora said, "The gizmo at the top doesn't catch. I can't reach it."

Rafe looked at her in annoyance. "Well, neither can I." As though to illustrate how simple it was, he pulled over a straight chair, stood up on it, did something to the gizmo, and then carefully adjusted the blind exactly half way to the top.

"Pretty slick," said Cora admiringly, thankful for the interruption.

"Yep, pretty slick. I hate slickness. I hate slyness. I hate having something put over on me."

"Who's putting over *what* on you? You said *last night*——"

"I know what I said. You were overwrought, talking your head off about a lot of idealistic crap. I wanted to give you a breather, give you time, give you a chance to think about my side of it for a change."

"Rafe I under*stand* your side of it!"

He went over to the closet and began to haul out blankets and sheets.

"Now what are you doing?"

"I'm going to sleep in the other room."

"Well, you don't have to drag that stuff out. The couch is made up. All you need is a pillow."

"Well, why didn't you say so!" As he swung around to replace the bedding a blanket came unfolded and caught between his ankles. His temper boiled over. He flung everything onto the floor savagely and strode down the hall into the other room.

He tore off the neat, dark-green corduroy spread from the couch and sat down with his face in his hands. He was shaking with anger, his palms were wet, and as he drew in his breath against them he imagined he could smell Ellie's perfume, the scent of her body, and behind his eyes her rich lips parted. With a groan he got up and poured a stiff shot of whiskey and downed it in a gulp.

"You going to take to drink?" Cora's voice, mildly mocking, came from the doorway.

"If I find it necessary," he said coldly.

"Who's overwrought now! It's better to talk, Rafe, than to take that kind of an out. We've got an emotional problem, darling, but it will never get solved if we get hysterical about it."

He poured himself another drink, but instead of drinking it, he held it in his hand as an act of defiance and an illustration of his control. Cora moved toward him, and he quickly avoided her, sitting down at the small desk, with his back to her. If she came close, she would know, she would misinterpret and respond, and put her arms about him tightly, and if she did, he felt that he just might take her by the throat.

The room was quiet. They fiddled with objects. Rafe put his glass down and lighted a cigarette. Cora ran a finger over a picture frame and looked at it for dust.

Rafe finally spoke. "I don't know. I don't know. It's me, I just feel so——"

"What?" Cora sat on the couch after she had folded up the spread. She drew her legs beneath her and crossed her arms over her stomach, waiting, wanting to listen.

"I'm trying to see," he said. "I grope around into my past and I can find no parents. I grope into the future and I can find no child of mine. I have no sense of perpetuity. I feel so goddamned alone." He glanced at her, at the absorbed, thoughtful face listening to him. And then the self-protective posture, the rounded shoulders, the folded arms, made him snap, "And you off in your little female corner, broody with your young. You're like a little animal, you disgust me."

Cora gave a low whistle of amazement. "You know, I ought to slap your face," she said quietly. "I would, except that I'm scared to. Frankly, you've gone all savage on me. Just remember something for a moment. I am your wife, I am pregnant against my will, I wasn't unfaithful to you——"

"You sure?" There was a glint of mockery, of cruelty in Rafe's eyes. "You mean there wasn't an iota of cooperation? You mean there wasn't some moment when you didn't get a hell of a kick out of being raped?"

Cora, stunned, shook her head. "Rafe, I guess I don't know you. You've never been cruel. You don't have cruelty in you."

"Oh, yes, darling. Every man has cruelty in him. Push him hard

enough, it'll come out. Let me ask you something. Once you sus-
pected you were pregnant, did you ever, for one second, do anything but plan on having it? Did you ever consider a bit of surgery
for my sake, for the sake of our marriage?"

"I don't think I weighed killing your pride against killing my
baby, if that's what you mean. I didn't think I'd have to. Nor did I
think our marriage hung in the balance, either. I think what was in
my mind was the fact that there was a chance it was yours. It's something I still think, still hope for."

Rafe threw up his hands. "You are so dense, so insensitive, it
appalls me."

"You want to pick a fight for some reason, Rafe. Now back off.
Let's quit this."

"I'll back off, you bet I will! You have your little bastard, knit
booties for it, think how cute it's going to be—but leave me out of
it."

In a rage he slammed out of the house, got into the car, and
roared out of the drive, squealing tires protesting at the speed when
he turned into the street. Once on the highway he took a sharp left
turn back into the desert, and the empty road stretched out, white,
luminescent, inviting.

The moon was setting, and the brilliance was gone when he came
back over the road. He stopped the car just short of the highway;
it was too soon to go back to his own house. He needed to think,
to gain control of this blind subservience to reflex.

He lighted a cigarette, blowing the smoke out in a relaxed sigh.
He was not going to be a hypocrite and feel remorseful or deny that
the past two hours had been thoroughly satisfying, his ego reani-
mated and restored.

The game was perfectly played throughout. The darkness and
secrecy lent its piquancy. Even the heart-stopping moments when
a small noise seemed to shatter the stillness and threatened to
bring on a light from the top of the hill. The gate creaked on its
hinges; his toe touched a flower pot and sent it rolling.

And when he saw Ellie standing in the open doorway of the guest
cottage, she whispered the correct formula: "What on earth are you

doing here?" There was nothing on beneath her robe, and he had not even bothered to reply.

The dizzying magic of newness, of unfamiliarity, was something to be consumed greedily; to discover the length of thigh, the flatness of bottom, the texture of small, firm breasts; the odor of skin and heavy hair covered his face, drowning him in fragrance as he lifted her, rocking on his feet, swaying, carrying her in the dark toward a single thin shaft of moonlight shining on a pillow.

He had winced a little when she said, "Oh, that was so great! Feel better?" He wanted to say, "Shut up now, just shut up!" And he hastened his dressing when she said, "Aren't you happy, darling? You're awfully quiet!" He tucked the sheet up around her neck, leaned down and kissed her forehead still moist with perspiration, and did the best he could. "You're beautiful," he said. At the door he gave a small salute and hastened in the shadows down the walk, cursing himself when he saw that he had left his parking lights on in the station wagon.

The landscape was graying noticeably. There were experimental calls that questioned the dawn. A squeak, a single pure note of song, a rustle of feathers in the brush, and then a waiting—as though to give the night workers a chance to vacate; to burrow down, to crawl under stones, to find refuge in hollows and holes.

A diesel truck shifted gears and rumbled on the highway. Rafe tossed out his cigarette and rubbed his jaw with a distasteful grimace, partly because he was bearded and felt crummy, and partly because he had come to no conclusion as to which came first, the chicken or the egg. He reviewed his anger with Cora; he heard himself saying preposterous words of cruelty. Cora had had her beating, and he had rushed into the barnyard and delivered a few more pecks and spur-thrusts just for good measure. Which had come first, the anger, or the desire for Ellie? Which was the cause and which was the result? Had it all been set up in the greenhouse with the simple invitation that Ellie had extended? It had only flicked his senses, even amused him at the time. A little tramp with other talents besides those of the drawing board. Ordinarily, as with others that flitted through his days, he could note and discard. Why not this time? Was she that attractive? No. What had made him want

Ellie so much that he had to raise himself to heights of righteous anger—or was it to lower himself to the depths of ego-wounding word-flaying? The hell with it.

At the house he pulled into the carport, not with stealth, but quietly, simply because he didn't want to wake Cora. He didn't worry about Maxie, who would lift his nose, sniff, and go back to sleep.

He went directly to the pool, and stripping out of his clothes, slid into the water's depths, shrinking from its chill. He leaned with folded arms on the ledge at the deep end, feeling cleaner, clearer in his mind, free of odors of perfume and sweat, released.

At the kitchen door he could see Cora, like a wraith in her soft white gown, and he had the feeling that she had died, that he was suffering the first acute stages of grief, and because he had not yet achieved the simplicity of sorrow, he was hallucinating. He played with the idea for a moment, watching the way the droplets of water clinging to his eyelashes added to the effect, blurring the outlines.

"I've got some coffee on," she said, and floated back into the house.

Suddenly he felt ravenously hungry; he wanted a plateful of pancakes dripping with butter and syrup, a slab of ham, a half-dozen fried eggs.

"Cora!" he shouted as he emerged from the pool. She appeared again at the door, not so pale and wraithlike now. The sun was sending some stabs of light between the mountain peaks, and everything had good everyday sharp outlines once again.

"What is it, Rafe?"

"I don't feel like going to sleep just for an hour or so. I'm hungry. Can you rustle up something?"

"You want some pancakes?"

"How did you know?" He tried to keep his gratitude from choking him. It was all out of proportion, out of scale.

"I didn't know," she replied. "I've been wanting pancakes for an hour."

"Be right in."

By the time he had shaved and dressed, the fragrance of bacon and the odor of coffee filled the house. He went into the kitchen. Cora was pouring out saucer-sized cakes on the griddle.

"Golly, you've made enough!"

She looked up, her eyes shining. "Don't they look wonderful? Made 'em with buttermilk. You watch these and I'll put the eggs on. You want eggs, don't you?"

"Yeah. Where's Maxie?"

"Under my bed. I let him in right after you left. He was barking at the moon and wouldn't shut up. Now he's afraid somebody will put him outside. Can't please him. . . . Damn!"

"What?"

"There's a piece of shell in this egg, and I can't get it."

She leaned over the spluttering eggs in the pan, fishing for the elusive fragment with a spoon. She closed her eyes for a moment as the stove seemed to tilt suddenly, and slowly the eggs began to rotate. She straightened up with a gasp and said, "Oh, damn! Oh, no! Oh, get out of my way, Rafe!" Gulping, she ran across the kitchen in the direction of the bathroom, and he heard the door slam.

Terry Ostander said, "You have a beautiful back, David." She ran long fingernails down his spinal column and finished with a sharp pat on the compact, solid buttocks.

"Hey," said the man, turning over quickly and grasping her hand. "Your nails are sharp, you know that?" He held her fingers, examined them, and then kissed the palm.

"I had a manicure yesterday."

"Dandy. Did you tell the girl to make claws? Just so you don't draw blood, I don't mind."

A fat white candle burned in a sconce on the wall by the long windows. It was the only illumination in the room, and it made jumping shadows in the breeze.

"I've got to go, sweetie. It's going to be light pretty soon."

"One cigarette, okay?" Terry stalled, reaching for the box on the bed table. Lighting two. "You always have to go. I hate it so. If we could just sleep—and wake at noon—and go for a swim in the pool—have *meals* together."

There was no reply. Terry turned her head on the pillow and watched the coal blooming on the end of the cigarette between his lips. "Wouldn't you like that?"

"Mm."

"What does that mean? You would—or not?"

"Oh, sweetie!" His tone was impatient.

"Okay, I'm sorry. I can dream, can't I?"

"Don't dream, Terry. Be satisfied."

"I guess I have to. It was all so much fun, so exciting till you had to go and mess it up."

The cigarette glowed angrily.

"You're going to drop ashes all over the sheet."

Quickly he stubbed the cigarette out in an ashtray, swinging himself off the bed in one swift movement, going over to where he had thrown his clothes over the back of a chair.

Terry bit her lips, pride holding back another apology. She had to watch her step with this man constantly. He was so young, so sure of himself with her. The wrong word, the wrong attitude, and he'd be gone. Without much imagination he had said, "I am what I am." In the same genre he might have added, "Like it or lump it." He was all body, and she'd bought it. Really bought it. Her tears and anger she had kept to herself. He was an animal she kept in the cage of her protection. Cared for, fed and clothed and pampered, sleek and beautiful. But with the cage door left wide open always, reminding him that it was open, that he was free. He was free or he never would have stayed.

She had held back the bit of gossip she had picked up from Amanda McWhorter, her manicurist. She was not sure of how it would affect him, so she had said nothing. It wasn't likely that he'd hear it. He rarely left the ranch except on nights when Paul and the boys were home, when he couldn't come to her. Then he'd appear at the kitchen door, ask for the keys, and take the pickup truck. And if, later, she asked him where he went, he'd say, "To the movies."

The time was short, the problem was painful, too painful to face continuously. Cora and Rafe had never indulged in the careless marital bickering that seemed to be the natural climate of so many marriages. They had air-clearing fights, but they were normally patient with each other's small moods. Cora could rail about the never-ending dusty sand that seemed to cover everything five minutes after she had swept, brushed, and dusted it all out in the morning. She could get angry and complain about "living out in the boondocks" when a plumber was vague about how soon he could get out to fix an appliance.

Rafe had his own problems of pressure and politics in his job. And money, always money. Often he came home with what he called his tired headache, and once Cora suggested that maybe he needed glasses. He yelled that he didn't need glasses, that he had twenty-twenty vision, and Cora replied that she had twenty-twenty hearing and went out into the kitchen, leaving him to argue with an empty room.

But they bore no grudges over a careless word; they wasted no time with the useless dredging up of ancient mistakes. They could argue heatedly over a difference of opinion, but they had the gift of listening, and each of them rarely attempted to convert the other to his personal opinion. Until now. The problem now could not dissolve in a permissive endowment of the right of each to act and feel as he wished over a belief, an idea, an attitude. One of them was going to get hurt, seriously, and each of them underwent a hesitating, bleak, and dangerous postponement. All the words seemed to have been said; all the arguments, the emotion-colored phrases, the flare-ups, and the "let's be sensible" talk-outs were over with.

Rafe took refuge in imaginary dialogues during his drives to the airport. Over the low music on the radio he would try out various approaches aloud. Usually he would try to console himself first with an image of Cora lying in his arms some night, whispering, "It just isn't right. I can't lie here with you and let another man's child grow within me. Help me face it."

It was a pretty thought, but he dismissed it. "Sentimental crap!" It was maddening that she seemed to be so unconcerned that she had been accidentally—criminally—impregnated. She even seemed surprised that it bothered him. Bothered! What a little word, he thought, for the way he felt. Was she completely amoral? Like a mare or a bitch? Perhaps he should have thought of it before. Earlier in their marriage she had always been disappointed when a menstrual period came along. Well, so had he, for that matter. Then, after a year or so, they just stopped talking about it. Maybe he should have suggested a stud for her. There were lots of guys at the airport, healthy, fertile animals. Not sterile like he was. His mind wrenched away from his own heavy sarcasm. Until last June she had shared the deficiency; to such an extent that they avoided a medical examination to find the cause, just out of fear that one or the other would have to take on the whole burden of the fault. Nobody wanted to feel that he wasn't a whole human being. He knew what it would have done to her; it would have just about killed her to say, "I can't give you a son—I can't have children!" Why, then, couldn't she understand how he felt? Now, damn her, she was going around proudly with heavy, tight breasts, a rounding belly, a look in her eyes full of a secret triumph. Well, so now she knew. But he'd be damned if he'd raise her bastard. He'd walk out on her first. He'd leave her, by God!

He shut the radio off to still the talking voice that had interrupted the music and his own conversation. He tried again, this time with the idea that the decision ought to be, *should* be, his. "I've made an appointment, Cora, for this afternoon. You're coming with me, and it will be all over before you know it. I don't want any further argument. This is what I have decided is best for us, and in time you will agree with me." And Cora would nod her head and say, "Of course, darling. I've been very foolish." He could almost see her, acquiescent, smiling bravely, putting her hand in his. But this exchange was lifted almost literally from another experience.

About a year after they were married, Cora had procrastinated about a painfully infected molar. The pain would go away and then come back, and she would go around with something in her mouth that smelled of cloves and holding a heating pad on her cheek. He made an appointment with the dentist at the clinic, Hugh Titus, and simply came home early one afternoon and rushed her, weeping in fright, to have the tooth extracted.

But this was no simple matter of a tooth extraction. If she yielded at all to the same technique of being rushed into a decision, she would be red-eyed, angry, and hating. It would be a Cora who would never recover, never forgive him, whose voice would sound bitter and ugly—"So that's what you meant when you said you'd take care of me!"

And the rest of the world was concerned about population explosion. Everywhere you turned you read about family planning, about the pill, about legislation for legal abortion. In their own town of Sabado they were attempting to give some birth-control education to the Mexicans, who went on grinning and singing and popping kids by the dozen. How rich they seemed!

He parked the car in the employees' area at the airport and wiped the perspiration from his hands. He sat quietly for a moment until his heart stopped leaping behind his ribs. He pulled a comb from his shirt pocket and ran it through the hair at his temples, patting down the cowlick on the crown and peering at himself in the rear-view mirror. He noted the deep furrow between the heavy brows and pushed at it with a fingertip to smooth it. Somebody would be sure to say, "Comes now Chief Thundercloud!"

He pocketed the keys and got out of the car. His attention was caught by a small plane making a final approach at the end of the runway. Under his breath he said, "Go around again, you stupid sonofabitch, you're comin' in high!" He glanced up at the dark-blue panes of the tower where he knew the same command was going out in politer terms. He took a deep breath, feeling lighter, almost happy to escape into the detailed problems of the day's work.

"Hi, Carl!"

"Hi, Rafe! How 'bout this weather!"

"It's really somethin' all right. Transmission from San Francisco still lousy?"

"Yeah, it's this end, though."

"It is, huh? Well, let's give 'em a call. If we shift to higher freeqs to get out the O.R.M. and tell Leather Lungs to send with his left foot, we can clear. We can check with San Francisco to see if their mast is cocked and tell them to give us an I.M.I. on their freeq before we shift. . . ."

As the sun neared its zenith in a cloudless sky the town of Sabado assumed an attitude of serenity. Almost any activity was useless, postponable. Cars stayed parked at the curb, their metal tops tossing back waves of heat and light. Children played in the house, and adults sought the coolest air-conditioned corners of their stores and offices, staring idly from closed windows, as isolated as though a snow storm were raging in the streets.

There was not even a sigh from the dusty plumes of the tamarisk. Lizards flattened in the shade of rocks; in the distance saguaros solemnly, reverently pointed to the source of light and heat, and the mountain ranges in their own calligraphy affirmed the statement in unyielding terms against the sky.

On the empty black highway an enormous truck, its aluminum sides flashing, roared toward the little tan Volkswagen coming from town, and Cora gripped the wheel as the slipstream pummeled the car.

A few minutes later she pulled into the carport, and when she switched off the key, the silence become absolute. The gravel crunched like thunder under her feet as she made her way to the kitchen door, a full grocery bag under each arm. The kitchen was dark and comparatively cool. There was a soft hum from the fan in the window, and the refrigerator muttered in the corner. Under the dining table Maxie's tail went "thump-thump," but otherwise he didn't stir.

Cora put away her supplies, folded the paper bags, and stuck them in a rack on the cabinet door under the sink, wondering, as she often did, why the kitchen didn't seem to bulge with overabundance after all the trouble and time and selecting and carrying. But as always, no cabinet doors had to be forced to close. The refrigerator shelves remained uncluttered, with almost every item in plain view. The pound of butter and the dozen eggs lay smugly in their compartments in the door; the carton of cottage cheese replaced one that had been rinsed and put into the trash. There was a new, slender bottle of olives—stuffed with onions. Uncle Dan had ordered them for her, since Rafe never remembered to pick them up in town. "Rafe likes them with his martini, Mr. Bruckner." "Why sure, Miz March, have 'em next time you come in. Me,

I never could take those martinis. Whoo!—get you drunk! Never take the place of a good cold can of beer. That's my speed."

"What Rafe likes," "What Rafe wants," had always been a pleasant concern for Cora. As simple as coffee black or steak rare, and as complicated and fussy as three bath towels on the rack, folded double. Now the smallest service seemed a currying of favor, a bribe for his good humor. In a salad dressing a hint of dill always brought an appreciative "Mm, real good!" and when he came home at night, she removed her apron as soon as she heard his car, even if she was wearing only dungarees and a clean white shirt, because he always gave her a fast up-and-down look before he embraced her, and his eyes said he liked what he saw.

But now there was no embrace. There was a "Hi!" and an immediate plunge into talk of the day's happening. The dill in the salad called forth a polite "Very nice," without the usual wink and a grin. Their eyes met rarely. The kiss of departure seemed to slip over onto a cheek.

The minutiae of daily living had absorbed all violence and emotional discussions as completely as quicksand, but the couch in the other room remained made up, and the covers were folded down at night with a brief "Good night, honey."

Cora felt as though she were waiting for the other shoe to drop, although outwardly she matched his tone and manner. The days went by routinely, empty of communication, but they *went by*; time was passing rapidly, and she wondered if she would be able to meet one last angry appeal, or what she would do if he made some kind of awful ultimatum—like leaving her. The very thought appalled her, and when sometimes it came, it overwhelmed her, and in her mind she groveled at his feet, weeping, crying, "I'll do anything you want. Just don't be like you are now. You've gone away, and I need you."

It was triggered by as small a thing as a slender bottle of olives— "with onions in 'em."

Slamming the refrigerator door, she walked out of the kitchen into the back yard and stood by the pool. She let the heat envelop her. In seconds the force had wiped out every trivial thought, every stray image or unformed word. The shadow at her feet was puny and distant. She raised her head and closed her eyes and licked her lips and they dried instantly. She felt weightless, diminished, transparent, as though everything had been consumed except her bones, and even they were white. Then there was a rushing in her ears, an anxious rhythm that became a pounding. She took a deep breath and turned back toward the house. The telephone was ringing.

"Yes?"

"Cora. It's me."

"Yes, Rafe."

"Honey, I hate to do this to you. You've been to the market already, I bet."

"Yes, I have. But what?"

"Brian Foley's here. He was in San Diego with some time on his hands. He hitched a ride to the airport here. And, you know. What could I do? Stay with us, is all I could say."

"Well, for Heaven's sake, don't apologize. From all you've said, he must be great, and I'd love to meet him. Now, let me see. . . . Oh, hey, I've got a couple of small fryers in the freezer—if you think that'll be enough."

"That's fine, honey. I'll pick up a case of beer—and—and I do thank you!"

"For what! No big deal—I'm not going to get flustered and clean the whole house if that's what you mean. One thing."

"Yeah, what?"

"Where do you want to put him? I mean, in the living room? Or shall I put fresh bedding on the couch in the other room? It's got the bath—and——"

"I agree. Also, no explanations."

"Right."

"What time will you be off?"

"Not till six. Brian wants to go into town and get a pair of dungarees and swimming trunks and stuff, but he'll be happy here till I'm through. He can jaw with the fellows, and there's a flight due in here from San Antonio. The navigator used to be on his run. We'll be home 'bout six-thirty. Maybe not completely sober. You know how it is."

"I know how it is. I'll keep the chicken in the oven in case you're late."

"You're quite a gal. I'm—I'm very grateful to you, Cora."

"Oh, come on! See you later. 'Bye now."

She cradled the phone, puzzled. What was all this gratitude and thank you and you're quite a gal stuff? He'd brought people out before, for pot-luck and poker, with no more than a "Carl and a couple of the guys are coming for a game tonight—what do you want me to bring?" Of course, Brian was special. Rafe had told her that Brian's capacity for beer was unbelievable, that he never got drunk, at least his sharp tongue never was dulled or his wit diminished. Cora knew Rafe envied his mind, his fresh intelligence that danced around and through a problem. "The Sarge always had the answers, but he acted as though you'd've come to the same conclusions if you'd had another minute to think. I mean, he never was a smart guy. We'd have hated him if he was. But he made us feel smart, so we were the smartest outfit in the Army."

Perhaps that was it. In some way, maybe Rafe was putting his gratitude into a future tense. Maybe he was saying, "Remember what I've told you about this being a shrewd cookie. I'd be grateful if you behave so he isn't aware of our trouble."

She got up, smoothing her dress, smoothing her thoughts, turning them to little things. Defrost the chickens. Make some potato salad. Is there enough mayonnaise? I think I'll do the candlelight bit tonight—and no muu-muus—thank God I can still get into a sheath. Well, just in case I might look a little thick, maybe the swing skirt with that boat-neck cotton blouse and those blobby white earrings and lots of eye makeup—get the attention up, up high. And then she sighed, thinking how wonderful it would be if Rafe would come in saying, "Sarge, this is my wife. We're going to have a baby, isn't it great?"

The station wagon pulled into the carport, and Cora rapped on the kitchen window and gestured to Rafe. "Don't bring him through the kitchen, you dope!" She saw him say something to a stocky man with flaming red hair; they both looked up and laughed and went around to the front. She wiped her hands and untied her apron,

and when she opened the door, they were standing on the veranda
with their backs to her, looking at the view. The man had his hands
on his hips, shaking his head, and Rafe was pointing out the different mountain ranges, which still looked unstable and wriggly in the
heat.

When Rafe saw her, Cora noticed the flicker of acknowledgment
that she looked lovely, and smiling, he said, "Darling, this is Captain
Foley. Sarge, my wife."

She held out her hand. "Well, that's a bit confusing. Which is
it, sergeant or captain?"

She felt her hand disappear into a huge paw as the man said,
"Brian will do, ma'am. I'm happy to meet you."

Although his greeting was warm, Cora caught a speculative glint
in a pair of cold blue eyes. There was a fine tracery, the spokes
of glare wrinkles at the corners. His face was wide, and freckles were
strewn over his forehead and the bridge of his nose, which was
blunted from some early barroom argument. Of medium height, his
body was heavy in the shoulders, and he carried himself like a man
in excellent trim. The red hair was curly, threatening to pop loose
in ringlets from the dressing that held it flat. From his looks it
would have been no surprise to hear a brogue, but there wasn't
a hint in a voice that was soft, musical, as though he were a trained
singer.

"I was saying to Rafe, I'm sure that all the words have been used
up to describe the beauty of the desert. What an experience to live
here!" He swung an arm in an arc, and Rafe moved back out of
the way.

"Careful, Sarge, that's a deadly weapon you're waving around!"

Cora said, "It's pretty hot just now. Most people can't take it. You
should come in the spring, when the flowers are in bloom."

"It's beautiful then, too. I've seen it." He said softly, "I learned
to fly out here. A long time ago."

For a while they simply stood and gazed, absorbed, at the dis-
tances. Finally Foley said, "It looks as though something tremendous
had happened—just a moment ago, or an eon ago—and the place
was stunned into silence." And then he shook his head and a

curl popped loose. He smashed it back into place with his palm. "No, it's a mistake. One shouldn't try. There are just no words."

Cora said, "It's a highly personal experience, you know. It won't permit you to be indifferent. I have a very good friend who lives here who still says, 'It gives me the willies—all that waste.'"

He turned, almost angrily, to her. "You know better, don't you? There is no better example of thrift. Every cubic inch is used. It's full of life and great ingenuity—hoarding every drop of water, manufacturing protection from heat and dryness, even the sand itself is used as a weapon. Ever watch a kangaroo rat kick sand into a snake's eyes?"

"Ever shake a scorpion out of your boot?" Cora said jokingly, and they all laughed.

Foley said, "That—I'll admit—will give you 'the willies'!"

They moved into the house, and Foley looked around him and patted Rafe on the back and said complimentary things about their house, and then Cora left them to go back into the kitchen while Rafe showed his friend where he would sleep and where to put his things in the other room.

"We got time for a swim, Cora?" asked Rafe.

"About twenty minutes, okay?"

Cora opened the oven and turned the chicken with a pair of tongs. It smelled delicious, and she noticed it was coloring nicely. As her hands mechanically attended to other little jobs she pondered at the phenomenon of how human beings can be totally different to different people. From Rafe's reminiscences, "the Sarge" had emerged as an archetypical tough Irishman, quick-tempered, with a sarcastic tongue and a big heart. Perhaps. She wasn't so sure of that big heart. The look he had given her had been cold, faintly hostile, faintly superior. He seemed much older than Rafe, although she knew it couldn't be more than two or three years. Perhaps it was a hangover from their relative positions in the Army, but she didn't much care for Rafe's somewhat obsequious attitude. He al- most—damn it, she thought—he almost fawns on him! She hated to see that. It weakened Rafe, he lost dignity, and there was no need for it. She wondered how long Foley would be staying, feeling slightly disappointed that she hadn't liked him immediately, as she knew Rafe wanted her to. For then he would sense it and try to make up for it. She sighed and shrugged. She would do her best.

Dinner was mostly reminiscing and catching up. Cora listened and smiled and wished she had cooked three chickens instead of two. There was a bond between these men, a friendship born of a common experience in the Army, and afterward they had been wise enough to keep it alive, in correspondence and in frequent visits between Foley's flights when he happened to be passing through Tucson. The last four years, however, he had been on the big Pan-Am jet flights to Honolulu, and their communication had dwindled to postcards.

One flurry of letters was exchanged just before Rafe married Cora, and regarding that time, Brian now said, "He was really scared, Cora, did you know that?"

"No, I don't think I did." She smiled and looked straight into Brian's eyes. Why was he baiting her?

"Well, don't hang her up like that, Sarge," Rafe said quickly. "Tell her what I was scared about."

"As I remember," Brian said slowly, carefully filling his glass so that the foam headed gently to the rim, "it had to do with whether such a poor specimen of a man should endanger the life of such a fragile, other-world creature, a being of such perfection—" He grinned at Rafe. "Well, you asked me!"

"Hell, I didn't sound that asinine. I was a loner scared of marriage."

"And you were feeling trapped."

Rafe's face darkened. "That's not true, Brian, and I think you're making Cora uncomfortable."

Quickly, Foley put his hand on Cora's. "I'm sorry. I'm teasing Rafe, not you. I don't know you well enough to tease you! No, the real truth is he was questioning his ability to be a good husband to you, that's all there was to it. I was someone who had known him for a long time, and he wanted me to reassure him."

"Well, you weren't very reassuring." Rafe laughed. "What was it? 'All you have to be sure of is that you want to take a chance.'"

Cora smiled to herself, thinking she knew almost to the day when

Rafe received that letter. She remembered a conversation on the unfinished veranda of the house. A lovely night. A long time ago.

They were all silent a moment. Rafe reached for a humidor on the shelf of the divider beside him and offered Foley a cigar.

Accepting, Brian said, "Thought you were a pipe smoker, Rafe. Did your wife object?"

There it is again, thought Cora, mystified.

"No. And I am a pipe smoker. I got these for you. Remember, the skinny panatellas?"

"I think there's something you did forget, Rafe," Cora interjected.

"What's that?"

She put her hand to the side of her mouth and whispered in mock secrecy, "Beer!"

Rafe bounded up from the chair. "Oh, my God—that was . . ."

"The last of a six-pack."

"I'll run down to Uncle Dan's. No, don't get up, Brian. It'll only take a minute."

"Don't go to any trouble, man!" Foley protested.

"No trouble. We got to have beer, that's all." And he was gone.

Foley turned and looked at Cora.

"I'll help you with the dishes. May I?"

She shook her head. "Sit still, finish your cigar. All I have to do is pop them into the dishwasher."

Cora kept her eyes on her folded hands as the silence built between them. She thought, "He expects me to ask 'What have you got against me?' and I'm not going to fall for it." Aloud, she said, "Did anyone ever call you Red?"

He smiled. "Not more than once. Not because I'd mind, but that was my father's name. Is, I should say. He's not dead, although he might as well be. Big Red, Big Mike Foley, one of the really great fliers."

A warmth crept into the voice that she had not heard before.

"He was a part of the breed which was to aviation as the astronauts are to the space age. He was of the leather-jacket-and-goggles age. He flew DC2's and DC3's on the mail routes. Later he was on C-47 transports out of Goose Bay during the war. Cargoes, personnel."

He squinted his eyes through the blue smoke.

"Red Foley was a lucky pilot. It was a reputation that made him very uncomfortable. True, he never even dented a prop. But it wasn't true that when you flew with Foley bad weather dissolved and recalcitrant engines sang sweetly for him. It was no mystery. In spite of his rather untrustworthy appearance—sloppy, unshaven, red hair flying in all directions—he was a cautious man, a studious man. Deep down he trusted no one, and he never took anything that flew for granted. And he had guts. Man, he had guts! The stories I've heard about him. Some fellow will come up to me— 'You're Red Foley's kid, huh? Let's have a drink and let me tell you about the time . . .' So it goes."

"Is that why you went into the Army at first?"

He peered at her as though he'd forgotten she existed, and then he chuckled. "Yes. You're right, you know. It's a little hard to be somebody's kid! Although he was a hero to me, and I wanted to fly. Eventually I got around to it. But never in his class. Never!"

"What happened to him? He's still alive, you say."

"He's in a sanitarium in New York—had a stroke a couple of years ago—can't talk." He shook his head miserably. "Funny thing —he'd just got married to this chick—my mother died about ten years ago—can't talk." He shook his head miserably. "Funny thing he was retired. I was afraid that his illness would blow the marriage, but she's with him all the time—loves the guy."

"And that's hard for you to understand."

"Yes. It's tough. The age difference. And before the honeymoon is over he becomes a helpless human being. What kind of a marriage is that for her?"

"I don't think marriage has to be perfect in order for it to work."

"Is yours working?"

The question came suddenly. She wasn't quite prepared for it, but she replied with a shrug.

"Let's put it into your language. Let's say maybe one engine isn't singing quite as sweetly as it should."

"I thought not." He got up, crushing his cigar into a glass ashtray on the table. "Do you want to put these . . ." He waved at the table.

"Let's just blow out the candles and maybe they'll go away. I've got some brandy in the living room if you'd like it."

He followed her, saying, "Thanks, but I'll wait for the beer."

Cora opened the front door; a breeze had risen and it was considerably cooler. She looked out into the darkness, listening for Rafe's car. She was deeply uncomfortable with this man, especially as she was not sure what or how much Rafe had told him.

Now he flung it at her, like a knife. "What have you done to my friend, Cora?"

She whirled around to face him. The words had been softly spoken, but his smile showed he meant to hurt.

Then he held out his hands in apology. "Oh, you must believe me, I'm as confused as you look. I can find no hint of the kind of woman I expected to meet after the few hours I spent with Rafe today."

"What kind of woman?"

He sat back and fished for a cigarette in his shirt pocket. "There is a breed of female, pretty hard for a man to spot, but they're deadly. They consume a man. They emasculate him. For what reason, I don't know. They say it's kind of sex hatred, a desire for power. Maybe it's as simple as the fact that the chase is over, that after marriage a man stops pursuing. I don't know. But Rafe is a different man. He's *less* a man than when I knew him."

Cora frowned and moved over to the chair opposite him. "Is he so changed?"

"Yes. Deeply changed. Oh, I don't mean that Rafe ever was a man to flaunt his virility. Never a scrapper or really very aggressive. I don't mean *that*. But there was a quiet sort of confidence about him, self-sufficient, richly emotional, but hard to upset. Very bookish man. Even on the long marches when we were together, I'd catch a glimpse of him with that damn pack on his back, and he'd be reading some technical book as we went along. I'd ask for a communication. He'd make it and then go right back to the book. I've felt that he was happy in his job here. With his kind of men, talking their kind of esoteric jargon."

Cora persisted. "But in what way does Rafe seem changed? Why do you think it has to do with me?"

"Ah, it's none of my business. Except—that I hate to see a man deteriorate. He's anxious, unsure, he's lost pounds. I understand at the airport that he's pulled some bad goofs. I want to help him, that's all. I wish I were going to be here longer."

Cora was disturbed that Foley had observed something about Rafe that she was unaware of. Outside of the unresolved domestic chill that had settled into their relationship, to her he seemed the same, and she was distressed that their personal problems were affecting his work, his job, and his health, perhaps—but at the same time she felt no compulsion to defend herself, or make any explanations, or even admit that she might have some part in what Captain Foley called his deterioration. Mostly she hated the temptation to say, "What about me?" She wanted no part of the childish competition, the silly game of "Who is suffering more?" For the winner of that game was not necessarily the one who got the most sympathy. Besides, sympathy was not the prize she longed for. Now that she knew, knew for certain that she had passed her own point of no return.

She reached for a cigarette. Foley snapped his lighter to it, and she drew in the smoke. It tasted good. The annoying headaches and faintness, the morning nausea, had disappeared within the last few days. Her last visit to Dr. Titus had been brief, and he had said, "Yes. Yes, indeed. Everything's fine. Quite normal."

"You're not angry with me?"

Cora shook her head, in denial as well as to bring her thoughts back. "Why should I be angry? Have you insulted me, Captain Foley?" She smiled coolly.

"It was my intention. To shock, rather than insult. I apologize. Especially after such hospitality, and such an excellent dinner. As a matter of fact, I'm beginning to feel very badly. I'm on the wrong track entirely somehow. But I *am* disturbed about Rafe. For that, I offer no apology, because I am his friend, and as his friend I claim the right to try to help." He pulled at his chin. "Is there another woman in the picture?" he asked.

Cora laughed. "What is it with you? Why does the culprit have to be a woman? For all you know, maybe he's robbed the bank to pay a gambling debt. There are all sorts of colorful suggestions I might make."

"They wouldn't be any good, Cora. Maybe it's hard for a woman to see, but a man can—can *smell* it. It makes the hair rise on the back of his neck in a combination of fear and contempt. And it's sexual in nature. If there's anything a man is really afraid of it's losing his—his sexual identity."

"I see. And I thank you for your delicacy. Your manners have improved."

"They had to. You're a very subtle, very formidable woman, Cora. For that very reason, you're not entirely off the hook."

She leaned forward. "You know, you're prying, Captain Foley. If Rafe hasn't chosen to discuss his marital difficulties with you, I see no reason why *I* should."

He stiffened slightly. "You're quite right. I'll stop. And please, I'll stay stopped even if you decide to be friendly enough to call me Brian."

"Fine. And now—I'd like to offer you a beer, if I knew where it was. It, and Rafe. He's been gone a long time."

At that moment Rafe's fist smashed into bone and cartilage. His opponent howled and staggered toward him, spurting blood. Then arms and hands detained them both, and Rafe felt himself pushed up against the side of the station wagon, breathing hard, a red veil gradually clearing before his eyes.

Someone was saying, "Hold it, hold it, Rafe. He's drunk. He don't know what he's talkin' about!" The speaker was also drunk, happy drunk, distressed because a little kidding had gone too far.

There were others, there was laughter, there were obscenities, somebody said, "Let 'em fight!" and a woman shrieked.

The bartender from the establishment next to Uncle Dan's came charging out, insisting that they take their fight someplace else or he'd call the sheriff.

The peacemaker opened the door of the car and shoved Rafe into the seat. "Go on, go on, Rafe. You okay? That stupid bastard, runnin' off at the mouth. Shouldn' pay any attenshun to 'im."

The other man, now quite safely restrained by his friends, continued to yell about what he would do the next time he saw Rafe— "You think you can take a poke at me and get away with it . . ." The next time would be the following Monday morning, when, behind the news counter at the airport, he would have only a vague remembrance of the encounter, saying, "Morning, Mr. March," making change for Rafe's copy of the paper, glad that a dark-green visor on his head concealed a pair of purplish eyes and there was a bandage over the bridge of his nose.

On the ten-minute drive back to the house Rafe sucked at his bleeding knuckles, took long breaths to calm himself down, tried to think of what he would tell Cora and Brian, and then got angry all over again.

It was the case of beer that started it. Rafe was carrying it and a cold six-pack across the sidewalk from the market and putting them into the rear of the station wagon when half a dozen of the fellows he knew from the airport came out of the cocktail bar and greeted him jovially.

"Hey, you havin' a party, Rafe?"

"Where ya goin' with that case of beer, man?"

He had smiled and said, "No party—just a house guest. We ran out of beer."

Then Bennie, the news vendor said, "Who's the guest? That big-shot pilot I saw you with, I know!"

Dormeyer, from TWA reservations, said, "Fellow by the name of Foley, isn't it?"

Bennie said, "Whyn'tcha ask us up to meet him? You got enough beer, an' we'll pick up some scotch."

Rafe slammed the rear door of the station wagon and shook his head, smiling. "Not tonight, Bennie—some other time." He tried to move past the group to the front of the car. He had to shove a little, for the men were leaning unsteadily against it, and there were protests.

"Ah, come on, Rafe, there's no place to go in this stinkin' town."

"Whyn'tcha drive us back into Tucson?"

"Nah, I c'n drive. We're all goin' in my car. Wanna come with us, Rafe?"

"No, thanks, I can't. Really, I can't. Captain Foley and my wife are waiting for me."

"Alone!" Bennie hooted.

Rafe, impatient now, tried to open the door, but Bennie blocked him, grinning up into his face. "You better hurry! 'At's why he doesn't want to go with us, fellows, he don't trust his wife!" And even though a warning bell was ringing, Rafe took him by the shoulder and spun him back toward the middle of the sidewalk, with the approving remarks of his companions.

"'At's a hell of a thing to say, Bennie!"

"Cut it out, Bennie, you're drunk!"

Bennie shrieked, "I am not drunk! Everybody knows all about his cute li'l wife!" There was a kind of sudden deadly silence, and Bennie felt he was losing his audience. "Well, what the hell, she got knocked up by a Fuller Brush man, didn't she? Or was it the milkman?"

Had Brian Foley been present he would have altered his opinion of Rafe as a nonaggressive, quiet man. Quiet, perhaps, because he said nothing, simply took two steps in a red fog, with his eyes on the grinning face, and then his fist slammed home.

The sound of pleasant laughter from the living room grated on Rafe's ears as he came into the kitchen. He awkwardly sought the light switch with his elbow. The case of beer was cradled on his forearms, and the six-pack mounted on top underneath his chin. Just as he found it Cora opened the swinging door from the living room, flipping the switch on that wall. So the light went on and off, and Cora laughed and Rafe said "Hey!" and when Cora switched it on again, she said, "'Scuse me!" and laughed, and it sounded like a silly giggle to Rafe, who was in no mood for giggling, silly or otherwise. He said, "What the hell is so funny!"

Brian came through the door, saying jovially, "I'm parched, my good friend. Where the hell have you been?"

Rafe had his back to them, prying off the bottle caps from three of the cold ones. He held one out to Brian. "Here. There's a glass in the cupboard, if you want it."

Brian took the bottle with one hand and caught Rafe's wrist firmly with the other. "What happened to your hand?"

Cora moved quickly to him. "Rafe, you're bleeding, what happened—and, my God, look at your shirt!"

"Looks like you struck a gusher, Rafe," said Brian, leaning against the dining table and putting the bottle to his lips.

"Yeah, I popped the sonofabitch in the nose."

Cora was unbuttoning the shirt, pulling it out of his pants, and Rafe yelled at her, "What are you doin'?"

"Take it off, please. I want to put it into cold water. It's a brand-new shirt and it'll stain." Growling, Rafe submitted.

"There's some Mercurochrome in the medicine closet," she said as she took the shirt out to the laundry tray.

As she passed Brian he looked at her and said, "Nonaggressive!" with a wry smile, and Cora laughed.

Rafe, running water from the faucet over the caked blood on his knuckles, looked around quickly at them and said, "What's the joke?"

Brian studied him for a moment, and then said, "Only a few minutes ago I was telling Cora of your virtues as I remember them."

"My *virtues!*"

"Yes, a nice quiet guy, not the brawling type."

"This wasn't a brawl. The guy was drunk and said something out of line and I popped him, is all." He reached for the beer on the sink and put the bottle to his lips, drinking until it was half empty.

Cora, returning, picked up the remaining bottle, saying, "What was it all about, Rafe? Tell us."

He replied by glaring at her and shouting, "Get a *glass*, Cora! Don't drink it like that out of the bottle. You look like a goddamn tart!"

In the silence that followed, Cora quietly took a glass from the cabinet, poured out the beer, and sat down at the dining table before she sipped it. Her eyes were lowered, her face cold.

Brian was with it. "Something about Cora, huh, Rafe?"

"Yeah."

"Who was it, Rafe? What did he say?" Cora had a pretty good idea by now, and she realized Rafe was trying desperately to recover from anger that went very deep, that had not been relieved by a one-punch fight.

"It was a jerk named Bennie. He has the magazine stand in the waiting room, and frankly I don't think I want to tell you what he said. Okay?"

"Bennie Rousch?" Cora persisted.

"Yeah. You know him?"

"No, I don't. He's Alice Gordon's nephew."

"Who's Alice Gordon?"

"Oh, you know. She runs that small notions shop. I was in there just the other day. Miss Gordon is always going on and on about her nephew, Bennie Rousch, how he isn't really appreciated and so forth; and you just go on listening and pick out your pins and needles or whatever it is. I think Bennie lives with her, and he's 'so good about bringing home his pay——' "

Rafe interrupted, interested now.

"Cora, you weren't *gossiping,* were you?"

"*Gossiping!* You think I'm crazy or something? I was looking at some white wool."

"What *for?*"

Brian, listening quietly, decided it was time he either left the room or reminded them of his presence.

"Look, why don't we adjourn to the living room, where we can all sit down? I sound like the host, but really, why don't we?"

They didn't hear him. Their eyes were locked in quiet combat.

Cora was saying, "White wool. I like to knit."

"Since when? I never saw you knit."

"I used to. I haven't forgotten. It's natural for a woman to want to make some things for——"

"Shut up, Cora!"

Brian rubbed his forehead uncomfortably, tried to get a word in, and gave up.

"I believe it was you who suggested it, if you remember." Cora's own temper had risen at the tone of Rafe's voice.

"*Wasn't* it you?" she said, heading for trouble and not caring. "*Wasn't* it you who suggested I knit some booties for my little bastard?"

Rafe's shoulders dropped, and he muttered, "Oh, Christ!" and flashed a look at Brian.

Cora followed the look, took a deep breath, and said quietly, "Brian is a friend of yours, Rafe. It might be a very good idea for you to cry on his shoulder. Now, I'll tell you what *I'll* do. I'll go to bed, and you can take Brian into the other room where I won't hear you. I don't think he's read the papers, and it might be fine for all of us if you'd fill him in." With considerable dignity, she added, "Good night, Brian. I hope Rafe lets you get some sleep." And then she went out of the door.

For a long time the two men stood silently drinking their beer and smoking.

There was a note of authority in Brian's words when he spoke, a sound of the superior who was accustomed to problems—and to straightening out unproductive behavior.

"Whatever this is all about," he said, "I don't quite know why you have to act like a horse's ass. This petty, niggling, comic-strip-level bickering is ridiculous."

Rafe shook his head miserably. "You don't know, Brian. You don't know what I'm going through."

"Shit! You sound like a self-pitying fag. Now knock it off. If Cora's two-timed you, kick her out, or kill her. Or if you can't do that—why, swallow it. But, buddy, don't you try to cry on my shoulder."

The swinging door whooshed behind him, and Rafe heard Brian shut the door to the bathroom in the other room. He looked around, surveyed the dinner dishes still on the table, and began to carry them over to the sink. He scraped the remains of the food into a colander and turned on the tap to rinse the dishes before putting them into the dishwasher. The water splashed onto his pants, and he reached for one of Cora's aprons from behind the door. He hung the bib around his neck and tied the strings and went on clearing off the table. He got the place tidied up in a few minutes, and he was about to turn on the dishwasher when he realized Brian might want a bath, and there wouldn't be enough hot water. He took a sponge mop from the broom closet and ran it over the floor in front of the sink, and suddenly he realized how he looked. He saw his reflection in the windows, his naked torso partially covered by a dainty, flower-sprigged apron, a mop in his hands, his hair tousled, his heavy eyebrows colliding on his nose. He laughed, and the sound of it was a snort of self-disgust. Deliberately he went about finishing up the job, even though he wanted to tear the apron from his neck, smash something, run, run until he was exhausted.

Everything was put away now. Cora was the kind of cook who cleaned up as she went along, so there was little else to do. He lined up the bottles in the beverage compartment of the refrigerator, took out two of the three remaining cold beers, and flipped off the caps. He removed the apron, reviewing something Brian had said about Cora. He was damned if he'd cry on his friend's shoulder, but he couldn't let that one impression go by without straightening him out.

Brian was sitting up reading by the light of a small Tensor lamp perched on a bookshelf beside the couch. He was wearing pajamas embroidered with two dark-red heraldic dragons rampant on the jacket. As Rafe came in with the beer Brian looked up and said, "Ah, thanks, man!" and then, "How do you like my personal rebellion against uniforms?"

Rafe nodded. "Very sharp," he said absently, giving the dragons only a cursory glance. He pulled up a chair and put his feet up onto the end of the couch. "Sarge," he said, without looking at him, "Cora didn't two-time me. She was raped."

Brian patted the head of first one dragon and then the other. "I think they're rather nice. This one's Huntley and this one's Brinkley." Then he looked at Rafe with very bright blue eyes, took a drink of his beer, and said, "Go on."

After two hours, several trips to the bathroom, and more beer, during which Brian had not said a word, and Rafe had begun to repeat himself, Brian leaned back against the pillows and with his hands clasped behind his head, said, "All right. Now, first of all, I'm not very impressed or shocked by this—ah—enormous tragedy. But that's because it's not me that it happened to. I don't know how I'd feel. I'm damned if I'd let it destroy me."

"What's destroying me, I think, is that I don't know what to do about it."

"Let it happen. As near as I can figure, there isn't much you can do about it now anyway, is there?"

"No. Cora's won, just by doing nothing."

"And you feel this has *reduced* you? Nuts. You just didn't pick the winning team."

"What the hell was I supposed to do? Tell her, 'It's okay with me if you want to have a baby by another guy'?"

"I don't believe she *wanted* to, and I have no opinion on the moral aspects of the case, whether or not she should have had an abortion. I have a feeling if she had, you might have had a more serious problem on your hands. From the few hours I've spent with her, she surprised me. I expected something quite different. She is probably one of those women who, the first time they become pregnant, find that the world about them is relatively unimportant. And you can flap your arms and scream and yell, and nothing disturbs that inner purposeful calm. *Women*, I'm talking about, not those sharp predatory babes who are full of ambition, who are out to prove they can handle a man's world. That kind we can lick, hands down, but not the Cora kind." He laughed softly. "I just hope they never find out."

Rafe said, "If they do, we'd really have a population explosion."

"No, no, that's not the point. Think a minute. What do you love about your wife?"

"I don't know—lots of things. From the first, she seemed like— the other half of me." He blurted it out defiantly, daring Brian to laugh at his sentimentality. Brian didn't laugh.

"You bet. And not the better half, or the weaker half, but the full, individual complement that functions just as strongly as your half."

"You've never married, Sarge. Why not?"

Brian looked up quickly, wondering why Rafe wasn't following his thinking, and then shrugged. "As long as we're full of beer and confidences, I'll tell you. I think my mother died of sheer loneliness for my dad. He was married to flying. Like the old sea captains, he was just never home, and he had a gal in every airport. I'm the same way. I don't want roots. I couldn't stand your kind of life, settled in one place, content in your job."

"It's not dull. Cora and I have a few good friends. We both love the desert."

"That's better."

"What?"

" 'Cora and I.' Defend her, don't fight her. Defend yourselves as a unit. I don't mean that you ought to go around popping creeps like Rousch, or Lousch, or whatever his name is."

"Brian, if the people in this town are gossiping, I want to know about it!"

"And what? Screw the town! It's none of their goddamn business. I know, I know." He waved a hand. "It's easy for me to say screw what people say and then fly off in my shiny fat airplane."

"That's right. We live here."

"That's right." He gave an enormous yawn. "Sorry, kid, I'm beat. Butt out, now will you? Go to bed with your wife. It'll solve a lot of things."

"Yeah. Good night, Brian. Tomorrow's Sunday. Get up when you feel like it. I'm off till Monday. We might go fishing, if you'd like it. There's a place about an hour from here . . ." But Captain Foley was snoring softly.

The light of the morning sun was just beginning to slide down the eastern ranges, slanting in at the living-room windows and promising another day of heat, when Brian Foley walked in quietly on his bare feet, looking for the telephone. The red curls stood up on his head, and there was a pink crease along his cheek where he had slept on it, but he was wide awake and alert. He spotted the phone and then went to close the half-open door to the bedroom. As he reached for the knob he saw the sleeping figures in the gloom, the sheet pulled up halfway over their naked bodies, their arms wound around each other. He pulled the door shut carefully so as not to snap the latch.

He scratched his head and yawned and placed a reverse-charges call to Newport Beach, California. Then he called Tucson International Airport, and as he waited for some information Rafe stuck his head out of the bedroom door.

"What are you doin' up so early, Sarge?"

"Good morning. Sorry, I didn't want to wake you. Hold it a minute. . . . Ten-thirty?" he said to the phone. "What's the flight number? Okay, I'll be there. . . . That's right, Captain Foley, F for Freddie."

"What are you doing?" asked Rafe sleepily, tying the strings of a robe around his middle.

"I'm sorry, I have to leave you. Something's come up."

"Well, Jeez, just like that? I thought you were going to have at least a week."

Brian lighted a cigarette, shook out the match, and said, "There's a girl, her name's Linda, and she's gorgeous."

"Oh. Well, I'm disappointed. I bored the hell out of you last night. I'm sorry."

"No, no, no, Rafe," said Brian almost too emphatically, and went on to explain. "Linda and her husband have a place, a great big ranch or something in Hawaii. She's not nuts about island life, and once in a while she comes over to the mainland to stay with friends in Newport Beach. And—once in a while I give her a call. I just took a chance this morning."

"Sure. Sure, I see."

Rafe turned back into the bedroom, and Brian heard him waking Cora, her exclamation, "What? He's leaving!" and quickly he made his way back to the other room to get showered and dressed.

In spite of his insistence that they go to no trouble, that he could get a cab, that he could get coffee at the airport, and by the time he and Rafe were through arguing about it, Cora had eggs and bacon and hot rolls and coffee ready.

They drove him into Tucson International in the station wagon, making no further protest at his leaving, sticking to the rule of "Speed the parting guest."

As his flight sidled up to the ramp he clapped Rafe on the shoulder. "It was great to see you again, kid. And Cora"—he took her hand with both of his—"thank you. You're a lovely person. Take care, now!"

"Captain Foley, would you care to come aboard now, sir?" asked a young man in uniform.

"Well, I don't know. Depends on who's flying this heap."

"Captain Holsenbeck is our pilot, sir. He told me to tell you he'd be back to see you after we're airborne."

"Fine, fine, and you are . . ."

"Norman Dewitt, co-pilot."

Brian made the introductions to Cora and Rafe. They said good-bye again, and he was saluted and ushered up the steps of the plane. The stewardess smiled broadly, and Brian greeted her and touched the tip of her nose with a forefinger. When he turned to wave at Cora and Rafe, the sun tangled in the braid of his cap and sparkled on the wings of his jacket, and Cora said as she waved and smiled, "Wow! Glamor boy!"

"Yeah. I'd like a cup of coffee. How about you?"

They went into the coffee shop and sat at the counter, watching as the ship lumbered out to the end of the runway.

Cora said, "I was going to ask Terry Ostander for dinner. They'd have made a good combination."

"What do you mean!" Rafe said. "She's a little old for him, isn't she?"

"She'd have amused him. I'm sure they'd have found a lot in common."

Rafe, with his eyes on the ship, said, "It's very peculiar. I didn't know I bored him. We've always been able to talk. I wanted to go fishing today."

"He doesn't know what he missed. Whoever Linda is——"

Rafe turned to her with a quick laugh. "Oh, I'm sure she's a doll—and prettier than a fish—but a guy comes to your house with a big suitcase and hangs up clothes, puts things away in a drawer—looks like he's going to stick around for a while."

"I don't think you should be offended."

"I'm not offended. . . . Wonder why they're using that runway. There's a hell of a crosswind."

"How can you tell?"

"Honey, the dust! It's all blowing out that way towards the grove of paloverde, see?" He watched intently as the plane gathered speed. "Get up, get *up*," he whispered softly. "Boy, I bet Brian's sweatin'. Especially after jets, these things must feel like—oh, boy!" He gripped the edge of the counter and then relaxed as the ship soared up onto the step and began a gentle right turn to the west. "I'd never make it up in traffic," he said. "I'd have a permanent sinking heart."

They made their way back to the station wagon, and the wind blew wisps of hair into Cora's face and ballooned into Rafe's sport shirt. They hurriedly ran up all the windows on the car and turned on the cooler. Rafe drove in silence for a few minutes, watching traffic, looking around at the disappearing horizon.

"You know, Brian's changed a lot."

"Well, so have you probably, but I still say you shouldn't be offended, because it was me he didn't like."

"Why do you say that?"

"And after you had your little confab with him, he liked me even less."

"That's ridiculous. He never said anything that wasn't——"

"I'm sure he didn't. But he's a glamor boy, Rafe."

"Well, I don't know what that means. He's damned attractive, I know that. The thought crossed my mind that you might fall for him."

"I think it crossed his mind, also. And an itty-bitty, quick, non-involving conquest of his friend's dull little country wife would have been just right for his ego. But after your little heart-to-heart last night he probably decided he preferred an atmosphere not so fraught with complications."

"Maybe so. I shouldn't have spilled my guts, but . . ."

"Of course. What's a friend for? I thought it would do you good, and I think it did. He went on a lot to me about being worried about you——"

"He did?"

"But I guess it was just curiosity. There was too much 'I want to help my friend' stuff. People who talk a lot about helping others rarely seem to have time to do any helping. Once his curiosity was satisfied as to what it was all about, Linda and Newport Beach sounded like more fun."

The wind took the car and shook it, and Rafe gripped the wheel. "Boy, we're not going to have any visibility at all in a few minutes."

They were just coming over the rise that led back down into Sabado. On the right was the dismal junk heap of a carwrecking concern. Bits and pieces of metal and plastic covering and leather clattered and spun free in the wind, and a hubcap glistened as it rolled across the road. Rafe applied the brakes to avoid hitting it, the rear wheels locked in the sand, and the car veered around sickeningly as Rafe cursed. There was a screech of metal as the rear bumper hooked into an upright of the chain-link fence that fronted the yard. The car rocked once on two wheels and thudded hard as it righted itself. Rafe turned the key, saying, "You okay, honey? I'm going to take a look." He pushed the door open against the wind and made his way around to the rear to examine the damage.

Cora sat with her eyes closed, shaken, feeling faint. She unfastened the seat belt and touched the button that lowered the window. She felt suffocated, sick. But the wind blew a cloud of sand into her face, and she hastily ran the window up again.

Rafe got back into the car and switched on the engine. "It's amazing—not a scratch except for the bumper. It's pulled loose, but I'm not going to fool with it now. Hey, what's the matter—scare you?"

"No, I'm all right. I wasn't scared. We've skidded on sand before. . . ."

"Cora, you don't look good. Darling?" He took her face in his hands. It was drained of color.

"I'm okay. Let's just get home."

Rafe eased the car back onto the highway and made the drive to the house almost by instinct. The wind was blowing steadily now, the sand obliterating landmarks, drifting across the highway in sheets.

"You want me to help you put the tarp on?" Cora yelled as they got out of the car.

"The hell with it. Let's get into the house."

The house seemed dim and quiet, except for a caterwauling around the eaves. Maxie greeted them with the condescension reserved for people who don't know any better than to be outside in such weather.

Cora reached up to switch off the fan above the sink. "This isn't doing much good," she said.

Rafe looked over as he was going through the door and then stopped. "Cora! Cora, there's blood on the back of your dress!"

She turned around, her eyes wide. "I thought so. I'm having awful cramps." Her hands went to her belly. "I think I'd better lie down." There was a puzzled look on her face, and Rafe made it in time to catch her before she fell. As he lifted her and kicked the door open she mumbled, "You better call Doctor Titus . . ."

It grew dark very early; a somber, dun-colored gloom. The wind had diminished, but still wailed around the windows. The shade of the lamp beside the bed was tipped, and the light shone on a small enamel tray of hypodermic syringes, broken ampules, cotton swabs. There was a sharp odor of alcohol in the air.

Rafe, grateful for something to do, was wringing out cloths from a bowl of cool water to keep on Cora's sweating forehead. The doctor had deliberately given him the little task to occupy him and divert Cora so that he might concentrate on important matters.

The pupils of Cora's eyes were dilated, and they never left Rafe's face. They had both been told not to talk, that Cora must stay as quiet and calm as possible.

"I would like to knock you out," Dr. Titus said, "but I can't because of the baby, see? Hm. Yes. Now please breathe lightly again, through your mouth."

He held a stethoscope on the white skin just below the tanned area on Cora's belly. Her nightgown was tucked around her breasts, and a sheet covered her still-shivering legs.

The doctor listened intently with closed eyes, moving the stethoscope half an inch at a time, finally holding it still. Then he spoke, and his voice was loud, like a deaf person's, because of the instrument plugging his ears. "There it *is!* That's better. Mm hm. Quite clear."

"You want to listen? It's very interesting," he said to Rafe.

"To what?"

"The baby's heart, of course. You're used to isolating sounds you want to hear, aren't you? Hm. Yes. Well. You'll hear quite a lot of . . . static. Ha, Ha! But listen for a ticking, very fast—faint, like a watch, but it's quite strong," he said proudly, as well he might. He had been fighting for that beat, irregular and weakened by deadly contractions, for four hours.

Rafe moved around and stood beside him and put the ear pieces in place as the doctor held the disk pressed to Cora's flesh.

Rafe's eyes widened as he listened to the multitude of loud hissings and gurglings and cracklings, and he said, over the racket, "I wish I had a fine tuner!"

The doctor nodded and moved the disk fractionally. There were more poppings and hissings, and Rafe shook his head, smiling, indicating he couldn't sort it out. Then his smile faded, for vaguely, as though it were at the end of a busy tunnel, he heard an insistent ticking. Immediately his experience blotted out all extraneous sounds, and he concentrated desperately. Static. A voice. A voice echoing out of the skies. Fading. Blurring, clearing. He pressed the ear piece tighter. Luff-dupp, luff-dupp—Mayday, Mayday. There. Now. Clear. "We read you. We read you—five by five!" he said aloud.

He stood up, pulled the instrument loose from his ears, and looked at Cora. "I heard him, darling. I heard him," he said, in wonderment.

Cora smiled; her lips were dry and cracked. "That's good. I'm so glad."

"Now, I'm going to leave you for a while. I'll be back in—" Dr. Titus consulted his watch—"one hour. I want to make sure those contractions don't start up again. I don't think they will. But you *must* stay quiet, Mrs. March. You'll keep her quiet, won't you, Mr. March? Hm. Yes."

He moved into the living room, and Rafe followed him, asking the inevitable question, "Will she be all right now, Doctor?"

"Yes, I think they'll both be all right now. But she'll have to stay in bed—week maybe. Miscarriage from here on in can be very bad business. Very bad sometimes. Lose the mother from bleeding you can't get at except by surgery—too late sometimes—go into shock— *pfft!*"

Rafe shuddered at that casual snap of the fingers. "You'll be back then?" he asked, scared all over again.

"I'll be back, and I won't be far away all night. You stay awake, okay?"

"I will."

"Little brandy and coffee will help that. But keep *her* quiet—mustn't get out of bed. You got a bedpan?"

"I'll find something. What can I give her to eat?"

"She won't want much. Jello, little soup. No coffee or tea or alcohol, naturally. See you later, Mr. March." The door opened and the windy night absorbed him.

Cora basked in the luxury of loving attention—from Rafe and from Constanza, who came to care for the house and to be with Cora while Rafe was at work.

The wind had blown itself out, left the sky brilliant, and brought the first hint of lower temperatures. On the highways campers began to make their appearance, and business picked up in Sabado. Like migrating birds the tourists had a sure instinct for a time and a place where they would be comfortable.

During the week Rafe, after doing some marketing, walked into Alice Gordon's notions shop, looked about him, and felt as though he had stepped into the past. It was a tiny, two-counter affair, with an aisle down the middle and a short stairway leading to living quarters above. There was the musty smell of yard goods arranged in bolts high up on shelves that were reached by a traveling ladder. Under glass cases were spools of thread, embroidery hoops, tatting shuttles, crochet hooks, darners, black- and white-headed pins, tape measures, and other treasures of the needlewoman.

He fingered the pages of a patterns magazine while he waited for Miss Gordon, who had caroled "Just a minute!" from the stairs.

As she appeared, puffing a little, Rafe hesitated. He really didn't know what to ask for. He had not consulted Cora, for he wanted to surprise her. All he could remember was "white wool."

"My wife was in here the other day—Mrs. March—you may remember, she was looking at white wool."

For a second Miss Gordon looked as though she were about to say, "Well, I'll be damned!" except that such words never crossed her careful lips. She certainly did remember. She and her nephew Bennie's girl friend, Amanda McWhorter—such a sweet girl—had had quite a talk about it. It had given her an opportunity as an older woman to impart a few words of advice on some of the less romantic aspects of sex. Nymphomania in particular. Poor Amanda had been shocked—absolutely shocked—Miss Gordon remembered with satisfaction. These young people! They thought the Aunt Alices of the world were some sort of neuter gender, born middle-aged, uninformed, and emotionless. Overindulgence, she explained to Amanda, that was the cause of women becoming as animalistic as men were naturally. Girls should be taught *very early* in life— in that respect she was *quite modern*—of the dangers of yielding completely to the sexual impulse. Even if they found that they enjoyed their husbands' attentions, which, again being very modern in her thinking, she conceded *might* make for a happy marriage, nevertheless it was just as well to restrict such indulgence. Mrs. March was a case in point. You could tell, you could just tell, with those heavy-lidded eyes and that full underlip of hers, that she was—well—*oversexed*. Rape, indeed! If she had been raped, they would have found the scoundrel. Living in that remote part of the area—nearest neighbor was a half mile up the road—it was well known that she walked around in her yard without a stitch of clothing on her back, or anyplace else for that matter, ha, ha! Why, any passing stranger would be bound to take it as an invitation. Men being what they are.

Amanda had listened attentively. Privately, she didn't know just what she would say to Bennie the next time he came to take her for a Sunday-evening drive. It usually ended up in a motel someplace because Bennie was thoughtful enough not to take any chances of being caught in the back seat of a car. And, she thought with a shudder, she liked it. She enjoyed it, but she didn't quite see how she would ever think of any other man but Bennie. And they were going to be married. But if what Aunt Alice said was true, that wouldn't make any difference! It seemed hard to believe such things occurred outside of movies and books. Of course, if a girl had heavy-lidded eyes and a full underlip and beautiful hair and a cute figure—like in the movies—she could understand how it might happen. And there she was, that poor woman, Mrs. March—pregnant by some unknown man. According to Aunt Alice, she apparently had fooled her husband, but she couldn't fool the rest of the town! Aunt Alice had had it straight from Lillian Titus, the wife of the doctor who was taking care of Mrs. March. The doctor also knew there was some reason that Mr. March couldn't have children, probably some injury or something, the poor man.

It hadn't fooled Alice Gordon for a second when Mrs. March came in the other day to pick up a yard of narrow elastic, the quarter inch. She sat on the stool at the counter, leafing through a knitting magazine, and she asked, "Do you have the yarn for this pattern?" and Miss Gordon had showed her that indeed she had, and when Mrs. March said she might make it up for her sister in San Diego, it just made her want to smile.

"White wool?" Rafe repeated, noting Miss Gordon's confusion with deep satisfaction. "Something she wants to make for our baby."

"Oh, the *white!* Yes, for the crib blanket. Well, I think I have the full supply here now. It isn't *exactly* a white. There's the teensiest pinkish tone to it, you can't see it except when——"

"Well, whatever it was she wanted. I want to pick it up now."

"Do you know if she has number eight needles?"

"I don't think so. Look, could you just give me whatever it takes to make it?"

"Of course, Mr. March. Now, here is the sheet with the picture and directions, and let me see. Number three plastic crochet hook for the edging. When do you expect the baby?"

"March."

"Yes, I know your name. I said, when do you expect the baby?"

"In March."

"In March. Oh, isn't that funny, now! Well, I suppose that ought to mean good luck or something!" She went about gathering up skeins of yarn and putting them into a large cardboard box.

"I was born in March also," he volunteered. He wanted dearly to say, "It's a good month for bastards. For lucky bastards," but at the moment he was feeling much too kind. Also a little sorry for her because of Bennie's busted nose.

"Is it going to take all that wool for one little blanket!" he exclaimed.

"Oh, yes. Yes, it calls for sixteen skeins. Of course, if she knits looser than four and a half to one inch there may be a skein or two left over, which she can return, of course. Now, if there's anything else?"

"Not unless you can think of something."

"Well—now, there is something—a new kind of winder. That is, unless you're a very patient person, one who doesn't mind sitting for half an hour with a skein of wool around his thumbs."

This was pretty esoteric for Rafe, and then he remembered from somewhere, and he held his hands out as though he were describing the length of a fish. "You mean this business? While somebody winds it up?" She nodded. "No, thanks, I'll take the winder." She showed him the gadget, and immediately he began to figure how he could wire it up to a small motor, how much current for it to make how many revolutions per minute, and then he said suddenly, "Fine, fine. How much do I owe you?"

There were still heavy blue shadows beneath Cora's eyes, and there was a transparency to her skin, but she was beginning to find the confinement to bed a nuisance. She was restless and bored.

She heard Rafe's car and sighed with relief, murmuring, "There's my darling," and reached for a comb.

He appeared in the doorway with the huge box, grinning. "Think you're going to lie there forever and do nothing, hey? Well, let me tell you, no woman of mine is going to have idle hands. I've just come from a place where they've got all kinds of work for idle hands. And empty heads. God, how women can fuss with this kind of itsy-bitsy stuff." He pulled the string loose and dumped the soft, silky woolen skeins onto the bed.

Cora purred. "Oh, Rafe, how beautiful—for the crib! Honestly, your memory is frightening! And you went to Alice Gordon's for it? What did she have to say?"

"She didn't have anything to say, except I think I gave her something to confuse her. To spoil her gossip."

"What? What did you tell her?" Cora asked with delight.

"Nothing much. She asked and I told her that our baby was going to be born in March. She stuck to the March coincidence, but she heard the 'our' part, that I know."

"Propaganda, that it?"

"Propaganda. I've been spreading it all week. At the garage where I had the car fixed, at the barber shop, at the airport. Very simple. I just talk about it before they do. We had a car accident and my wife nearly lost our baby, and yes, she's doing fine now, and yes, I was damned worried. As simple as that."

"As simple as that," Cora murmured, rubbing her cheek with the wool.

Rafe sat on the edge of the bed. "I know it's a switch. It's hard for me to understand how it happened."

"I just hope you stay feeling this way. It's going to make things a lot easier for me. It was a pretty big price to pay—to lose you—for a child I didn't want."

"Ah, you'd never get rid of me! Not a chance."

"I don't think I'll ever forget the expression on your face when you heard the baby's heart beat. What did you expect to hear? Or didn't you know it had a heart?"

"No. I heard just about what I expected. But you know how— well, say if you've lost something, mislaid something, you'll go back to the room and kind of go through the motions of what you were doing the last time you remember having whatever it is you lost?"

"Sure, I know." Cora nodded. "Association, mnemonics. Like remembering names."

"Well, I don't know. You always haul out a word like that, one that's not in my vocabulary."

Cora laughed. "Oh, for Pete's sake, don't make yourself sound ignorant! You speak a whole language I can't make head or tail of!"

"Now wait a minute, wait a minute. I'm trying to tell you something. It was the earphones. The stethoscope that was like earphones. It hit me the same as when you latch on to a guy who's lost his bearings in the night. And we on the ground know damn well that underneath the dry, repeated signal, he's scared and praying somebody will hear him. Maybe he's got a cabin full of passengers. His instruments have fouled, and he's off course. All kinds of things. And I know that there isn't a man in my business under the circumstances that isn't going to use every skill at his command to get that guy in safe. And what's more"—he laughed with some embarrassment—"we don't give a damn *who* he is, or who his father is!" He placed both hands gently on Cora's belly. "What's his name, Cora?"

"His name is William Reedy March," said Cora, who was blinking hard.

Rafe smiled. "Bill March. Good ole Bill! We'll bring him in!"

Then they both laughed, and Cora put words to what they had both just thought of. "It could be a girl, Rafe!"

"Well, *hell!* Billie March, then." They laughed some more, and then Rafe said, "But I don't think so, no." He stood up, taking one of the skeins of wool into his hands. "It's a guy, I'm sure. You really going to make this stuff into a blanket?"

"Yes, it's easy. And it's going to help me for the next few days while I have to stay in bed."

"Are you going to make anything else?"

"I don't know. Babies don't wear all those fancy knitted things any more. And I'm not that good, anyway."

"We'll have to get the other room fixed up for him. You got any ideas?"

"Have I? You can build shelves and things, can't you?"

"Sure."

"Well, it's very simple. And it won't cost too much. I don't want it to be all pretty-pretty with fluffy curtains and Mother Goose characters and junk."

She went on describing a practical, comfortable room in which to care for a child, and Rafe said he would "bug the place" so they could hear the slightest sound with a flip of a switch.

"I can put an extension out at the swimming pool. I can rig the whole thing myself, and you can hear if he's crying without having to run in in a wet bathing suit."

Cora said, "You aren't a bit superstitious, are you?"

"Why?"

"We've got a long time to go, you know. Lots of things could happen."

"Nothing's going to happen, Cora. I promise you."

She held up her arms and he sat beside her. She buried her face on his shoulder. "If being happy has anything to do with it, nothing will."

Cora was happy. Cora-happy meant Cora-healthy, and that really was what Rafe wanted. He tried to reinforce his feeling of acceptance with every device he could think of, but the heartbeat known as William Reedy March was still the enemy. No longer to be considered either as nonexistent or merely a growth to be excised. Rafe's one headlong plunge into fright and panic, followed by the serenity of acceptance, was not the stuff of daily bread. And though he did his best to promote the image all over town, he himself was not transformed into a proud prospective father.

He tried hard to turn on a light when someone inquired after Cora, but it flickered badly.

Charlie Eldridge hailed him from his car one afternoon, passing him on the highway near the turnoff to "the Mansion," as Sue called their place.

"Come in and have a drink, Rafe. Haven't seen you for a while."

A blazing bougainvillea concealed most of the drabness of the house's stucco exterior; it caught the eye with the same effect that Sue had achieved so successfully indoors. Dead-white walls with a single huge, bright abstract painting, one wall of the kitchen knocked out to make a service bar, a freestanding fireplace, bright scatter rugs on a painted floor, music coming from a built-in unit, changed the conventional boxiness of the dwelling into a warm environment for work, for study, and for conversation.

The usual greeting came from Sue. "Hi, Rafe, good to see you. How's Cora?"

Rafe turned on the light. "Oh, she's fine. She's doing fine, just fine."

Charlie said, "Well, that's just fine. How are you doing, just fine, too?"

Rafe heard it and let the light go out. With these people he didn't have to try so hard. He grinned and said, "I'm okay," and swung a leg over one of the tall rattan stools at the bar. He accepted his drink, a scotch on the rocks. They chatted comfortably for a while, and then Rafe looked at his watch.

Sue said, "Why don't I call Cora and tell her to join us?"

"Thanks, Sue, but I'm tired. I'd rather get on home. If you want to, you could phone her and tell her where I am and that I'm on my way in a minute."

"Will do." Sue left the two men and went into Charlie's study to phone.

Charlie said, "You look beat, Rafe. You having a rough time?"

Rafe swirled the ice cubes in his glass. "The only rough time I'm having is trying to act as though it weren't rough."

Charlie Eldridge kept listening, looking at him through heavy-lensed glasses. Rafe didn't elaborate, just went on rotating the glass. Finally taking a swallow, he said, "I better go, Charlie. I shouldn't hang around people who listen. It's too much of a temptation."

"To what? Talk? Talk's good."

"I'm inclined to feel sorry for myself, Charlie, and I hate that."

"Yeah, that's kind of a waste of time, isn't it? But you can talk *about* feeling sorry for yourself, and that might help."

"I don't know. I tried it not long ago. With a guy I thought was my best friend." He told him of Brian Foley's brief visit. "I really don't know why he acted as he did. It was as though he had been inexcusably bored when he had hoped to have a little fun. I don't know. But I feel as though I talked myself right out of a friendship of long standing."

"Red Foley's son, eh?" Charlie mused. "Red was a great man, Rafe. I know a lot about him. For some reason the greats impose a heavy hand on their offspring—too much to live up to, and they are aware of their comparative mediocrity. It can be painful. I think it quite possible that your friend just plain ran away from too serious a situation. Not consciously probably. But something that made him uncomfortable even to listen to."

"But that's all I wanted. Even Cora understood it. 'Talk to your friend, it might be good for you,' she said."

Charlie shook his head. "No. You picked the wrong audience. I'm dead sure that if he had had the same experience you have been through, he would have lighted out for parts unknown the following day. Let me suggest something to you, Rafe. You might try on a little better opinion of yourself. Both Sue and I admire you a hell of a lot."

Rafe reddened, and he stared at Charlie.

"That's no bull, Rafe. We know what's going on. We know how people lick their lips over misinformation that renders them in some small way superior. But you keep on, going about your job, taking care of your wife, being very much of the man they whisper that you're not. That's tough to do, kid!"

Rafe swallowed the remainder of his drink in one gulp and stood up.

"Sue!" called Charlie, "Hey, Sue! Rafe's leaving." He shook his head. "I think she's gone back to her goddamn pottery wheel. She's been taking lessons from an old Indian woman, and she's up to her hips in adobe mud most of the time."

"Thanks for the drink, Charlie. Heard anything about your book?"

Charlie held up two crossed fingers. "They're considering it."

"Well, that's just great, isn't it?"

"I'm superstitious. It helps me pretend I don't care."

"Well, let me know what happens, will you?"

"You know it. Say hello to Cora for us. Tell her to let us know if she needs us—and you too, Rafe."

"I thank you, Charlie."

Rafe went to his car, whistling a little and saying, "Whatta y'know! Whatta y'know!" Thinking, "I'm not as tired as I thought I was."

Cora was happy. And even though she was aware that some of the people in Sabado had given her the appellation "The March Woman," she carried herself tall and proud, chin up, face serene. All that mattered was what Rafe called her: "Hey, You" or "Honey" or "Fatso." Something in the tone of his voice made her feel warm and contented.

There were those who said she seemed to "flaunt herself." It irritated them to see no sign of guilt or shame; no lowered eyes, just gaiety, making jokes. Jokes! Laughing about it. Sticking her belly out as though she were proud of it!

"You'd better hold the door for me. It's pretty narrow for me *and* these packages. Even for me without the packages, for that matter!" "Uncle Dan, you got any candied ginger?" "Ginger? Candied?" "I could eat a pound of it right now!" "Well, Miz March, I thought ladies usually had a hankerin' for pickles!" "Nope. Candied ginger and black-walnut ice cream."

It was all pretty disgusting. As though—well, as though she'd *enjoyed* it. Enjoyed getting "that way." And elbows dug into ribs in front of the soap-powder shelves, and snickers went into cupped palms.

She placed her market bags into the trunk of the Volkswagen, and removing the heavy sweater she had worn when she left the house, she put it on the front seat. She was about to get into the car when she remembered she had promised Rafe to stop at the hardware and feed store for a Phillips screwdriver.

Rafe was on a temporary night shift, and in the afternoons he was putting in time on his redecorating project of the other room, which was no longer spoken of as "the other room" but as "the nursery." The TV set and the portable bar had been placed in the living room, the couch dismantled, wrapped, and stored in the cabinet next to Rafe's workbench in the carport.

He whistled and swore at his work, and because he was a perfectionist, he was as temperamental as a prima donna. Today it had been the Phillips screwdriver that he had blown up about.

"I keep things right where I can put my hands on them. Now where the hell is it? Just when I need it."

"Maybe you loaned it to somebody, Rafe."

"Why would I loan it to somebody? Everybody has a Phillips screwdriver. You don't borrow something like that!"

"Well, I haven't seen it. I don't even know what it looks like. Can I pick up one when I go into Sabado? Just tell me what size, what to ask for."

He told her and added, "And wear a sweater, it's cold outside. And drive carefully."

The store had a wonderful smell, and while she was waiting for change, she sniffed the odors of grain and leather. She reached into an open sack of wheat, stirred through the grains, and nibbled on their chewy substance.

She said "Thank you" as she received her change and dribbled the coins into her purse. One of them dropped and rolled across the floor toward the rear of the store, and a cowboy in jeans stopped it with his toe and said, "Hey, you shouldn't throw your money around like that!" As he leaned over to pick it up she stared at him

because she had recognized the voice. Quickly she turned, pretending not to have noticed, and hurried out the door.

A half block away she sat at the wheel of her car, the engine running, her eyes on the entrance of the store. She had to be sure, completely sure.

In a few moments the man came out, a heavy sack on his shoulder.
She put the car in gear and moved ahead cautiously, wanting to get
nearer, but not near enough for him to notice her. She could see him
clearly now. He was deeply tanned, and the white-blond hair was
longer now.

He hoisted the sack into the rear of a small black panel truck and
slammed the doors. He stopped to light a cigarette, turning his
profile to her, and if he turned another inch, she was ready to push
the accelerator down to the floor. But he got into the front of the
truck and drove off, and Cora moved into the place he had vacated.

As she went back in, Cora smiled at the clerk and said, "I don't
think I picked up all my change. Did I leave a quarter on the
counter?"

"No, ma'am, you dropped it. Here 'tis. Fellow in here picked it up.
Called to you, but you didn't hear."

"Oh." Cora's voice encouraged him to elaborate. "That's funny."

"Yeah, that fellow from up at Ostander's," he volunteered with
neighborly garrulousness, and Cora stood quietly and listened, knowing she would hear more.

"Durrell, his name is. He trains Mrs. Ostander's show horses. She's
got two boys, you know. They're crazy about riding. Don't see Dave
in here often, of course, he bein' head man. Usually sends in one
of the hands for supplies."

Cora nodded politely, smiled, put the quarter into her purse,
and said, "Well, thanks a lot!" Coughing a little to cover the shaki-
ness in her voice.

Rafe had just lighted a fire in the fireplace when she got home.
There was a fragrance from the burning greasewood twigs he had
used to start it. He had put some coffee on. The house smelled cozy
and warm, and worry and fear had no place in it. She was quiet while
he helped her put away the supplies, and he chattered on about

what he had accomplished, about some glue that had to set before he could sand the pieces, and what did she think about new tile?

"It looks bad where the couch was. You can see the difference, and they've got great stuff nowadays. You don't even have to wax it. . . . Cora? What do you think?" he asked, when she made no comment.

"It's pretty expensive, isn't it?" she said after a moment.

"All right. What's with you? And don't give me that 'nothing' stuff."

"Pour me some coffee first. And let's go in and sit by the fire."

When they were seated in the big chairs that flanked the fireplace, she lighted a cigarette with a steady hand.

"His name is Durrell. He works for Terry Ostander." Rafe didn't need to be told whom she was talking about.

She told him the incident in detail, and she was relieved to see that after the first shock Rafe didn't explode or seem to have any inclination for precipitate action. He shook his head, puzzled.

"I can't figure it. You say it was the same truck? How could it be?"

"There's only one explanation. The police found the wrong truck. Don't you see? If it had been a truck belonging to the Ostander ranch, it would have been traced to Terry—and to Durrell."

"Of course. Now wait a minute. A man by the name of Robinson bought a secondhand black panel truck in Bisbee. He drove here and ditched it—for some reason—and hitched a ride. Now, why wouldn't he have been picked up? They checked every car——"

"Because, mightn't it have been earlier—in the morning maybe—however long it takes to drive from Bisbee?"

Rafe nodded. "And Durrell's been here all the time. Not five miles away. What about Terry?"

"I don't know. It probably never occurred to her. Maybe it's because you never bring anything like that home to yourself. Remember I said he was freshly sunburned? Reddened? That was one of the things that made Gus say he wasn't from around here."

"Might have been newly hired. Eastern. Lives on the place in a bunkhouse, and of course, the truck that was found wasn't hers. So even if she'd given it a moment's thought, it couldn't have been Durrell. . . . There's only one thing."

"What?"

"The ropes. Gus took them with him. I wonder if he's still got them. I'll just bet they'd trace out to the Ostander's barns."

"Probably." They sat quietly and drank their coffee, watching the fire.

Rafe put his hands to his face, rubbing his forehead at the hairline with his fingertips. He muttered, "Goddamn it, both of us had put him out of our thoughts—pushed him out like a nightmare. I'd give my right arm for you not to be so positive. You are sure, I suppose."

"I'm afraid so, Rafe. I made sure it wasn't a trick of the imagination. I wanted to run like hell, but I waited outside the store, up the street, to get another look. I wasn't more than fifty feet away from him—in the sunlight. The store was a little dark. Maybe that's why he didn't recognize me."

"Are you sure he didn't?"

"He didn't *act* as if he did. But that doesn't mean anything. There *was* something. I'm guessing. He took a long time lighting his cigarette. You know, 'Take a good look!'"

"Why would he want you to see him?"

"I don't know, Rafe! I was scared, confused. I was thinking of what he might do if I ran right to the sheriff's office and said, 'This is the man!'"

"He'd say you were crazy. A silly, hysterical, pregnant woman."

She gave a short laugh. "That's about right. My word against his. And I doubt even Gus would support me. 'You're a friend of Terry's. You've been to her house on numerous occasions in the last six months, and you've never seen this man before.' It is peculiar, you know."

"Not really. The corral and barns are a good quarter of a mile away from the house."

"Yes, that's true. You can't even see them from the terrace. That grove of trees around the pond. And I doubt if any of the hands ever comes near the house."

"Well, honey, what do you want to do? What do you want me to do? I think we could nail him. Get Gus to question him, find out where he was that day. There's the pocketknife we found behind the bed. There are the ropes. And I'm sure Terry would help us."

Cora rubbed her forehead. "Oh, Rafe, I don't know! Right now—I don't feel like stirring up things. I don't think I feel up to a hassle. Accusations, denials, courtrooms, newspapers—I don't think I could take it!"

Rafe got up to kick a log back onto the coals, and it sputtered like a firecracker and burst into flame.

"I know what I'd like to do. I'd like to catch him on a dark night and beat the hell out of him."

Cora sighed. "That sure would do a lot of good."

"It would me. It's like a hunger that's never been satisfied."

"Sure, I know. That's why we still have wars. Men and their itchy fists."

"Well, now, Cora," retorted Rafe, wanting to argue, "it's the very essence of maleness. It's the nature of man to fight for what belongs to him, whether it's possessions or ideals. Look at these non-violent kooks! They grow long wavy hair and play a lute like fools in a medieval castle. Mental eunuchs. They're not using reason and intellect to prevent wars; they just want to sit around on their ass and wave a placard with 'protest something' written on it. It takes *men* to get to the moon, it takes *men* to fight if and when it's necessary."

"Oh, I realize that, darling. You don't have to sell me," Cora said in a soft conciliatory tone. Then she added with a smile, "And the symbol of their power, the missile, the rocket—have you ever noticed? —it's almost aggressively phallic in design."

"Cora! Really!"

"What! *You?* Shocked? It's true. Straight up and stiff!" She laughed, and her laugh was a taunt.

He said, "Stop it! You'll give me ideas, and you know we can't do anything about it." He knelt at her feet and put his arms around her hungrily. In a moment he controlled himself and gently put a hand on her bulging form. "How's Bill? Kicking a lot?"

"He never stops, seems like. He wakes me up in the morning, stretching. 'I'm awake, so *you* better wake up.' Which reminds me, I'd better wake up and do something about dinner."

"What are we going to have?"

"You want to barbecue? I've got some ground sirloin."

"Good. I'll start the coals."

After dinner, although the black starry night was chilly, they sat out by the radiant warmth of the charcoal brazier. Rafe had lifted it from the tripod and placed it on the concrete beside the pool. They had put on sweaters and held mugs of mulled wine, which Rafe took great pride in preparing.

They sat quietly, with Maxie on his rug between their chairs. They sipped their wine and yawned loudly.

"Damn!" Cora said.

"Why 'damn'?"

"Oh, I'm still bugged by the thought of Durrell. Wish I'd never seen him."

"Forget him. I don't honestly feel as though we owe society or justice or whatever, anything that might harm you. All *I* care about is you and Bill. To get you both landed safe and well. I'm sure we could stir up something. But I agree with you. In your condition, I don't think you should be exposed to a lot of emotional strain."

Cora shuddered. "The thought of it gives me goose pimples."

Rafe was silent for a long moment. Cora reached out a hand and said, "Now what are those troubled thoughts I hear?"

"It seems a little soft."

" 'Soft'?"

"Yeah, soft! I should be wanting to take action against that man. Do something. Haul him up in front of a judge and say 'This sonof-abitch has got to be punished for what he did to my wife!' I don't feel that way. It bothers me. I'm scared. Oh, not of him, but I'm scared that something might happen to you. Somewhere along the line I got turned to water."

"You? Ho-ho! Now that's a real dandy self-image. If you're building up something like that, it'll wreck you. It's false as hell!"

"You think so?"

"I do indeed. I think that pride is necessary to health. Emotional and physical health. So don't indulge yourself."

"Indulge myself? In what?"

"In that kind of talk. 'I'm scared. I've been turned to water.'"

Rafe smiled in the darkness. He was remembering what Charlie Eldridge had said about having a better opinion of himself. It wasn't easy.

Cora held out her cup. "Can I have a little more? About half?"

"Let me warm it up first. Sure you're not cold?"

"I'm fine. You have to go pretty soon, don't you?"

"Yep. Getting that time. Next week I'll be on day shift. But I have to work Saturday and Sunday."

"Then you'll have Thursday and Friday off, is that it?"

"That's it. What are you going to do all evening? I hate to have you alone at night."

"I won't be alone tonight. The Demings are coming. Maybe we'll play a little gin or something."

"You going to tell them about Durrell?"

Cora shook her head. "No, I don't think so. I know they can be trusted not to repeat anything, but I don't think I should burden them with this. It's a pretty tasty bit, you know. And they're human. And Myra loves a bit of gossip."

They were moving back into the house. Maxie stretched and went off to sniff at the bushes to see if any messages had been left since he last checked.

In the house Cora perched on the edge of the tub while Rafe shaved. He could see her in the mirror and turned around. "Cora, don't."

"Don't what?"

"Don't sit there. It's slippery. Put the lid down and sit on the john, will you? You make me nervous."

"You're interrupting me. I'm telling you what Myra said."

"Okay, go ahead, but sit over there like I told you."

Cora complied. "Now, where was I?"

"You were quoting Myra as saying that somebody had said to her that people in Sabado were very tolerant about you."

"That's it. It was the word 'tolerant' that got her mad. She said she lost a perfectly good sale because she practically went into a lecture about tolerance. She told me that she said in her most smiling sarcasm, 'Well, *isn't* that *nice* of the Sabadoans! To be tolerant, to be so forbearing!' "

"She's right, you know. It's the racist who is tolerant, the Pharisee who says he's clean. But I hope she didn't lose too big a sale. Hey, isn't that the phone?" He turned off the tap so they could hear. "You want to get it, honey?"

Cora went through the bedroom, saying, "Probably Myra—can't come or something."

It wasn't Myra. The pleasant voice on the other end made her catch her breath.

"Terry! How *are* you? I haven't talked to you in ages!"

"Yes, and you ought to be spanked. Why don't you ever come up here? What do you do, sit around in that little shack of yours all day?"

Did Terry know? And what would that mean? Rafe heard the nervous pitch in her voice and appeared at the door, wiping his face with a towel. Cora looked at him, communicating her confusion, and then answered a question of Terry's.

"Oh, I'm feeling great now, thank you. I'd have been up to see you, but the doctor doesn't like me to drive too much. I go into Sabado for my groceries, and that's about it!"

"Well, you know perfectly well that Paul or I will come and get you any time you say," Terry said. "That's what I called about, anyway. Can you and Rafe come up Sunday afternoon for cocktails and a swim? I'm having a few funsy people, the Eldridges—Charlie sold his book, you know——"

"Yes, I heard, isn't it wonderful?"

She went through a small list of congenial people including Professor Liebig and that "nifty-pie illustrator of his, Eleanor Girard. She's going back to New York on Monday, thank God!"

"Why?" Cora laughed. "Competition?"

"You bet! I caught Paul drooling one afternoon when she was lying around here in a bikini."

Cora said, "Wait a minute. Let me talk to Rafe. He's about to take off for work." She covered the mouthpiece. "She wants us for cocktails on Sunday. You think we should go?"

"Tell her we'll come. I think it's a good idea. Tell you why in a minute."

"Fine, Terry. And thank you, Rafe says. We'll be there."

After a few more pleasantries she hung up.

"I thought you had to work Sunday?"

"No, the *following* Sunday. This is fine. I think it's a good idea. We shouldn't change any of our habits, and Terry's a good friend."

"Do you think she knows?"

"Impossible! What makes you think that?"

"I don't know. I've got a funny hunch."

"Cora! You're out of your mind."

"I guess so. But with Durrell up there . . ."

"Why should you be more apt to run into him than you have in the past? We had dinner with her and Paul Holloway up there, when was it? About a month ago?"

"Yes, I know. But I feel different. I'm afraid it will show."

"My darling, you play a very good game of poker—for a woman. If you do happen to see Durrell, you can look through him as though you'd never seen him in your life. I'm sure you can do it."

He went back to get his jacket, and Cora sat thinking, worried. The child gave a throbbing series of kicks below her ribs, and she murmured, "Quiet, Bill, be quiet. Oh, God, I don't know." And then she composed her face into a smile and went in to the bedroom.

"Why doesn't she marry Holloway?" Rafe asked.

"Paul? I don't know as she wants to. She's awfully cagey about guys wanting to marry her for her money."

"For Jack Ostander's money, you mean."

"Yes. He left her every dime. All the property, the livestock, the office building in Tucson. Paul's a fine man, she's lonely and likes being waited on, being adored."

"Funny, he doesn't look like that kind of a guy."

"Oh, I think he pays his way. He's even got his own office at the ranch—handles all the business of the place, besides whatever you have to do about an estate."

"But he was a perfectly respectable lawyer, a friend of Jack's, and after Jack died he just moved in."

"So? It's a big house, Rafe."

Paul Holloway listened to the decibel level of the party with an experienced ear and decided it was going well. There were screams and shouts from the pool; in the paneled bar a dozen people talked loudly about Vietnam, the Government, Civil Rights, and the fishing off Baja. Nobody was listening to anybody. It was a mixed crowd, a shotgun party designed to clean up all entertainment obligations so that the coming holiday season could be started fresh and selective.

Everybody said what a marvelous hostess Terry was, but it was Paul in the role of host and social secretary who engineered it. Somebody had to do something besides make endless phone calls and invite people. He made out guest lists and put them at Terry's elbow, hoping she'd stick to them. He hired the extra help and ordered food and drinks and flowers. And finally greeted people at the door—with the apology, "Terry will be down in a minute," managing to give the impression that she had been working so hard in preparation that she was late in attending to herself. The truth was that she usually had to be reminded that there was a party. "What's all the goddamn noise downstairs? Trucks coming and going, and I wish someone would fix that damn service gate—it bangs!" When he told her, she would say, "Today! Oh, God! Can't we call it off?" After a shower and a bloody mary she would take off for a ride or a drive because she couldn't stand all the hullaballoo.

Today she had been out riding until so late that Paul had begun to bite his nails in exasperation. And not only figuratively. A compact, quiet, self-contained man, Paul Holloway gave the impression of always being in control of a situation. He edited his own speech and came out with few words. No gesture was superfluous; his expression was pleasant and friendly—always. He wore lightly tinted glasses with wide black ear pieces and heavy rims, and they served him as a mask. He put horrible-tasting stuff on the tips of his fingers so he wouldn't forget and spoil the whole picture with his filthy habit of nail-biting. But he usually cheated and left one thumb clean. That way he could hold a cigarette between his two fingers and almost unnoticeably work on the thumb nail.

It helped. It helped the waiting. Jack Ostander had been dead nearly two years now, and Terry regularly promised to marry him—

someday soon. Terry was a disease that Paul had contracted the day he first saw her—a brief meeting in Jack Ostander's office in the capacity of the company lawyer. That was a year or so before Jack's death. They met again in San Francisco quite by accident at the Mark Hopkins. She was on a shopping trip and Paul was on business, and it was the most natural thing in the world to take her to dinner and the opera. And then lunch the next day. And dinner in Chinatown that night. And then *not* to say good night after a nightcap in her room at the Mark. It was exciting and wonderful to find that one wasn't anywhere near being middle-aged. Back in Tucson it was Terry who insisted that she couldn't break it off, that she would tell Jack—someday, that they would be together—someday. And Paul's disgust and self-hatred began when he realized it was the danger, the surreptitiousness, and the almost-getting-caught that excited Terry. She even contrived situations that brought out a dark look of suspicion in Jack's eyes.

Then it was all over—the game, the deception and, Paul guessed, the fun for Terry. For Jack simply slumped over during a board meeting, and he was dead. And to Paul Holloway fell the job of taking over the reins of the Ostander enterprises, temporarily at least. More permanently, the consolation of the widow who seemed for a time to be inconsolable.

Much to his surprise, Terry grieved, loudly and sincerely. She got drunk, and he sat up with her night after night while she told him of how wonderful Jack had been to her and all about the first days of their marriage.

Jack had been in the meat-packing business in Chicago when he met Terry. She was a cocktail waitress at a hotel; Jack had decided that she was too lovely for such a background, and that he was the one to take her out of it. She told Paul how kind Jack had been, how safe he had seemed, how he had taught her everything she knew without ever acknowledging the cultural gap between them in a condescending or hurtful way. He merely thought of it as "lack of information" that could easily be supplied, in books, in contacts with the right people, by traveling, by being curious, and by learning. Terry had been curious all right, and she had learned, and the veneer was thick and shining. She had borne him two boys, and they completed her security.

After the first two years Jack had decided to move to Arizona and raise beef rather than pack it. He loved the desert; it had been his home originally, and now he wanted to build his own place, with horses and cattle, in the land he loved. Jack had been afraid that his wife, as a city-bred girl, would be unhappy, but to his delight she thrived on it. To her it was the easing of pressures and standards of social life. You could have all kinds of people around regardless of who they were. The watchful eyes of Chicago hostesses were lifted. The tight little circle in which they lived had been a great strain. She didn't have to attend lectures and be on committees, things for which she had little taste.

The only drawback was that there were fewer men to acknowledge and pay homage to her dark beauty. As the years went by there were even fewer, and Terry at forty-five had a slim figure, not from discipline but from nerves. Terry's friends thought of her as generous, funny, and warm. But Paul knew that her generosity had a hook in it; while her laughter was hearty, her humor was nil, and her warmth was merely heat.

Paul Holloway carried the two-sided coin with him always. He despised Terry, and he loved her and wanted her to marry him, and he knew he was stupid to think marriage would make him possess her more. The only way to possess Terry was to make himself useful to her, to be available at all times, to provide her with attention and flattery. He was the mediator between her and the boys, for she was inconsistent and unpredictable, at times a tyrant and a penny pincher, and at others, overindulgent. He was nursemaid to her hangovers, chauffeur, bed companion and back scrubber, and responsible for the handling of a fortune. He submitted completely—and bit his nails.

He looked for Terry by the pool after seeing she wasn't in the bar. He was stopped by the bartender, who said they were running low on vodka, and he gave him the key to the liquor closet. He was about to go over and relieve Rafe March, who looked uncomfortable talking to that little bitch, Ellie Girard, when he realized he had been careless in handing over the key to the liquor closet. The fellow was a new man; he had better go and keep him honest.

Ellie was pouting, and Rafe's face was stony. She had him backed into a corner, her arms held wide with a drink in one hand and a cigarette in the other. She was saying, "You just don't care for art, is that it? Of course, my work is not really *art*, you know. I'm really a draftsman, but I have a great appreciation for non-representative painting. To you it just doesn't mean anything, is that it?"

"I think it serves its purpose," said Rafe, squirming, and keeping a lookout for Cora.

"*Your* purpose, perhaps?"

"And yours, I'm sure."

She shrugged elaborately, spilling a little of her drink.

"Dr. Liebig often speaks of you. He said to me, 'I wonder why those two charming young people don't come to see me.'"

"My wife hasn't been too well."

"So I noticed. But isn't that a bit *trying?* I mean, I think it would put you under a terrible emotional strain."

"Nothing I can't handle." Rafe was getting fed up with the silly game.

"I would have been glad to help. Of course, I'm going back to New York tomorrow."

"So I understand."

"And I won't see you again."

To Rafe's relief, Paul Holloway moved in quietly. He removed the cigarette, which was about to burn Ellie's fingers, and dropped it into an ashtray on a table beside them.

"Have a fresh one, Ellie," he said, offering her one from his case. "Menthol—cool you off." He smiled at Rafe, and while holding a match to Ellie's cigarette, he said to him, "How's your wife? I haven't had a chance to talk to her." Ellie sulked.

"Oh, she's fine, thanks, Paul," and his eyes emphasized his gratitude.

"When's the baby due?"

"About three months now."

"That's great, just great."

"I seem to have lost her in this mob. You know where she is?"

"No. Oh, yes, I remember. Terry was taking her upstairs."

Rafe frowned quickly.

Paul said, "Oh, she was all right, don't worry. Probably off to the loo or something."

Ellie was looking with distaste at her menthol cigarette, but Paul, disinclined to offer any more services, spoke to Rafe.

"We've got a new baby too, you know. Skydiver threw her foal yesterday—beautiful chestnut filly. Want to come and have a look?" He glanced at Ellie. "I'm sure you wouldn't be interested, Ellie. You'll excuse us?" He took Rafe's arm and they moved toward the door. "I promised Ray Weeks and Jed Schember I'd take them down. Let's round them up."

Rafe was relieved to be free of Ellie, but he had mixed feelings about going down into Durrell territory. If he saw him, that is, if Paul brought him into the group, he wondered if he could keep from staring, from losing all control and leaping on him like an animal, his hands curled for the throat. He shook his head at the vision and brought his attention back to Paul, who was going on about the bloodlines of the Blue Sky stables. There were Skylark and Skyrocket and Skydiver, three great brood mares, bred only to the finest stallions in the West. Bred for power and speed, blue-ribbon jumpers, all of them. They were going to have a fine turnout in the spring show, Paul was sure.

Stone dolphins formed a leaping arch over a fountain in the cool inner patio; the arch was repeated at the open end toward the mountains, which were now beginning to be touched with salmon pink and shading off into deep-blue shadows. The sound of the fountain echoed pleasantly around walls garlanded with vines. It was too cool and shaded even for guests who might be seeking a quiet place to talk. A flight of steps led to the balcony that ran along the second floor of bedroom suites. They were designed to catch the early morning sun and then heavily curtained against it.

Terry closed the French doors and turned back to Cora, who was standing before a tall antique pier glass.

"From this angle I look like an amphora," she said.

"A what?" asked Terry.

"A jug."

"You look pregnant, that's all—just great," Terry commented absently.

"I love this room, Terry. It's so huge, so quiet. It must be wonderful to sleep here—the sound of the fountain and the odor of jasmine, and the view! You should ask Sue Eldridge to paint it—the way it's framed by the eucalyptus grove, and that little bit of red-tile roof down there." She looked more closely, moving over to the door. "That's a corner of the stables, isn't it? Funny, I never noticed that before."

Terry lighted a cigarette and settled herself in a deep armchair. "Sit down, Cora, put your feet up. I don't think we'll be disturbed. And these walls, as you noticed, are soundproof. We don't have to worry about being overheard."

Cora had a sensation of skin prickles on her neck, but as she turned back she kept her features in order, a pleasant, inquiring smile pasted on her face.

"What are you going to do about it?" asked Terry in a level tone.

"About what?" The question was automatic and inane, she thought; but then she repeated, "About what?" because it suddenly occurred to her that she wanted very much to know why Terry's attitude seemed hostile, threatening.

Terry made a shoo-fly gesture. "Let's skip the cover-up—with me, at least. Dave said he knew you recognized him at Foster's." She laughed. "He said it was so funny. You ran like a scared rabbit, and then outside, you watched him from your car. He drove around the block and saw you'd gone in again, obviously to find out who he was. Must have been a hell of a shock, huh? To find out he'd been up here all the time while you and that western-movie sheriff were scouring the desert? Now, I want to know what you intend to do about it."

"What's it got to do with you, Terry?" There were some wild guesses in her mind.

"I think you know. How come you didn't run right up to me and tell me I was harboring a criminal?"

"I wasn't ready to run and tell anybody."

"When do you expect to be *ready?*"

"I don't know. Rafe is anxious about me, my health. We had

one scare. I was pretty sick." She knew she was floundering in her confusion.

"Did you tell Rafe?"

"Tell him what?"

"That you recognized Dave?"

"Well, of course!"

Terry swore.

Cora waited until the miasma cleared and then said, "Why should it matter so much to you, Terry? Did you cover for him? Is that it? What kind of a story did he tell you?"

"Oh, shut up, will you, for Christ's sake? Let me think."

"Okay. Why don't we talk about this another time? We both should get back to the party."

"Screw the party! Sit still. We've got to talk about it now. I promised."

Cora, knowing Terry, thought perhaps she had become involved out of a misplaced generosity. Maybe Durrell had told her some distorted version of the episode, and because she liked him, or felt sorry for him, had agreed to a cover-up. Everything had gone fine, the whole business had quieted down, and then Durrell made a rare trip into town.

She said to Terry, who had left the soft comfort of the chair to do some pacing, "We don't want any trouble, Terry. It would be pointless now, months after the event. But you'd better tell Dave Durrell that we won't stand still for any crowing on his part, or manufacturing lurid gossip that has nothing to do with the truth. We could still make a lot of trouble."

Terry whipped around to stare at her, and involuntarily Cora leaned back as though expecting a blow. The look on Terry's face was anguished, frightened, full of hatred. She stood trembling, and the two women stared at each other silently. Then Terry regained her poise, and quietly spoke.

"Cora. You listen good, now. You listen good, because I mean every word. If you so much as *peep*—if you identify Dave Durrell as your attacker, as a rapist—whether you can prove it or not, I will kill you and take the consequences."

It was said so quietly, so undramatically that a chill went over Cora because she knew Terry meant it. She made an attempt at unbelief and managed a laugh. "That's a hell of a thing to say, Terry. This is Cora, your friend!"

"Friend, my ass! I mean it. I won't lose that boy!" Tears glittered in her eyes.

Cora screwed up her face. "You're in love with *that*—that kind of an animal?"

"I know all about what kind of an animal he is. Maybe I like it. You wouldn't understand things like that. I know that he likes to hunt. But I've got him hooked with money and a soft life. And I'm going to keep him. Is that clear?"

Cora said, "It's clear. It makes me want to vomit."

Terry waved a hand. "There's the bathroom. Be my guest."

"Does Paul approve of all this?"

"Don't waste your sarcasm on me; you know better. Paul runs the joint. I don't know what I'd do without him. And he loves me. He's not a suspicious man. But I need more than unselfish devotion in my life."

Cora said "Why?" and then wished she hadn't. She was sure a discussion of philosophical values was impossible at this moment. She was right.

Terry gave her a look of pained impatience. "Listen, sweetie, I saw to it that I would have a lifetime of security when I married Jack Ostander, and here it all is." She waved her arm around, presumably to encompass the great house, the land, all that it meant in terms of money. "This is my little blue blanket. But I can't just sit and chew on it."

"But an affair like this—with the risk it involves. I should think you'd be on your way to a nervous breakdown!"

"Of course. You *would* be. You and your ordinary little moral mind! Your meat and potatoes values. You noticed the sound of the fountain and the odor of jasmine, and all it means to you is something to go to sleep by!"

"And to you it's an accompaniment for romance," said Cora with a smile.

"Don't sneer, sweetie. Don't sneer at the trimmings. Paul is often away on trips, or sometimes he stays at his apartment in Tucson to keep up the fiction of separate residence for the boys' sake. And when he does, I shed about twenty years. I come alive. See that candle sconce in the corner by the window?"

Cora looked over at the wrought-iron fixture into which was set a fat white candle halfway burned down.

"When the coast is clear," Terry continued, "I light it. It can be seen from the stables. That's all. It's an invitation. He can come to me if he wants to, or not. He usually does."

"If he isn't out—hunting."

Terry was about to reply with fury, when there was a knock at the door, and she directed her venom toward it instead. "Yes! What the hell is it now?"

A chubby little Mexican girl, big-eyed, dressed in a black and white maid's uniform, opened the door uncertainly.

"Meester Holloway, he say de Congressman Slade, he is here."

"Well, now, that's exciting news, isn't it? I'm thrilled! You tell Mr. Holloway to give him a big hug and a slug of bourbon and branch water. Okay?"

The girl looked puzzled, and then smiled. "*Si, Senora!*"

Terry said quickly, "Wait a minute! What are you going to tell Mr. Holloway?"

"You be down soon."

"'Atta girl, you're really very bright!" She patted the girl's red cheek, gave her a little shove, and closed the door.

Cora had risen and picked up her handbag, but Terry waved a hand like an order to a hound. "Down girl. Just sit down. I'm not finished. I want to set you straight on a few things."

Cora said firmly, "I don't want to hear any more about it. I've got the idea. You don't want your boy friend sent to jail. I can't make any promises. Rafe has done a magnificent job of staying sane during all this, but I'll have to go along with whatever he does, whatever he wants."

"You tell him what I told you. He'll think twice before shooting off his mouth!"

"I'd go slow, Terry, if I were you. Nobody likes threats."

"That's the point, you idiot. Don't you understand? It's me that's threatened!"

"What do you mean?"

"You might not be able to prove a thing, but you could make a hell of a stink. Dave wants it spelled out for him. He wants everything nice and cozy and reassuring, or he'll cut out. He told me, he said, 'I'm tired of ducking that dame on the streets of Sabado. Who the hell ever thought she'd come into a feed store?' You don't know what it's like, Cora, trying to hang on to a guy like that. It's like being blackmailed." She put shaking hands over her face for a moment, pressing at her cheeks until they were distorted. "I'm hooked. If he leaves, I'd have to follow him no matter where he goes. I'm telling you, Cora, don't do anything. Don't scare him off. That's what I'm afraid of—of having to live without him."

She got up and went to her dressing table to repair her makeup. Cursing under her breath, she dabbed some lotion on a pad of cotton and wiped off mascara, and then with a small brush she re-applied her makeup. Finally, she took a deep breath and looked at Cora and laughed. "You oughtta see your face!"

"I was just remembering something. You invited me up here to stay at the house with you. I thought it was generous and kind of you. What if I'd accepted?"

"You'd never have laid eyes on Dave, believe me. This is a big place. It would have been an amusing idea." She shrugged. "You see, as soon as they found the wrong truck, we were in the clear. God, that was funny! I even called up that hick cop, what's his name, Gus Boyd, and offered the help of 'my man, Durrell,' which he declined with thanks. My kids were begging to do some sleuthing, and Boyd let them help in the search on their motor bikes." She went on laughing at the joke.

Cora's hands were clasped tightly in her lap, and she said, "Did you think it was funny, what had happened to me?"

Terry gave her a level look. "In a way, yes. A bitter-funny way. You see, he'd only been out here a couple of weeks. And I hadn't been able to—ah—fulfill a promise I had made to him last spring. The kids were just home from school, Paul was floating around, and there just hadn't been an opportunity for us. He was keyed up and sore at me. When he told me—that awful afternoon—what had happened"—she crushed her cigarette out in an ashtray and went on crushing it even after the coal was out—"we were down in the tack room, and I was crying and cussing him and saying why didn't he go to one of the houses around here, that I could have understood that, and he said he didn't like that kind of a whore."

"Where in the world did you pick him up, Terry?"

"I didn't 'pick him up,'" she answered heatedly, and then laughed. "Well, maybe I did, at that. Except that it was in the house of friends." She started pacing again, her arms folded, hugging the memory. "It was at one of those big hunt meets on Long Island, where all the horsey people get together—pink coats and hounds, the whole bit. Lots of people from ole Virginny, some from England. A big excuse to drink and eat and get your neck broken. Dave was hanging around. I think he'd crashed the party, for he wasn't riding, even though he looked very dashing in jodhpurs. I saw him at the bar, and he was trying to mix one of those Black Velvet things. He wasn't pouring it slowly enough, and the stuff was foaming up like soapsuds. I took one look at him and decided I'd rather help him mix Black Velvets than ride. I waltzed up to him, *exuding* charm, and I said, 'You've got to pour the stout into the champagne, you know.' 'No,' he said, 'it's the other way around,' and I said, 'Are you sure?' and he looked at me—and man, that was it." She turned away from Cora and went to the bed table. Picking up another cigarette, she puffed at it until it looked as though it would burst into flame.

"Anyway," she went on, "I found out he was a trainer, that he was broke and looking for a job. I asked him if he'd like to come out west, that I had a few show horses and did some breeding, and he said, 'I think I could satisfy you.' And I said, 'I'm sure you could,' and we laughed like hell."

Cora shifted uncomfortably in her chair. Powder-room confessions always embarrassed her, and she had the feeling that Terry might go on to more intimate revelations.

"Well, that's fine, Terry. So you had a little fling, but well, haven't you looked ahead at all? The situation is preposterous. The man's a creep."

Terry shook her head and squeezed her eyelids shut. "I don't want to look ahead—not any further than the next time I hear him coming up those steps from the patio and walking through that door and into my bed. And I want to see him smiling and eager, and you'd just better not louse it up."

Cora laughed softly. "I don't have to louse it up, Terry. You know the answers."

"I know. I *have* looked in the mirror lately."

"I didn't mean that. You're an attractive woman. You're attractive enough to do better than Durrell."

"You don't understand at all, do you? You don't understand how two people, regardless of age or social position——"

"Can be made for each other! Oh, spare me, Terry!" She got up and walked to the window, and they said nothing for a moment. The fountain below chuckled in the silence.

Terry said finally, "Anyway, it's me that'll do the kicking-out. When I'm tired of him."

"You're not very consistent, Terry. One minute you're going to follow Dave Durrell to the ends of the earth, and the next——"

"All of that's none of your goddamn business! I asked you up here to tell you something. Now, I've told you. I don't think I can make it any clearer, and you'd better read it like it is, or it means your goddamn hide. Nothing else concerns you!" Her voice was getting loud and shrill.

"Nor you, apparently."

"What do you mean?"

"Have you thought about anyone else but yourself?"

"Don't moralize to me, Cora. This is beyond morals. You wouldn't understand that, of course."

"No, I wouldn't. I think I'd consider my children, anyway."

"Do you think a drug addict moralizes about his needs? Oh, he may give it a fleeting, remorseful thought, but it's pretty pale stuff."

"Your boys, their life, their future, is 'pale stuff'?"

"Can't I get it through your head that I *know* I'm wrong? I know I'm a sex-starved middle-aged bitch; I *know* I must seem pathetic to you; I know that my hold over Dave is only good so long as he's safe, but I also know I'm absolutely helpless. I'm hooked on this man, like I've never been hooked before. As far as I'm concerned, he *invented* sex, and nothing, but nothing else, matters to me."

She was pacing around the room in long strides, her hands on her hips. Cora sat motionless, concentrating on the gentle sounds of the fountain, waiting for the storm to subside. Finally, Terry swung around to face her.

"Well, say something, goddamn it! Don't just sit there like a goddamn fat Buddha with your hands on your fat belly!"

"What do you want me to say, Terry? And I think you'd better hold it down. I'm not sure you can't be heard in the patio."

That took Terry out of her pacing circle, and she strode over to the windows and flung them open. She stepped out onto the balcony and looked over the railing. "There's nobody there," she said, coming back into the room. Then she stopped. "Wait a minute." Returning to the balcony, she called out, "Paul?" Below, there was a door to the living room that was open, and curtains moved in the air. She raised her voice. "Paul?" He appeared at the door.

"Yes, my love?" he called back. "Are you going to stay up there all afternoon? Some people are leaving. You should come down."

"In a minute, Paul," Terry replied, and came back into the room again, looking worried. "I hope to God he wasn't out there all this time. He moves around like a cat. Always appearing over my shoulder—gives me the creeps."

Distractedly, she picked up a comb from the dressing table and ran it through the black mane of her hair. She gave a small shake to her head so that a few locks fell forward on one side. Then she placed black, goggle-like glasses over her eyes and turned around with a smile.

"Now, then," she said, as though she were soothing a naughty child, "you don't have any intention of talking to our friend Gus, do you, darling?"

Cora smiled back. "To our 'western-movie sheriff'?" Then she said seriously, "I don't know if I have the legal right to keep quiet, Terry."

"Nuts. You not only have the right, but you'd better keep your mouth shut, especially if you consented to the act." She gave a laugh that was more of a yip. "I think that's what they call it, isn't it?"

"Rafe knows I didn't consent."

"Oh, you mean, if you *don't* accuse Dave, Rafe may think you're keeping quiet because you *did* consent. Well, now, that's an angle that hadn't occurred to me!"

"No, no, no. I don't mean that!" Firmly she kept herself from telling Terry the unpleasant details. The memory of Rafe's face when he first saw her came into her mind, how he cut her loose and washed off the blood. "Rafe knows what happened," she said dully. "Terry, I don't know that I could *ever* talk about it. You can tell that to your boy friend, can't you? Maybe that's enough to satisfy him."

"I doubt it," Terry said carefully, "because I'm not sure it's true."

There was a knock at the door.

"Come in, damn it."

Paul came in the door, which she yanked open. "What's keeping you, Terry?" he said with irritation. "You must come downstairs!"

"My little friend Cora here has a problem," she said confidingly. "She wanted some help. I'm *sorry!* But I think we're all right now, aren't we, darling?"

Cora had risen. "We sure are," she said, smiling at Paul as she passed him and went out in the direction of the staircase.

It was a long fifteen minutes before she could locate Rafe. He wasn't out at the pool, but she had to stop and talk with several people, refuse a drink, refuse to "come and sit here with us." It takes time to say "No" pleasantly, to answer, "Oh, you're not leaving so soon!" At her question, someone said they had seen Rafe in the bar. She was getting very tired.

In the smoke-heavy atmosphere of the dark-paneled game room and bar she found Rafe deep in a poker game with three of the richest ranchers in the area, and she wondered what he was using for money.

She put her hands on his shoulders and he looked up, his mind on the cards. "Hi, honey. I'm showing these guys how the game is played."

She leaned over and whispered, "I've had it. Let's go."

"You'll just have to wait, honey. I'm ahead, can't you see?"

She pulled up a small chair and sat near him. Somebody put a drink into her hand, and she said, "Thanks, I need that." She took a big swallow.

Rafe snapped his head around to look at her. His lips formed, "You okay?" over the hubbub, and she shook her head. He turned back to the men at the table.

"I know I shouldn't, but my wife . . ." The ranchers were gallant and understanding. "We'll get you next time, Rafe." "You go right ahead, your little lady looks a bit peaked." Somebody volunteered to play out his hand, and they said their good-byes and made their way from the room.

In the hall, Rafe said, "We should find Terry."

Cora picked up her shawl from the back of the tall mahogany chair where she had deposited it. It was a modified rebozo, of dark-blue wool, and she wrapped it around her shoulders with a slight shiver. "We don't have to find Terry. I said we were going."

Rafe said, "Here's Paul. . . . Sorry, we have to get home, Paul. It's been a very nice afternoon."

Cora held out her hand to the little man, with a new feeling, wondering why she had always thought of him as a "little man." He was quite average in height and weight, but he was colorless. His hair was sparse and gray-streaked. He affected a well-trimmed, thin mustache, which followed the outline of his upper lip, and he had a look of fastidiousness. No one ever saw him in a bathing suit; he wore thin tropical linen suits, and if he was without a tie, he wore a knotted scarf.

"I'm sorry I kept Terry so long, Paul. It was all my fault."

"Why, that's perfectly all right, Cora, my dear. I thought she'd gone off to take a nap. She's like that, you know. Gets bored and leaves the party to me." He patted her hand, and for the first time Cora noticed the nails were bitten to the quick, and she realized this was a man in hell.

"She could do worse, you know, Paul." She smiled into his eyes. "Terry's parties are always beautiful, and I know why."

Paul stopped just this side of being phony-modest, and said instead, "Thank you, Cora. You sure you won't stay for supper? Maybe you don't like venison, though. We've had it in the freezer since the hunt last season up north. The chef is fixing it sweet and sour, like sauerbraten. It should be magnificent."

Rafe looked as though he would like to stay. "Sounds wonderful," he said.

Firmly Cora wrapped the shawl around her and said, "It does, but thank you, no, Paul. And stop drooling, Rafe!" They all laughed and said good-byes, and Cora and Rafe after some trouble extricated their station wagon from the parking area.

When they were finally out upon the road that led down to the highway, Rafe settled back and said, "Well, I had a good time, much better than I expected." He looked at Cora's profile in the fading light. "You're tired, aren't you, honey? Wasn't so bad, though, was it? I went down to the stables with Paul and Ray Weeks and Jed Schember to see the new foal. And I didn't see anybody that could have been Dave Durrell. Couple of colored boys walking some horses in the corral. Then there was a very old geezer with whiskers and a Mexican boy carrying water. You should have seen that foal, honey— great big brown eyes and long toothpick legs."

The encounter with Terry seemed almost too melodramatic and fantastic for Cora to know how to begin to tell Rafe. For tell him she would, no matter if Terry thought she was idiotic.

"Rafe, I'm curious," she said finally, interrupting his description of beautiful horseflesh. "How do you think of Terry? I mean, we've known her a long time. If you had to tell someone about her, what would you say?"

Rafe thought a moment. "Gee, I don't know. Well, let's see. She's attractive. Works at it a little too hard. Tries to show how much she's 'with it.' Dresses too young. You know, that long hairdo, for instance. Doesn't go with a neck that's getting scrawny. She's got a nice body—athletic, trim. She's very easy to talk to—I don't know! What are you after?"

"Would you say she was, well, oversexed?"

"Oh, honey, I wouldn't know about that!" He laughed.

"I don't mean like, well, like Ellie Girard, for instance."

Rafe made no comment. He didn't care to get on the subject of Ellie Girard.

"I mean the real, highly sexed kind, that's got to be involved in some elaborate, dangerous love affair, for kicks, for constant sex."

"Me, I'm a country boy. I've never run across that kind. Only in books. My wife is sexy enough to suit me." He put an arm around her shoulders and pulled her over closer to him.

Cora put her head on his shoulder. It felt so safe, so good, so *normal*. She murmured, "Do you think she could kill anybody?"

"No, of course not. . . . What!" He withdrew his arm, pushing her away from him so he could see her face. "What in the hell are you getting at?"

Cora told him what she was getting at, interrupted by comments of disbelief and astonishment, and questions about Terry's state of, or lack of, sobriety.

"I believed her, Rafe. And I'm sure you would have, too."

"But a guy like that!"

"Can't tell, maybe he's her Heathcliff. Women are apt to get romantic around that time. They figure it's almost over for them. In a few years men start looking through them instead of at them."

"Maybe she's just got to cheat. Maybe that's her idea of fun. She cheated on Jack with Paul Holloway. Now she's cheating on Paul with this one."

"Well, whatever it is, if we do anything to scare off Durrell, she's going to make some kind of trouble with me."

"I don't believe it, I just don't. Terry's been a good friend. But I'm like you, I sure as hell don't like threats. You know what we ought to do?" asked Rafe.

"Yes, go right to Gus Boyd and tell him the whole deal."

"It wouldn't necessarily mean you had to prefer charges, you know."

Cora drew the shawl tighter around her shoulders and shivered.

"Oh, Rafe, I don't know," she said wearily. "It's in the past. I wish it would stay there. And I'm not too crazy about the idea of one more person knowing who Durrell is. This town—things get around."

"Not with Gus."

"Oh, I don't know. Gus has a deputy who's got a girl probably.

And Gus has a wife who knows everybody in town. Nope. It's not for me. Not because Terry said she'd kill me, either."

"Terry's not about to kill you or anybody else, honey. So put that out of your mind."

"You mean you don't think she'd show up at our front door with a pearl-handled weapon and pump a few slugs into me?" Cora laughed, and Rafe joined in.

"Let's forget it! And now that you talked us out of a good venison dinner, what have you to offer in its place, my lovely?"

"Chops."

"Chops! What kind? Pork, lamb, veal?"

"Hey, I've got some veal in the freezer. How about some veal parmagiana as a consolation?"

"You're wonderful. But it's frozen."

"Won't take long. Has to be pounded and stuff."

Rafe put an arm around her. "Tell me honestly, now——"

"Keep your eyes on the road, Rafe!"

"I am. How do you feel? Did you get very upset? Did it bother you a lot?"

"Well, it did, yes. She scared me, the way she looked. And I got caught up into the emotional attitude. She was screaming at me. I thought sure somebody would hear her. I've always felt I was pretty easy-going in my speech, but you should have heard the stuff she spouted. Genuine waterfront."

"You should have belted her."

Cora laughed. "That's what I like about my man!" They were turning into their driveway, and Cora, looking at the house, sighed happily. "Ah, dear little grass shack, dear little gray home in the west, you're so corny and sweet and square, I just adore you, don't you, Rafe? Don't you think it's nicer than that great big place of Terry's?"

"Yeah. From a distance it always reminds me of a desert outpost of the French Legion. All they need is the tricolor flying from the roof."

That reminded Cora of the location of Terry's bedroom. "Hey, did I tell you," she said as they got out of the car, "did I tell you how she lets her boy friend know that the coast is clear?"

"Don't tell me she hauls up a flag!"

"Honey, you won't believe this! She lights a candle in the window!"

"You're kidding!"

They both exploded into laughter and lewd remarks, and they were still giggling when they reached the kitchen and heard the phone ringing.

"I'll get it, I'll get it. You feed Maxie, I bet he's starved." And Cora, wiping tears from her eyes, picked up the phone and said gaily, "Hello, hello!"

"Cora?"

"Yes, who's this?" There was a long silence and the sound of heavy breathing. "Hello?"

"Cora?"

"Yes, this is Cora March."

"It's Terry."

"Yes, Terry," she answered, and Rafe appeared instantly at the kitchen door. To him she said, "She's plastered. . . . I'm here, Terry, what do you want?"

"Djoo tell Rafe?"

"Yes, I did. I told you I was going to."

"You are an utter poop, aren't you! If you were a fire hydrant, I'd pee all over you. You're so icky, so town-of-Sabado and environs."

Cora held the phone away from her head and looked at Rafe. "No sense at all!" He leaned over her shoulder so he could listen.

"I just want to reiterate"—there was considerable difficulty with the word, which had to be repeated syllable by syllable before it would come out right—"that . . . I wasn't kidding. I wasn't drunk when I talked to you. I had had one shot of cognac, my best cognac, I mean Jack Ostander's best cognac, out of a beautiful cobwebby bottle. I always have a shot of cognac before an interview. Not because I need any Dutch courage, you unnerstand? But so I can blow expensive breath at shits like you."

"Terry, where are you telephoning from? Where are all your guests?"

"Where am I? I'm in my li'l workshop, honey! Lying *flat* on my great big king-size workbench. My guests are stuffing themselves under the superior guidance of Mr. Paul Holl'way. That answer your question?"

"Yes, Terry. You just get some rest, now. I have to go and get Rafe's dinner. I'll call you tomorrow, shall I?"

"No. You don' call me. I'll call you. An' I intend to keep calling you. You know what a shiv is, darlin'? I gotta shiv. A lovely thing. It's one of those pretty things you press a button—and blip!—there it is, all ready to sever a car—car—carotid artery. Read it like it is, baby. You dig?"

"Yes, I dig, Terry," said Cora in a soothing tone. "I'll talk to you soon. You call me whenever you want to, okay?"

"I don't intend to *call* you!" She suddenly burst into loud sobbing, and over it Cora could barely make out the sense of her words. ". . . why did you have to? It's my darling's baby you got in your belly. What do you want with his baby? I swear to Christ I'll kill you. If you make Dave nervous, I'll kill you, so help me."

Rafe took the phone from her.

"Terry, this is Rafe," he said. "I want you to listen to me!" But all he heard was a sound of weeping and the phone being cut off.

He cradled the phone, and they stood looking at each other.

"Scary, isn't she?" Cora pushed a strand of hair back from her damp forehead.

"She's drunk! I don't like this. I don't like it at all." Rafe walked around clenching and unclenching his fists, the black brows crowding the bridge of his nose. "I don't like having you upset. I don't like to think what that dame might do when she's drinking."

"Wonder if Paul could do anything," Cora said, remembering the bitten nails, the eyes that betrayed suffering behind a facade of sweet cordiality. "I bet he knows more than Terry thinks he knows. He's a lawyer."

"Well, what's that got to do with it? Why drag him into it? You know perfectly well he would say that if we've got a complaint, we should file it with the district attorney."

"I don't know. I just think lawyers are people who are supposed to act unemotionally, logically. Of course, if he *doesn't* know, it would hurt him, and he looks to me like a man that just couldn't take one more hurt."

Cora moved out into the kitchen, leaving Rafe lost in thought, sitting on the arm of the couch. She went into the laundry area where the big freezer stood, opened the lid and leaned over, pushing packages aside until she found the veal she was looking for. Because of her increased girth, it was difficult and she breathed heavily, and the child responded with a few adjustments of its own. She put her hands on the quaking surface of her body, saying, "Poor little bastard. Everybody wants you dead!"

"Who you talking to?" called Rafe from the living room.

"To Bill, who else?"

He came out into the kitchen and leaned against the frame of the doorway. Cora glanced at him as she went on with her preparations.

Finally she said, "Go on, think out loud."

"I'm wondering," he responded, "just how safe it is to say, 'Oh, Terry's drunk, she'll forget all about it in the morning'—things like that. She and Durrell might easily have some kind of a spat and then she'd blame it on you, fortify herself with a few drinks, and waltz down here with that shiv in her handbag. I don't know about you, but I'm not sure I want to live with that kind of suspense."

"I don't like it either." She had been running water over the small package, and was now trying to separate the thin slices of meat. "Funny."

"What's funny?"

"Oh, how we live in an era in which the whole world is anxious, threatened, uneasy. But for real kicks it's the immediacy of the one-to-one relationship, the thought of one silly, menopause-Minnie with a knife in her hand just outside your door that packs the wallop."

"Well"—Rafe scratched his head—"I'll tell you. Soon as we finish dinner, I'll call Gus and ask him to stop by, that we want his advice on something. Maybe he can offer protection or *something*, without taking any official action. Just as a friend."

Cora wrinkled her face in distaste and disagreement.

"Oh, Rafe, let's not! Let's take the chance. People are tired of gossiping about me. It's become a 'who cares?' kind of item. I don't want to stir things up again. Oh, damn it!" She sat down hard onto one of the dining-alcove chairs, overcome by tears.

"Honey!" Rafe went to his knees in front of her, his hands firmly on her shoulders.

"It's nothing, darling, it's just pregnancy tears. They're hard to hold back. I just want to have my baby in peace and quiet. I wish we could take a trip. No, I don't. I don't want to have to run away. I don't want to be scared or threatened, I just want a little peace!"

"You'll get it, goddamn it, you'll get it! Now, how 'bout that parmagiana you promised me? And shall I open a bottle of Chianti?" He got to his feet, went over and opened a drawer, and picked up a small wooden mallet. "Here, take this," he said. "Now get up there and pound the hell out of that veal. Do you good."

Rafe provided the peace he promised Cora. The surface was combed and straightened and patted into place, but he raged inwardly as he went around securing windows with new locks and putting a chain on the front door. He called Myra Deming and Sue Eldridge and suggested they make a point of spending time with Cora because, he told them individually, "She's been pretty nervous lately. I worry about her being alone." And for sheer luxury he arranged for Constanza to come daily, for four hours, so Cora could have breakfast in bed.

But it was all he could do. As long as he chose to stand still. During his drives to and from work, the only times when he was actually alone, he fretted and fumed, his thoughts bursting into words. "How long can I take it!" For months he had been frozen, immobilized into a do-nothing agony. "My wife is raped, and I stand still and watch while others go after the man with the gun I should be holding." Cora comes home and informs him as to the identity of her assailant, "And what do I do? I go to a party where the guy hangs out, and I get nervous for fear I might run into him." Not in fear for his own safety, but for its consequences, for what it might do to Cora. And now this. "This—this *tramp*—saying she'll take a knife to my girl, and I go around locking the doors." Oh, it was kind of Charlie Eldridge to say he was being a man by minding his own business, by taking care of his wife, by doing the right thing. Action might be wrong action, so better take no action. Maybe it was his Latin background. He saw himself sitting against a wall with his arms folded, a serape around his shoulders and a sombrero pulled down over his eyes. The image disgusted him. It was Latin, too, to have a knife concealed under that serape, with fingers curled around it, ready to—to what? For Christ's sake! Was he unable to do anything except indulge in a boy's daydreams?

He took it out on the car, pushing down on the accelerator till the needle touched ninety, and then braking hard, pulling over to the side of the road, lighting a cigarette with shaking fingers, trying forcibly to put his mind on the day's work ahead. But his mind refused to take orders and continued to hop around in the exciting, kaleidoscopic field of colorful, desirable, unattainable goals. He fiddled with the knobs on the instrument panel, pulled out the one that turned on the window-washer, watched as it piddled on the glass, then turned on the wipers. That left the rest of the windshield in a dusty contrast, so he got out and with a wad of paper toweling wiped off the rest.

What did he want anyway? Was it to be a hero? To be approved? He Walter Mitty-ed his way into listening to dramatic conversation.

"My God, Rafe, if we hadn't stopped you, you'd have killed him!" (Gus)

"So you're Dave Durrell. I think you and I have something to settle!"

"Take it easy, Rafe. I'll handle this, legally." (Paul)

"Rafe, forgive me. I never meant it. I was drunk!" (Terry)

"Not that one, Rafael! It's too far out. You'll fall!" (Sister Agatha)

Sister Agatha! Clear and sweet came the memory, full of the smell of ripening apples and burning leaves, the feel of rough bark on bare legs. The wind swaying a branch, sickeningly, as he groped for the bright golden apple, Sister Agatha's face upturned beneath him, holding out the folds of her habit like an apron. He could feel himself grin in seven-year-old triumph as his fingers clasped the yellow fruit, gave a little twist, and tossed it down. He cautiously slid back along the branch, reached the trunk, swung on a lower branch like a trapeze, and let himself drop. It was a bigger drop than he anticipated, and the thud shook his bones all the way up to his skull, but Sister Agatha was smiling, saying how smart he was, how brave, how proud she was of him, and that they would have beautiful pies for supper. Then as they walked back to the kitchen together she lectured him gently, "You must learn to be more cautious, Rafael. Nobody gives medals for prudence, but most of the time it is the wiser thing. You must learn that." He had barely listened, trudging along in a dream, clutching one fold of her habit with a sweaty, sticky hand, looking worshipfully up at her face, which appeared and disappeared like a white cameo behind the headgear.

"The wiser thing," he said aloud. "Well, I've learned it, Sister. Maybe you'd be proud of me now. I'm not. I'm not proud of me at all. I'm a male that's not a man. Maybe I'm not even a male." He switched on the engine, holding down the accelerator, making it roar, drowning his thoughts in sheer noise.

A few days before Christmas Myra Deming came by the house, bearing gifts and gossip.

Cora was alone, straightening up after Constanza, who had left for the day.

"She has a genius for putting things back where I can't find them," she told Myra.

"Getting a little fussy, girl?"

"Oh, no, I'm not a pernickety housewife. She puts the soap powder up on the same shelf with the cereals, and——"

"'Pernickety'! I haven't heard that word since I don't know when!"

Cora laughed. "It was a favorite of my mother's. She used to say I was so pernickety about my books. She'd come in and dust the room and shake out all the little blue slips of paper I'd put in them as place marks for references, and I'd raise hell. . . . What is *that?*"

"It's for the baby. I just couldn't make a decent Christmas package out of it—too many bumps."

"I still can't make out what it is."

"Does it have to have a *name?* Call it a mobile if you want to. You hang it over the crib, just out of reach, and all the little thingamajigs move around and catch the light or jingle or rattle, and he's supposed to watch in sheer delight."

"Let's take it into the nursery. How do we hang it up?"

Myra unwrapped a length of wire, some painted dowels, and a small rubber suction cup. "We stick this on the ceiling or beam or whatever. My dear Joe made the pulley with his own little hot hands; I hope it works. It's so you can raise it out of the way when the kid gets bored."

When they had untangled and installed the mobile, Myra backed down off the stepladder, puffing a little. "I'm too *fat* for this!"

They stood back to survey their work. Myra had selected all sorts of objects from her shop: Indian feathers that caught a breeze, tiny little bells on a string, pieces of bright glass and metal. "It's sort of an infant's TV," she said.

"It'll be pretty when the morning sunlight shines on it," added Cora.

Myra looked around. "You know, this room is just wonderful—all those shelves! And new tile! I had no idea Rafe was such a handy-man."

"A labor of love, for me." Cora had a note of sadness in her voice that Myra caught.

"Well, dear, of course. Don't expect too much, Cora. I think he's really doing a job!"

"Oh, I know he is, Myra. Come on, let's have some coffee." They went back into the kitchen and sat down at the table. Cora got out fresh cups and poured the coffee. "This is still fresh. I keep a pot going all the time."

"Shouldn't drink so much coffee."

"I know. Rafe's always telling me that, too. And I try not to tell him I wish he'd stick to coffee."

Myra raised her eyebrows. "What's he doing, belting 'em a little?"

"At night. Oh, I can't kick. Especially since he's the type that gets quieter when he drinks. The only thing is, I'd rather he'd talk out his problems instead of drink them out."

"Maybe he can't."

"Myra, we've *always* talked! We've had talk-fests that lasted all night. It was wonderful. But now we don't talk, we don't argue. He's tender and solicitous, and he drinks too much."

Myra listened, stirring her coffee thoughtfully.

"Cora. You are very lucky. Let him. Let him ease his pain anyway he pleases."

"I know. I do. But I wish I could let him know that I understand. My God, I never wanted to have him hurt."

"I don't think any woman can understand Rafe's particular problem."

"Oh, Myra, that's the complaint of our time! Everybody bleats about wanting to be understood. But suppose our abilities were heightened and clarified, suppose we could take a drug that made us understand—constantly and completely. Would that make us yield to the other's needs more readily?"

Myra thought a moment. She wanted to say that it should, that nobody had to take a drug in order to understand Rafe's needs completely. But she agreed. "I suppose not. We'd still want everybody to think the way we do. Give us what *we* want." Although she wondered if she would have been able to do to Joe what Cora had done to Rafe. Had she *looked* at him lately? Didn't she realize that Rafe would always feel that Cora's first thought in a crisis had not been of him? Cora was pouring more coffee into her cup, and she held up a hand. "Enough, dear."

"Part of Rafe's difficulty is that he lives in two worlds," Cora went on.

"Oh, is that it!" Myra said to herself. She disliked Cora when she became pontifical. As though she liked to hear herself talk. Well, let her talk!

"The airport where he works is an extension of the big cities of the world. It's a small, unimportant tendril stuck out here into the desert. It feeds from cities. It takes on the color and tensions of people, of crowds. He talks in jet-age language to the men he works with—electronics, the space programs. Then he gets into his car and in a few minutes he's in Sabado, which has only barely heard of progress, rigidly conservative, where the social revolution is something that is like a television story. That's where the people of Sabado see it, in the news along with the westerns and the suspense stories and the soap operas, and it has about the same amount of reality."

"Oh, I don't know, Cora. I don't think we're that isolated. I think we're involved in the world. But—what are you getting at? What is your point?"

"Myra, the big deal today is involvement on a universal level, but 'cool' when it comes to personal problems. Now, Rafe just isn't cool about our situation. How can he be? We live close to nature. We sleep in the silence of the desert night. We watch the subtle seasons. The primitive, the natural, the animal—is very close. Nothing that Rafe feels is unnatural. It is intensely natural. Jealousy, possessiveness, the desire to kill the interloper—it's all very acute. I think if we lived in a beehive in one of the big cities, if we were around other young people, they would hear about a situation like ours and say, 'So? It's happening. Let it happen.' Other things would seem more important."

"Yeah, I know," said Myra. "I'm not so sure as I care for this new morality they talk about."

"It isn't a matter of agreeing with it or not. There is no doubt to me that if we didn't live here in our quiet little home, we would be on the go, listening to other people, caring less about ourselves, perhaps. We would also be caught up into unrest and constant anxiety and tension. I couldn't live that way. I'd rather have one big important problem, a real one, and breathe clean air and sleep nights the rest of the time."

"You should say these things to Rafe, Cora."

"I can't. He's too caught up. He can't see things that way. It's pretty tough, Myra. He takes me into his arms and—" she placed her palms on her body and laughed—"and what does he find? His whole damn problem pressed right up against him!"

Myra joined in her laughter and then sobered. "Oh, dear, I shouldn't laugh, really—poor Rafe. You, you *female*, you've got it just the way you want it."

"Yes, but my God, I hope I'm not smug about it. I don't really think I am. Because don't think I wouldn't rather be having Rafe's child. That part of it is still very bad, and I try not to think about it." She began to push the cups and saucers around distractedly. "There are lots of things I can't think about. Because I couldn't kill, I'm stuck with a life I'm not sure I want. But my body says, 'Be selfish!

Soak up all the care and attention you can get, there's a job to be done!'"

Much as she loved Cora, Myra felt like saying, "You're trying hard not to be smug, but you are. You're like a queen bee, with your wretched sterile drone of a husband knocking himself out to see that nothing happens to you."

Aloud she said, "Maybe it would help if you two would laugh a little more. Maybe Rafe needs to be jollied up."

"'Jollied'!" Cora frowned. "What do you mean, Myra?"

"I'm just going by my own experience. Joe was deeply depressed when he first got sick, and even more so when he recovered and found he would be paralyzed. Of course, we'd never particularly wanted children. But even so, now we couldn't. And this got to Joe, and he moaned around a lot and felt awfully sorry for himself. I just went on a strict schedule of poking deliberate fun at him, easy kind of fun, you know, *loving* fun—finding things to laugh at. It became a kind of habit. He never got a chance to brood. If he did, I'd say, 'Are you going to bore me with that kind of truck?' And I'd swear at him and say, 'I'll be damned if I'll be a nursemaid to you and say "How are we feeling today?" Nuts to that!' You know what I mean?"

"I suppose so," said Cora, nodding. But her response was politeness. Rafe was not Joe. To Rafe, laughter was always a surprise. He didn't find much that was funny. He could see the point of a joke easily and quickly, but he analyzed it before he laughed at it. Myra's word "jollied" made her wince a little. She realized Myra was making an offer of help, however, and so she said with a smile that became a dismissal of the subject, "I'll think about that. Maybe it's a good idea."

Encouraged, Myra went on to give some specific examples and some more suggestions. Cora picked up the coffee things and washed them out in the sink, and Myra took a towel to dry the cups and saucers.

"Another thing, you know, you probably haven't even thought of it," Myra went on, "but you've heard of childless couples, people who've adopted a baby, thinking they could never have one, and then very soon afterwards they find out one of their own is on the way."

"Yes, I've heard of that. It would be wonderful if it would happen to us. But it's nothing we can count on, Myra, don't you see?"

"But you could say to Rafe, 'When we have more children . . .' or 'The next baby I have . . .'"

"I know, I know, but anything I *say* is just a palliative. Rafe can't be kidded out of this, and he would spot any phony jollying up or talk about children, anything like that. He'd resent it."

"It doesn't have to be phony, Cora. Not if you believe it."

"I'm not sure I do. I'm not even sure if it is necessary for me to believe it or to count on it. What I have to believe in is what is happening now. Me going around grunting and short of breath, and trying to be patient, and wishing it were over, and watching Rafe about to pop a cork, and at the same time being so considerate, so thoughtful—more than any woman could ask—" She listened as a car outside sounded its horn. "That's the mail."

"Let me go get it for you, then I'll have to run," said Myra.

They walked out to the veranda together.

"Myra. It's good to talk to you. Don't be mad if I don't listen very well."

"Oh, pooh! Hey, I think Cecil's got packages for you. He's waving."

Cora cupped her hands and shouted, "How's your mother, Cecil?"

Myra was on her way, but she called back over her shoulder to Cora, "Talk about booze! She's been drunk for a week! . . . I'm coming, Cecil!"

One of the packages contained a lovely sheepskin rug, a ten-pound note, and a letter from Cora's father from Alice Springs. In it he said how happy he was to hear about having a grandchild, and that he was touched that it would be named after him if it were a boy. His letter also contained news of her mother's remarriage.

It was indeed news to Cora. She had not heard from her mother for some time. Her father had heard about the wedding through his lawyer, who informed him that he wouldn't have to pay alimony anymore. In his letter he said that maybe Bess would be satisfied now that she had hooked a rich man.

"I'm forever indebted to you, my dear Cora," he said. "That little crack of yours you made at the dinner table one night about ships leaving San Francisco was the turning point. Besides setting me free, it also made *me* a rich man in many ways. The Clarks and I have a fine prosperous station—sheep in all directions!" He suggested that after the baby was born and old enough to travel, she take a trip to visit him; he would send her plane fare and meet her with their private plane in Sydney. "Would you believe it? Your old man is quite a flyer now. We've got a four-place Cessna. Of course, it's a must in the outback." The envelope contained a snapshot of him holding a struggling lamb. It was a picture of a much younger man. He was bearded, grinning, and Cora shook her head in unbelief because she hardly remembered ever seeing him even smiling. It would be nice, she thought, to take a trip. But not without Rafe.

She needed Rafe. She sat with the sheepskin rug over her knees, running her hands through the wool thoughtfully, the bright December sun warming her face, the distant horizons resting her vision. She needed Rafe. He locked doors for her. He lifted things up onto shelves for her. He put an arm around her when she took walks out into the desert; he held her, supported her. He *supported* her. Instead of the expected wave of warm gratitude from the stimulus of the word, she felt a vinegary kind of contempt.

"Now, what the hell is the matter with me!" she thought.

An open convertible was kicking up clouds of dust beyond the fence. For a moment it seemed to slow down, then there was a crunching shifting of gears, and it roared on toward the highway. Cora couldn't see who was driving, and the outlines of the car were lost in the pattern of the cottonwoods. But her heart upped its rhythm, and she hurried indoors and locked the door behind her. The new locks Rafe had installed.

Of course it hadn't been Terry. Terry coming around in broad daylight—with a *shiv!* She laughed out loud and went to the kitchen to find something to eat. Of course it was ridiculous. But a drunken Terry could be a nuisance, and accidents could happen. The thought annoyed her. She got out a large jar of peanut butter and slathered a slice of bread with a huge quantity of the spread. There were some ripe olives. A glass of milk into which she stirred a chocolate mix. She chewed and swallowed angrily, thoughtlessly.

Why was such a problem allowed to remain so unresolved, so raw? Surely Rafe could—*should*—think of something. Why didn't he go up and talk to her? Give her a small scare of her own to think about? Of course, then he'd be on Durrell territory. Well. So?

She hadn't been sleeping well. Rafe would awaken nervously when she got up. Usually she stayed up only long enough to have a cigarette, stare at herself in the bathroom mirror, and brush her teeth. But tonight she couldn't go back to sleep. Rafe found her sitting in the living room, with reddened eyes, a magazine in her lap, some chunks of greasewood burning brightly in the fireplace.

"Well, this looks cozy, but you ought to be asleep. You feel okay?"

"I was hungry," Cora answered. "I got up to get a glass of milk."

"Why didn't you wake me? I never heard you sneaking out. Come on, honey, come back to bed. You need your rest."

"I'd rather stay up awhile, Rafe. I feel nervous. I get halfway to sleep and I think I hear a noise, and right away I start getting Terry on my mind, and what she said, and even though I know it's foolish . . ."

Rafe was still bucking sleep.

"It sure as hell is. It's stupid."

"It's stupid in the daylight."

"It's stupid at night. When you should sleep." He gave a mighty yawn and scratched his leg.

"Go back to bed, Rafe. I'm all right."

"No—no, I'm awake now."

"But you've got to go to work in the morning."

"Look, do you *mind* my company? Think I'll fix some coffee."

"It's all made, ready for breakfast. Just plug it in. But I honestly think you should go back to sleep. Just because I've got the heebie-jeebies, no reason you have to stick around."

He looked back at her over his shoulder as he went toward the kitchen. He gave a little laugh.

"What's funny?"

"Your solicitude for my rest." She raised her eyebrows questioningly. "You've been building a fire, cracking up dried twigs, you've been rattling magazine pages, and walking around. And with the weight you're carrying, you do kind of shake the house. You want company. Okay, you got it." And he went into the kitchen.

Cora had to admit to herself that it was true. But not quite this kind of company. What she wanted was attention. She was becoming addicted to TLC. She said it aloud, calling to him, "I guess I'm hung up on TLC."

He put a head around the door. "On what?"

"Tender Loving Care—you know. I like it."

He grunted and disappeared again. She got up and put some more small chunks of greasewood on the fire. It crackled and hissed and gave off a faint, not unpleasant odor of creosote. Dark fantasies of Terry disappeared, and in all probability she could have gone back to bed and fallen soundly asleep. But she felt guilty at having waked Rafe. He was whistling tunelessly in the kitchen, letting Maxie out, and then letting him back in, and when he came in with the coffee, she had once again assumed an attention-getting troubled frown. "Faker! Phony!" she remarked under her breath to herself.

"What'd you say, honey?" he asked.

"Didn't you bring me any coffee?"

He sighed, put his cup down, and returned to the kitchen, reappearing with another cup.

"You know, Cora," he said, "now don't get mad, but I really think a lot of this fretting about Terry is part of your condition. I think, naturally, that since you've got something pretty unpleasant to go through in a couple of months, you're kind of finding something else to blame it on."

"Oh, please!" Cora laughed, "Don't give me any armchair psychotherapy! You're hardly qualified."

"I said, don't get mad. And I don't like that tone from you, Cora."

"You listen to me! That gal threatened my life. Can't you understand that?"

"It was booze talking. That I do understand."

"It was booze, and fear. And the combination makes a dangerous person."

"What the hell's she scared of? Durrell? That he'll walk out on her? She'd be a lot better off if he did leave. So would we all."

"You tell that to her. She's hanging on to youth and sex and romance and the whole big deal. It's all personified in Durrell, and if she loses him, she's got nothing left. Nothing that matters."

Rafe growled, taking noisy sips of his coffee, "She better grow up."

Cora slammed the magazine onto the table. "Honest to God, Rafe, don't you ever head into a problem? Do you ever do anything but *react*? You take the easy way out. You say, 'She better grow up.' That's the way *you* feel about it. But you tell *her* that. Tell her he's a criminal, that he's amoral, rotten, and you know what she'll do? She'll sing, 'He's my man.' She's one of those women to whom men can do anything—except leave them."

Rafe had heard the phrase "Don't you ever head into a problem" and little else. She was right. He was meeting problems in the station wagon, talking to himself. He was roaring down the highway, beating his fists on the steering wheel, glaring at an empty road.

"What do you want me to do about it?" he said. "There isn't much I can accomplish at three in the morning."

"I'm not asking you to do anything," Cora snapped. "Just don't say it's stupid if I'm a little jumpy because somebody said they'd take a knife to me."

Rafe got to his feet impatiently. "Oh, nuts! Nobody carries out threats like that."

"They don't? What little world do you live in? Rape doesn't happen either—except to someone else. And yet it did happen, right in there!" She pointed, stabbing the air in the direction of the bedroom.

"And I did nothing about it. Is that it?"

"Don't be childish. I'm not saying anything about that."

"I *want* you to say something about it." If Cora had the same opinion of him as he did of himself, then all of his efforts at peace and quiet were meaningless.

She went on. "You said things don't happen like that, like people carrying out threats and rape, and I'm trying to point out that they do carry them out."

"I know, I know. But I've done nothing—really nothing—about any of these unpleasant events, is that it?"

"Oh, you've come up with all the natural reactions, Rafe."

"Well, that is very faint praise indeed."

"What do you want, bouquets?"

"Just an occasional *Olé!*"

"For what?"

He was thinking of the picture of himself that had occurred to him in the car. He sat down again, drew his legs up under him on the chair, and leaned back. "I lean against a sunny wall, with my sombrero over my eyes . . ."

Cora looked at him sharply. "Yes," she said, "I'll buy that. And there's a shoot-'em-up going on down the street, and you don't even hear it."

"I'm not deaf."

"But you've got cotton in your ears."

"Well," he said, getting up to prowl around and light a cigarette, "I can't keep up with you. I don't know how to play metaphor, or simile, or whatever."

"It's just that you've accepted things. You've been asked to accept a great deal. And once you've got into the habit of acceptance— well, it's out of line for me to expect anything else. To you—maybe to us both—everything has become like a mirror that's been breathed on. The images aren't sharp and clear. They're soft and contain no threat."

"Leave it, I said! I can't play that game. Say what you mean. What threat? *What* do you want me to do about *what?*"

"Listen, I'm not about to call any tune and expect you to hop! I'm not that kind of a woman. You know perfectly well I'm talking about Terry."

"Terry. Okay. Even though you're not that kind of woman, you've managed to call it." He strode over to the phone.

"Now what are you going to do?" For the first time her voice was anxious.

"I'm going to call Gus Boyd. I'm going to tell him I know where those ropes came from. I'm going to tell him you've had threats on your life, and I'm going to put that sonofabitch Durrell in jail for one hell of a long time. Okay?"

"Wait a minute, Rafe. Don't. Don't call Gus. This time of the night."

"What the hell difference does the time of day mean? Let's blow the whole shmeer. Let's get it over with. Suits me."

He was dialing. She put her hand on the phone, breaking the connection. "This is crazy. I don't want this!" She wrenched the phone away from him, staggering a little, and quickly he put an arm out to steady her. They stood there silently, breathing hard, looking at each other. Then, quietly, he put the phone back on the table and replaced the handset.

"What are you goading me for, Cora? I don't need goading. I'll blow if you keep it up. You made a valid request for peace and quiet in which to have your child. I've tried to give it to you." He raked his hands through his hair. "What is this perverse thing about women? They urge a man, they tease him, they shame him into a fight, and then they say, 'Oh, don't hit him!'"

"I'm sorry, I'm truly sorry," Cora said softly. "You needn't generalize. Be specific. It's this woman, this particular woman—me. I don't know what has made me like this tonight."

"Just tonight? I can think back and remember quite a few small, contemptuous looks—looks that I thought were merely grouchy weather."

"Well, don't pay any attention to my looks. I look bad enough as it is. And don't try to interpret—*anything*." She started toward the bedroom. "Come on, let's try to get some sleep, and I promise—" she said sweetly, "I *promise*—not to have any more nightmares about Terry Ostander. Even though I do think it was her car that drove by today."

"Well, why didn't you say so? You're sure it was Terry?"

Cora went on into the room and climbed into bed, pulling the covers up tightly around her.

"Cora! Are you sure?"

"Of course I'm sure!" she shouted, sticking her head up over the covers. "Who else drives a Jaguar around here?"

"Well, that vet, what's his name, Saunders, Sanders? He's got his place down here at the end of the road—couple of miles—maybe she was out to see him about one of their horses."

"That's right, dear. Could be. Go to sleep."

He clenched his jaw tightly as he got in beside her. No more. No more tonight.

In the Ostander garage there were pinging sounds of hot metal cooling. A pair of Christmas-present-new Honda CL-160 Scramblers stood side by side in the garage, looking mean and proud and bright. Two tall boys stood and admired them, walked around and around them, touching adjustments, poking, kicking, caressing. They had discussed everything about them that was new and different and better, in what way they were an improvement on last year's model. They had tried them out on the highway and charged around the desert, shouting, kicking up sand, pacing a jack rabbit. There was nothing left but to sigh in satisfaction. And to stroll back to the house for something to eat.

"We'd never have got 'em without Paul, I guess," said Wynn Ostander, the elder of the two. Seventeen, skinny, with large hands and feet, brown hair worn shaggy enough to be "in" and short enough to avoid angry comments about getting a haircut, "or don't come around to the front of the house!"

Dudley (Dude) Ostander was fifteen, and in his mother's eyes, "a gentleman, like his father." Dude took the hint, kept his hair trimmed, his nails passably clean, saw to it that he didn't stink, and remembered to kiss his mother occasionally. It was Dude who politely asked for, and got, extra spending money. It was Dude who had worked on Paul for the new Hondas.

Dudley Ostander was also an excellent horseman, "a marvelous pair of hands," his mother said. Wynn was impatient with the discipline and schooling of the horses and hated the drone of the words, "Elbows in, hands down," from Dave Durrell. He also hated Dave Durrell. Dudley learned more quickly and was looking forward to the reward of blue ribbons and admiration. It was Dude who had smelled out the funny business between his mother and Dave Durrell.

"She's a slut, you know?" he said to Wynn. "We gotta face it, man, you know?"

Wynn screwed up his face in distaste, which hid some of the pain he felt. "Where's she get off with that stuff at her age!"

"Maybe she's just had the hots all her life."

"Maybe it's because she started late. She was past twenty-five when I was born." Over the hill, he indicated.

"That doesn't mean she hadn't started screwing, you dope! Don't you remember reading about rumble seats?"

"That was still earlier."

"Well, anyway."

"They didn't even have any pill then, back in those days."

"I guess a guy still had to wear something—*ee-uch!*"

They began loping toward the kitchen, swinging their new orange-colored metal helmets, with padded ear cups and crown pads and goggle snap tabs, specially fitted at fifty-nine dollars apiece. They were in search of a piece of coconut cream pie and a Coke.

Paul Holloway parked his car next to the twin Hondas in the garage. He smiled to himself at the sight of them, wishing he had the nerve to try one of them out, to go bucking over the desert and up a mountain. He wished he had the nerve to do a lot of things. He touched the handle bar of the one nearest him, twisted it a little, and because he was alone, he went "Rrrrr-rrrrr!" He laughed apologetically, as though someone had heard him, and then chewed on a piece of cuticle at the corner of his thumb. He turned to the pathway leading to the terrace and went into his office-living quarters from the outside door. There were checks to make out, and there was a package of books he was anxious to open. He had an hour or so before Terry would be demanding his company, his attention, his comments on her appearance.

Wynn and Dude had changed to bathing trunks. They deposited a plate of fudge brownies and more Cokes on a low tile table, and then Dude started pulling it over to the edge of the pool, the wrought-iron legs of the table screeching on the cement.

"Hold the Cokes, will you? Hold the Cokes!" he yelled to Wynn, a second before they would have toppled.

"Why do you need a table all of a sudden?" asked Wynn as he assisted.

"I dunno. Don't want the stuff to get wet when we dive in, I guess."

"Well, aren't you gonna eat 'em?"

"I guess. Leave 'em here, the ants'll be all over 'em before we could get out."

"There's no ants around here. They spray stuff all over."

Then it was joke time, having to do with ants in the pants and getting *them* sprayed, and they haw-hawed and hooted, and dangled their bony legs in the water, gulped their Cokes, belched loudly, and laughed some more. Their laughter sounded young and careless and spontaneous and happy. But the boys had learned that laughter stilled anxiety. It cleared away mystery. If you could laugh at something, it erased its importance. The funny business between their mother and Dave gave them emotions of pain and disappointment, not because it was sexual in nature, but because it had the smell of evil, of something greedy, grasping, consuming. As though they, in some horrible way, *fed* upon each other. It had little to do with sex as they knew it.

Sex was a shenanigan; it was a game you played with a chick during a giggling scuffle, with her pretending she didn't want it, and then you slipped it in and she'd shriek and you both knew she wasn't surprised at all. Sex was in everything you did. It was the power you felt between your legs on a bike, the smell of oil and hot rubber and the roar and the wind in your face. It was in the beat of the music, jolting your hips, getting sweaty, but it was never serious.

Sex had no right or wrong in it, because it was as the books said, "pure infantile gratification," and you knew that, and so what! You grabbed a hunk of it because you sensed you were in for a change. All you had to do was look around you. There was this metamorphosis into adulthood, and man, that was a drag, something to be avoided as long as possible. Because then everything got embarrassing. It was mysterious—and somehow pretty dirty. It got mixed up in things that were ugly, like marriage and divorce and possessiveness and who belongs to who. And people got hurt. It was real scary. And being scared or hurt was something you ducked.

Their mother was a slut to them because she was violating their concept of adulthood. She was staying in their world too long, past her time. Her bikinis exposed flesh that was droopy, that had no bounce, with muscles that were no longer lithe but stringy and tense. She looked hungry. She bared her teeth when she smiled at a man, like she'd like to eat him up. No wonder parents warned their children of the dangers of sex. At their age it *was* dangerous. *They* were the ones who ought to be careful.

"So where do you suppose she is?" asked Dudley. "Her car's in the garage."

"Well, all I know is that she wasn't in her room. She's prob'ly out riding with Dave."

"She's prob'ly giving him his Christmas present under a sycamore tree."

"You think Paul's got any idea?"

"Godamighty, no, man. You squirrelly?"

Wynn leaned down and held his empty Coke bottle under the water, listening to the gurgling as it filled. "I just hope he never finds out, is all. You know? I think there'd be real trouble."

Dudley said, "What kind of trouble?"

"I don't know. But I think it would bother him. And he shouldn't be bothered. He's a good guy, you know?"

The "you knows" in the boys' sentences were hardly words; they were sounds sprinkled through their conversation repetitiously, like oral commas or dashes, for lack of ability to verbalize. Sometimes the "likes" and the "you knows" became very thick: "It was, well, you know, like maybe—you know," often driving the adult listener quite mad.

"I wish she'd—like marry Paul," said Dudley.

"What good would that do?"

"Give him the right to fire Dave."

"Yeah, that would be great. But why would it?"

"Chee-*sus*, you're dumb!" Dudley slipped into the pool and hung on to the edge, squinting up at his brother. "Don't you like Paul?"

"Sure I like him. You mean for Mom? I suppose. He's the right age, anyway. Of course, Dave's not really young, either. Twenty-four or -five, but he's too young for her, you know? Paul seems a lot like Dad. Somebody you can talk to—a little, anyway."

The boys fell silent. Dudley held on to the edge of the pool and kicked his legs in the lazy crawl. Wynn was remembering a man whom you could not only talk to but a voice that was nice to listen to.

"Funny."

"What?" asked Wynn.

"How they—" grown-ups, teachers, parents, were always "they" —"how they think we can't *see!* That day I was cooling off Skylark in the corral. Mom and Dave were walking in front of the stalls, you know, and all of a sudden when they got next to the tack room, Dave grabbed her arm and she gave a little squeal, '*Eeee!*' You know? So goddamn *cute.* They both looked out toward me, but I wasn't givin' out nothin', you know, and he opened the door and pulled her inside and slammed it."

Wynn kicked the side of the pool and muttered, "Stinks! I bet it's a real drag to have us home for holidays. I bet when we're away and Paul's off on one of his trips to San Francisco——"

"Come on!" yelled Dudley, and with a few strokes he reached the diving board. He pulled himself up onto it just as Wynn reached it from the other end. They collided and fell in, came to the surface gasping, calling each other names, chased each other, and then settled down to real competition in backstroke.

They didn't notice, they couldn't have heard the creaking of the tall rattan peacock chair that stood with its back against a trellised red bauhinia. At right angles to the windows of Paul's study, the divider offered semi-privacy and filtered the glare of the sun.

Paul Holloway got up slowly, wiped his glasses, and folded the newspaper, tucking it under his arm. Glancing out at the boys, he turned and walked into the room and quietly closed the door. For a while he stood looking around the room as though he had never been in it before. Curious. It rocked gently, like a stateroom on a ship. He sat down in front of his desk, selected a cigarette from a dark-red crystal bowl, snapped his lighter to it, and let the smoke out with a sigh. He picked up a paper knife and slit open a few envelopes containing bills. He opened a wide drawer and pulled out a large, thick checkbook. As he closed the drawer his hand strayed to a lower drawer on the right side of the desk, and pulling it open, he reached and found a small automatic wrapped in chamois. He held it in his palm for a long moment, and the room rocked again. He checked the clip, rubbed the barrel gently with the chamois, and then replaced the gun carefully in the back of the drawer.

"For Cora and Rafe, with love from Mother." The card was enclosed in a tastefully wrapped box from a well-known jewelry firm in San Francisco. The card was engraved "Mrs. Thomas Christopher Smith," and a stroke of a pen through the name indicated with charming cordiality that the recipients rated a more intimate signature. The item contained in the box was a small but elaborately tooled silver tray, protected from marring by a soft purple flannel envelope.

"Now, then," said Cora to Rafe, "there's a present just full to brimming with Mother Love!"

Rafe was breaking in a new pipe Cora had given him, wandering around the house in new bedroom slippers and a new white terry-cloth bathrobe with his initials on the pocket. With one hand he pressed the bowl of the pipe against the side of his nose, rubbing it gently, and with the other he clasped a glass containing a very dark drink.

He said, "Mm. What do we do with it?"

Cora put one hand on her hip and held the tray up high, shaking it like a tambourine. "Too bad it hasn't got jingle-things on it. . . . Darling, we look at it and say, 'My goodness, Mother must have a rich man for a husband; look at that card, and that engraving and the name of that jeweler, isn't it just too impressive for words.' . . . Balls!"

"Cora!" said Rafe automatically.

The holidays had been mildly frenetic. There were many "Come for drinks" invitations from Rafe's friends at the airport and their wives. And of course the Demings had a party at the shop one evening that was crowded, smoky, and gay. Professor Liebig's party had been organized by his British bird-watching butler, who had carols booming on the stereo, a huge log in the fireplace, great basins of wassail made with Madeira and brandy, and who had also carefully locked the specimen cabinets and stored the camera equipment. After standing around for a while in the crush, Cora and Rafe had exchanged messages with their eyes and elbowed their way out. Cora looked at the flight of stone steps curving down to the parking area. "I'll never make it," she had said. "I'm pickled. Smoked by that Yule log. Or maybe it's the hot punch." "I'll carry you," said Rafe. "You couldn't! I'm too bulky!" But he had.

Rafe was firm about Cora's not going to the effort of giving reciprocal parties. Instead they had a kind of constant open house, which was almost as much trouble for her. Rafe was not very helpful, because as soon as two or three people arrived he settled down with a drink in his hand, and she had to do the tray-passing and fix more things to eat when other, unexpected people arrived. Of course, it was Christmas, but she couldn't remember that Rafe had ever celebrated quite as heavily during previous holidays. And after people had left and she was wearily straightening up the place, Rafe would say he was going to walk for a while and "clear his head." Once she made the comment, "You're kind of tossing 'em down, aren't you?" And he had shrugged and smiled and said, "Celebrating."

Rafe's head would not get very clear because he had stashed a pint in the pocket of his leather jacket. What he really asked of the air and the desert night was to wipe out the sensation of walking in syrup, to wipe out the smell of sweetness. Christmas. Love and kisses. Jingle Bells. The infant Jesus. The infant in Cora's belly. There were tiny things everywhere, it seemed to him. Being folded and patted and held up and admired and put away in drawers. It seemed also that Cora spent hours in the nursery, mooning and meditating, arranging and straightening, finding little jobs for him to help her with: "Rafe, I think it would be handy to have a lamp here behind the chair where I give the baby its feeding. One of those three-way bulbs or even a dimmer maybe?" He fixed a dimmer switch for her.

The desert was a well of black, a bowl containing the night. Rafe walked into its heart, occasionally stumbling into rabbit holes, weaving a little. His flashlight zig-zagged. He found a place clear of brush where he sat down, flicked off the light, and waited for his eyes to accustom themselves to the darkness. It was a starry night. The kind that poets sang about. Here there was no competition with a city's glow; the glitter and twinkle were extravagant. The clarity of the air gave the illusion of depth. Some of the brighter stars seemed low, and the path of the Milky Way seemed to swirl and shimmer off into a farther distance just beyond the mountains. The horizon was jagged with peaks, and at intervals the star shine sparkled on a patch of snow.

Rafe breathed heavily, as though exhausted. He tried to put the way he felt into words, and the phrase "mashed potatoes" came into his mind. Without any salt. Except for the air that bit sharply into his nostrils, he was unaware of the night and its glory. The wind skinned his cheekbones, and he shivered. He poured a swig from the bottle into his mouth and waited. Waited for the long rolling belch that would follow, to which he added vocal accompaniments —all the Army words that described men like himself, and men like Durrell. He spewed them out in disgust and contempt, and they weren't enough. The cadence of the speech of another expert in self-contempt ran into his thoughts: ". . . for it cannot be/but I am pigeon-livered and lack gall. . . . This is most brave . . ."

The ground was icy on his thin buttocks. He sat with his heels dug into the sand, his elbows on his knees, the bottle waving in one hand, his head bowed, occasionally taking a pull of the whiskey. Finally he tossed the bottle away, listened for the shatter of glass, and heard nothing. He got up and urinated in the direction of the Ostander ranch, and then, shivering, walked back toward the house, his head singing from the liquor.

He stood by the edge of the swimming pool and felt alarmed because he didn't know how he had gotten there. Then he remembered what he must do. It had worked before. He knew he mustn't distress Cora by his looks or what he might inadvertently say. He must get control again. He took off his clothes, placed them on a chair, and with a roar plunged into the icy water.

Cora appeared in a moment with towels and a robe, fussing like a little hen.

"Honestly, Rafe, what's got into you? What are you training for with these nighttime walks and swims and stuff?"

Sobered—almost—he blew and spluttered and puffed and spoke through the water in his mouth. "Hey, it's great! Feels marvelous. Been eating too much, need the exercise!"

"Well, hurry up now, I've got the fire poked up and some coffee ready."

"'At's my girl. Darling, darling, I love you so much!"

"All right, all right. Now get in there, scoot!"

Sitting in front of the fire, Cora glanced at him as she worked on her knitting. The white-wool crib blanket was finished, folded and patted and put away. She had enjoyed the feeling of doing something when she had to sit and rest from housework. Reading, the ability to concentrate on anything more exacting than magazine captions for photographs, had deserted her; knitting quieted her hands, held her attention lightly, and she worked on the simplest articles, like the small carrying blanket she had on her lap now. It was a daffodil-yellow, because she had decided that blue or pink was too old-fashioned.

Rafe sat with his head leaning back on the cushion, smiling gently, his eyes closed. It was an odd look, Cora thought. Almost a silly look. His lips were not full, his upper lip was long, and there was no dividing V-plane beneath the nose; his teeth didn't show, and so the smile was simply a line across the lower part of his face. The eyebrows disputed the smile. Black and bristly and tied in a knot above his nose.

"You want to go to the Eldridges New Year's Eve?" Cora asked. "Or would you rather just stay here?"

"Whatever you say, sweetheart."

"Oh, I think it would be fun. We wouldn't have to stay all night. I don't think I'm up to one of their swinging all night sessions with a ranch breakfast at six. Just do 'Happy New Year,' kiss everybody, and come home."

Rafe didn't answer. He just sat watching the firelight from under long, straight, black lashes.

A few minutes went by.

"What's happened to conversation?" asked Cora.

"Hm?"

"Oh, for Pete's sake, I like companionable silences as much as anybody, but I haven't had anything from you but basic communication for almost a week—more than that. You stopped talking the night we trimmed the tree, remember? Is there anything wrong? You're really very strange lately!"

"What do you want to talk about, honey?" Rafe sat up, all attention, pleasant, smiling.

"Skip it, love," Cora said in disgust. "I'm going to bed."

Rafe watched her go into the bedroom. He thought to himself, "I can't talk. I can't talk except with filthy words. You wouldn't understand why. Anymore than I do. I don't want to disgust you. I couldn't do that to you."

He got up and went into the kitchen and poured himself another cup of coffee—and added a dollop of brandy.

Carefully he saw that the cord was disconnected from the coffee maker, that Maxie was inside, that the kitchen door was locked, the carport light off.

He reached around and patted his own shoulder. "That's a good husband. That's all you have to do, Rafe, m'boy—just be a real good husband." Unexpectedly he broke wind, and the timing made him laugh.

He turned out the lights in the living room and sat down again in front of the fire. In a few moments he heard Cora come out of the bathroom, and from the darkness he watched her as she moved about the bedroom, slowly, heavily. Her night dress made her seem larger, bulging from breast to toe. Her hair hung around her face in heavy strands, and when she straightened and it fell back, the line of her chin was thickened, her cheeks puffy. He turned away, longing for his girl, his delicate desert flower.

After an hour Cora was still moving restlessly, trying to find a comfortable position. She was gaining weight very rapidly now, and Dr. Titus had pursed his lips disapprovingly when she stepped on the scales. She had said, "I'm hungry. I'm just starved all the time. I eat a big meal and I feel like a stuffed pig, and then in about fifteen minutes I'm hungry all over again." "More exercise," he had said firmly. But the pool was too cold for swimming, and it was difficult to find a place to walk. A rabbit hole or a stone was a hazard in the desert. A turned ankle might mean a jolting stumble or fall. Occasionally she walked the road in front of the house, but invariably a car would stop at the sight of a pregnant woman, and a shocked face would say, "You need a ride? Where's your car?" She hated explaining.

Now she lay on her back, her arms above her head, trying to relieve the shortness of breath. Then an ache in the small of her back began to be noticeable, and she turned slightly onto her right side. As though to grab a hand hold, the child within her began a tattoo on the left side.

"Oh, brother!" she sighed. "January, February, two and a half months to go." And then what? Then the big unknown, the un-experienced pain, and the question of how bad, how much, what will it be like. Nobody could tell her that. Not even women who had had babies. They all just smiled and said, "It isn't so awful, and it's over before you know it. And then you forget all about the pain because there's your baby!" They all seemed to have complete amnesia regarding the actual birth.

She began to breathe more slowly, and she relaxed and closed her eyes. Suddenly she popped them open. She waited to hear what had wakened her. There it was. A loud snore from the living room. The room would be getting cold, since the thermostats were down and the fire was going out. She felt she ought to go in and wake Rafe and make him come to bed or at least get up and cover him with a blanket. But the child was quiet, she felt warm and part of the bed, and she hated to move. She knew what was making him drink more than usual, and she didn't know quite what to do about it. Last summer's nightmare, a man by the name of Durrell —to her it was now all irrelevant. It had all disappeared in the day-to-day problems dealing with her tiny constant companion. If Rafe would only stop *trying* so hard. He was being *too* considerate, *too* thoughtful. Obviously to compensate for carrying the heavy burden of the thought, "It's not my child." Why couldn't he just forget about that? Or at least develop a healthy indifference? Of course, that might mean he'd be indifferent to the baby, and that she couldn't bear. She sleepily wondered if you could be selective about indifference. A cup of hot coffee couldn't be half hot and half cold—not in the same cup. And if it weren't all in the same cup, then it wouldn't be . . . and her eyelids dropped shut.

It was the middle of February when two technicians unloaded a large TV set, the latest model of the most expensive make, with the latest development in tuning, the finest cabinet work, and a note from Terry:

Darling Cora —
I'm sure your birthday is near—or past—or something.
I just want you to have a little giftie, with my gratitude.
Love, love,
Terry

At first, it made Cora furious. In front of the service men she had to be polite and interested and pleased, and that took some of the edge off her anger. After a powerful antenna had been set up on the roof and adjusted, the set was turned on, and there was a travel film of Japan in magnificent color. She sat for a half hour, hypnotized, completely absorbed, switching away from channels that had only dull black and white. Finally she turned it off and dialed the Ostander number.

"Yes, darling. Did you get my little present?" Terry's voice was warm and happy.

"Terry, you're out of your mind. I can't accept this thing."

"Why not, darling? Don't be an utter fool! I'm grateful that you've kept your dear little trap shut, and I want you to know it."

"But Terry. I don't want to be paid off! I haven't kept quiet about Dave because of your silly, drunken threats."

"Easy girl. Don't push your luck."

"I mean it. Rafe and I decided not to say anything because we don't want a hullabaloo. Because we want to be left alone. Because we're not vengeful people. We would have nothing to gain by exposing Dave. Not now."

"So what are you saying? Can't I share my own happiness with you? Everything is so heavenly. The boys are back in school; Paul's in Denver for at least three weeks. His brother's in some kind of financial bind, and he's trying to see what he can do to help him. And Dave's all calmed down and happy again. You could have blasted it, and you didn't, and I'm grateful. And I've got an idea for some other goodies for you."

"I don't *want* anything from you, Terry!" Cora almost screamed.

"Sweetie. I know how much Rafe makes. I know it's going to be a squeeze with the hospital and doctors and things. Okay, that's his job. To provide all that for you. Although it must gall him once in a while. I thought maybe it would make things easier if occasionally I see to it that you get a little cream, some of the funsie things."

"Don't do it, Terry."

"Well, don't you *like* the TV? I know we don't have many stations out here, but I thought since you had to stay around the house so much, you'd enjoy it." Her voice had changed to a wistful sound, almost hurt. "Please enjoy it, Cora, please."

"Oh, Terry. What am I going to say to Rafe?"

"That you got a birthday present! Call it a late Christmas present if you want to. It isn't the first time I've given you presents. I didn't make it at Christmas, I know, but I was so damn busy, I had eight parties in one week."

"And you weren't sure of what I was going to do."

"Darling, we are *women*. I was sure you knew how desperate I was. I said a lot of things I didn't mean, but I know you understood. I was scared when you said you'd tell Rafe. I was afraid that—well, you know how men go off the handle, clenching their jaws and drawing themselves up to their full righteous indignation. But I had a hunch you could handle him. And you *did*. And I appreciate it. And I count you as my friend."

Cora wanted to say, I didn't *handle it*, and you're not my friend. But instead she said, "Well, I don't know if I can handle *this*. Rafe may say . . ." She heard the station wagon pull into the carport.

"Say what?"

"I don't know. I'll let you know. Rafe just drove in. I'll call you, Terry."

"Okay, sweetie, bye."

"Cora! I'm home!"

"Hi, darling. In here."

"Whatcha doin'? Hey-y! Where'd that come from?"

"I thought you'd see the new aerial on the roof when you came down the road. It's from Terry."

"What for?"

"She's grateful!"

Rafe gave a short laugh. "Well, she oughtta be! It's nice to know somebody has gratitude these days." And after examining the set, turning on the controls, he said, "That's the best job that company puts out. Great for these fringe areas. Beautiful cabinet."

"But Rafe . . ."

"Hm?" He was absorbed in the color tuning.

"Should we accept it?"

He flipped the sound off and sat back on his heels.

"Why not?"

"Well, Rafe, don't you feel it's a kind of pay-off?"

"Are you feeling—corrupted?"

Cora nodded. "Yes, I am. And I don't understand why you don't feel the same way."

Rafe rubbed his chin. "Boy, I gotta shave again. . . . Cora, if you feel that way, just send it back. But you have no control over what other people think or feel. If Terry thinks you didn't accuse Dave Durrell because you were afraid of her, of what she might do, she's wrong, isn't she?"

"That's correct."

"If she thinks you withheld information because of sympathy for her, she's wrong again, isn't she?"

"Yes."

"Is it so important for you to set her straight?"

"I don't know. I'm confused now. She said she might want to send me some other goodies from time to time. If I don't send them back——"

"Let her! Let her get rid of her guilt that way if she wants to."

"But she'll think—and what will people say who know we can't afford a thing like this." She waved her hand in the direction of the set.

"It seems to me, Cora, that you've done a pretty heroic job of saying nuts to what people think. And people, if you care, know that Terry gets these waves of extravagance—'dear generous Terry.'"

Cora laughed. "I know, you just want to see *Bonanza* in color!"

"That's right, and the World Series. I could never afford this, and I think it's great." He flipped up the sound. "Hey, look! The news—in color—isn't that something!"

"I'll fix your drink, honey." Cora went off to the kitchen for ice and to continue her dinner preparation. There was the pleasant fragrance of a roasting leg of lamb coming from the oven. She put in some potatoes, which sizzled as they hit the juices. She cracked open a tray of ice and got out the thermos, still feeling vaguely troubled. She wasn't sure she liked Rafe's accepting so easily. She would have rather had to do some persuading. She liked the sudden flare that lighted up his black eyes at anything that touched his pride. Maybe—maybe he just hasn't got any pride left, she thought. But that wasn't it, exactly. He didn't walk around or talk like a man without pride—beaten, overhumble—none of that. He had stopped drinking so much; he never did any belting anymore. Indifference. That was closer. Way back in her mind it was a word she had thought of before, but she couldn't remember when. Selective indifference. She laughed to herself; *she* wanted to do the selecting! She didn't want him to be indifferent about her being mad that Terry had paid her off. Of course he had good arguments, but didn't everybody rationalize that way? Sure, the world is corrupt, everybody cheats and lies and steals, and everybody does it because it's the thing to do if you're smart. This was the era of being smart. From the other room Rafe called out something to her and laughed. She walked over to the door, where she could see, and he was laughing at a commercial cartoon—in living color—and for some reason she felt very sad.

During the late days of the desert winter, the days of warmth and bright clear air and chilly sparkling nights, the transient guest breathes deeply, cavorts in his hotel pool, gets a tan he can brag about, notices that his hangovers clear up more easily, and goes home extolling the beauties and the fun of what he is apt to consider an eternal vacation land. The residents, animal and vegetable, know better. They know it as a waiting time, a time of lying low. The charges are set for the explosion of color and heat to follow.

There is no wet or dry season in the desert six feet below the surface. No soft spring rain cues the carpets of yellow, purple, red, blue; the exotic fleshy pink bloom on the end of a dry stick, the surge of green at the base of the mountains. The programming has been completed, and soon it will be "Now—*Now!*"

A full moon made the land an empty whiteness; a shining glitter of a snowy peak accented the gray to black outlines of the horizon. And a single lighted candle washed out its whiteness in the oblong of a window. In the patio below, a fountain gently washed the backs of the leaping dolphins and pattered softly on a water-lily pad.

From a glass door in the living room Paul Holloway could look up and across the patio, and he could see, not the candle, but its light, wavering gently on the opposite white wall of the window embrasure. It made him want to laugh, to echo Wynn's "Where does she get off with that stuff at her age!" A light in the window, for God's sake! Why didn't she just use the phone? Of course there might be reason for that. The phone was in the tack room, and the bell was outside the door, a large bell made to be heard all down the row of stalls or clear over into the corral. Even so, it seemed pretty silly.

He had driven from his apartment in Tucson, parked in the shadows of the eucalyptus east of the entrance gate, and waited until the lights in the house went off: the floodlight in the parking area, the exterior garden lights, and after a while the lights in the servants' quarters. He had walked up the driveway silently, around to the pool, letting himself into the office with his key.

He waited. His feet got tired, he needed a cigarette, but he was afraid to leave his post to get a chair, and he had left his cigarettes in the car. Maybe it was all a lot of nonsense. In a surge of hope, sweat broke out, trickling down his back. He had been collecting evidence since the day he overheard the boys at the swimming pool. But he realized he was collecting evidence of guilt. Counsel for the prosecution.

He had made a complaint against Dave Durrell to Terry, a very weak complaint, something about the hired hands not liking him

—which they didn't—and Terry had said she didn't give a damn, she could always hire new hands, but a good trainer was not easy to find. And she was right, of course. And he might have only imagined her defense was a shade too positive.

Before they went back to school, he had heard the boys making jokes about a "light in my window," performing mock dramatics with a hand over the heart, collapsing in laughter. It didn't make sense to him until he realized one afternoon in Terry's room when they were having before-dinner martinis that the large candle in its ornamental sconce by the window was burned down about halfway. It was a purely decorative fixture. There were others about the house, in keeping with the Spanish ranch feeling of the place: two tall stands in the hallway, antiques from the altar of a mission, a great branch at the head of the stairs. But they were never lighted.

He had strolled over to the window and observed that the candle was in a direct line of sight over the archway of the patio down to the end of the stable where Durrell had his quarters. He had said nothing, because it was too easy for her to say she used it as a night light. Maybe she did. Maybe the whole thing was the imagination of a couple of damn-fool kids. How was it that they were aware of "something funny," when he had never seen a flicker of a look or a betraying word or attitude? Easy. He didn't want to see anything, and he was not a jealous person.

Then had come his family trouble, and the trip to Denver, the settling of a suit out of court, and Paul had been preoccupied for days. When he realized he would be back in Tucson sooner than planned, he decided to use the opportunity and do a little sleuthing and get the whole thing cleared up once and for all. There was no use accusing Terry. He had heard her lie with the face of truth too many times. She would be wide-eyed, insulted, and then she would laugh at him.

If the light in the window was a signal, the response was certainly delayed, which couldn't be very flattering to Terry. The whole thing seemed childish. The boys had obviously been making up things, and why the hell had he paid any attention to them? Surely a man like Durrell—brainless, coarse, smelling of horses and sweat—surely Terry was too smart to get involved with a man like that. She was fastidious, and even her overt flirtations were with someone who could pitch a good game. She liked a kind of dangerous, high-level bantering, someone who knew the rules. He had been amused when one of their ranch-owner acquaintances made a heavy-handed pass. She had turned to him, Paul, and winked at him, and then proceeded to destroy the rancher with a kind of cruel ridicule that left the man red-faced and silent.

But Durrell, with his empty face, empty head—and then Paul remembered seeing him on the chestnut yearling, walking around the corral. He was shirtless, in dungarees, and the sweat glistened on the muscles of his arms and back, which were tanned to a pure gold; his right hand was gently stroking the neck of the nervous animal over and over, and he was making low, soothing noises. He remembered that he had appreciated the sight as one might a beautiful piece of bronze and gold sculpture. He had turned to Terry, beside him, and he remembered her face was expressionless, her eyes masked by the black sunglasses. Her lips were slightly parted, however, and the tip of her tongue was moistening them. Then she said, "I'm thirsty. Let's go back and build a drink."

That was months ago. Of course, Durrell accompanied her on rides, but then, she had never liked riding alone. "It's foolishness," she had said, "like scuba-diving without a buddy. A horse goes lame, you can't sit out in the middle of the desert waiting for someone to show up—or walk five miles in the sun."

An hour passed, and Paul gave up his watch with relief. He would go back to his apartment and phone her in the morning, telling her he had just arrived. When he had about reached his car, he saw the lights of another car coming toward him, and he stepped into the shadows near the gate. Anyone on foot was suspect around here, and he didn't want a car to stop and offer a lift or ask if he'd had a flat.

But the car was slowing, and then as it turned it picked up speed and scattered gravel as it went through the gate. It was the ranch utility truck, and for an instant he saw its driver. Durrell. He was in a hurry, for the truck tore up the driveway. The moonlight was glinting on the black shiny top, which swayed on the curves.

He hadn't even been home! There was no point in following, Paul thought, he'd be seen, he'd have to go through it all again. He should have stayed. He got into his car and wondered why he felt rocky again. His lips dried, his head throbbed. His plans for a simple confrontation had seemed so reasonable. No dramatics. If Terry wanted her centaur, if she wanted a bronze body smelling of horse sweat, that was okay with him, and he'd close the books.

But he hadn't reckoned on what his imagination would do when he was back in his apartment in Tucson, of the agony he would live through for the next twenty-four hours. Just closing the books wasn't possible. He was sick of being "a darling" and "do this, do that for me," and being "an angel," of being used. He was slow to rage, and rarely gave it expression except in biting words. But the following night would be quite different, cold, planned, full of hate. And he would stand again, waiting, the whole night through if necessary, with a small gun in his hand.

A party was in full swing late the following night when Paul drew up into the heavy shadows of the eucalyptus outside the ranch. The moon had not yet risen, and in the blackness a mist from the warm water of the swimming pool hung above it like a small cloud shot with wriggling reflections of light. In the deep surrounding silence Herb Alpert's trumpet lilted lovingly through *Desafinado*. Voices brayed, topping the full volume of the stereo.

Paul pushed buttons that would raise all the windows, cutting out the distant racket. With the whisper of the air-conditioning he relaxed; disciplined to patience, he prepared for a long wait.

It was two o'clock before the first cars began to trickle down the driveway and out of the gate. It was two-thirty when the pool lights and the garden illumination went out. One more car, and then in rapid succession the lights in the house were turned off.

Finally Paul stood watching in the blackness of the open door of the living room, his eyes on the flickering candle in Terry's window. He looked at the greenish figures on his wrist watch: three-ten. In the distance there was a soft whinny from the stables, and the thought of how far sound travels at night in the desert passed through his mind. He decided it was time to go—to go to the second station of his vigil. The steps inside the house were deeply carpeted, and he ascended them quickly and noiselessly. In a guest bedroom next to Terry's he pulled back a satin curtain. From here he could see over the balcony down to the driveway and the branching gravel road that led to the stables.

He listened. There were frank, uncautious footsteps on the gravel outside the patio. A whistled tune kept the rhythm, unhurried, deliberate.

Swiftly Paul left the guest room, went down the hall, and opened Terry's door, quickly, silently.

"Not a sound, Terry," he whispered.

She gasped as she saw the wide-open, obscene eye of the gun upon her.

"I mean it!" he growled. "Now don't warn him in any way. I don't want to have to kill you."

Terry's face blanched and she looked all of her age. Her hands grasped her throat as though to keep it from screaming. She sat rigid, the sheet pulled up over her naked body, barely covering her full, pendant breasts.

Paul smiled and whispered, "Tell you all about it some day." Reaching out for a slipper stool, he sat down upon it in front of the closed door in an angle of the wall that concealed it from the balcony window. And the little gun, held gently in fingers that were bleeding at the tips, perched like a small black bird on his crossed knees.

They waited. Silence. Nothing but the sound of the fountain, which continued its purling song. The candleflame wavered. Held steady.

Terry's breathing came in rasping sounds of sobbing. Once, she started to speak, and Paul cut her off with a whispered, "Not a word!"

A soft wind passed like a lonely ghost through the patio, changing the rhythm of the fountain, lifting the leaves into movement. And then it was still again. Like an afterthought, the candleflame flickered madly, lay fainting, flat, and blue for an instant, and then grew tall and calm.

In the distance a motorcycle coughed and roared into life, and as the sound rose and then fell into the distance Terry began to laugh and cry hysterically.

Paul put the gun into his jacket pocket. "How did you do it? How did you warn him?" And then, sighing wearily, he said, "The way you looked, I suppose. He saw you. Looking scared."

Terry buried her face into a pillow and sobbed, rolling from side to side, saying over and over, "You sonofabitch! You sonofabitch!"

Cora was sitting up in bed with a book propped on the mound of her belly. It was a nice long spy story, number seven on *Time* magazine's best-seller list. It had an attractive, slick dust jacket, in which the artist had composed the U. N. building against a desolate background of burnt-out skyscrapers and a red sunset.

She had settled down once again after an argument with Maxie. Maxie was restless. She had let him out before she came to bed, waited, and let him in. Then fifteen minutes later he stood beside the bed, looking into her face and wagging his tail.

"What's the matter with your kidneys, for Heaven's sake!" But she got up again and let him out. He was gone so long she had to whistle for him, and he came loping back, ran into the bedroom, and jumped up onto the bed.

She yelled at him. "Maxie, get off the bed! You know you're not allowed up there! Now get off, get *off!*"

He slithered off the bed, rolling his eyes at her, tucked his tail tight, and wriggled under the bed. But when Cora got in, the gap between the springs and the floor became too small for him, and he wriggled out again.

She was deep into the third paragraph of the book when she caught his eyes looking at her coaxingly.

"Maxie, darling, you are an idiot. I can't read while you watch! Now please lie down and be a quiet boy." The tone of her voice sounded like an invitation, and he bounced up onto the foot of the bed, curling up quickly and putting his nose between his paws, almost smiling, with great charm.

"Off! Off the bed, Maxie! What's got into you? You know better than this!" He gave up and dropped off onto the floor, where he thumped his body down hard, groaning in disgust.

After about ten pages her attention began to waver. She couldn't keep track of who was who; the long Russian names didn't clue in the gender too well, and there was so much Comrade this and Comrade that, and when one Comrade said to another Comrade, "Comrade, there is no room for love, we cannot think of ourselves or of our personal desires," she shook her head. She hadn't realized one of them was a girl. Or was he? She? With a loud yawn she turned and looked at the clock. Rafe should have been at the airport long ago. He should have called by now.

She hated this shift. It was only five nights—*mornings*, rather— every eight weeks, and this was the last one, and then he had three full days off.

He always phoned as soon as he reached the airport, because she wanted him to. "Don't you want to find out if I'm asleep?" she had asked. "It's just silly—waking you up." But he always called.

They usually went to bed about ten o'clock, and when Rafe rose at three, she could never "stay asleep with you tiptoeing around." After he left, she read or knitted until he phoned at four, and then she went back to sleep.

This morning she was far from asleep. Bill was scrounging around inside of her, and the book kept tilting from one side to the other. She sat up straighter. No good. She removed a pillow and tried to lie flat. No good.

Her last visit to Dr. Titus had been disturbing. There was another doctor, a good-looking young man, whom he had introduced as Dr. Wells. "This is your obstetrician. He'll deliver you when the time comes."

Confused, she had said, "But I thought——"

"Oh, I'll be with you," Dr. Titus had assured her. "I'll be assisting. But Dr. Wells is on the staff of the hospital, and I want you to be in the best and most experienced hands." He laughed his gravelly laugh and said to Dr. Wells, "That right, Doctor?"

She still didn't see why, although she knew she would not be delivered in the clinic except in an emergency. Cora finally guessed that it had to do with hospital policy or medical ethics or something —none of which she understood, but the hell with it. She had not developed any sentimental trust and confidence in Dr. Titus. He was brief and vague and full of *hum*'s and *ha*'s. Dr. Wells had examined her and the two doctors couldn't agree as to when the baby would arrive—two weeks, three weeks, any time.

Dr. Titus said, "Well, according to the date of conception—around the end of June, wasn't it?"

And Cora thought, "You louse! You too! Did you *have* to tell him?" And she said, coldly, "I haven't the slightest idea. My husband and I have always had fairly regular marital relations. I missed my period the first week in July."

And Dr. Titus hurriedly said, "Mm. Ah. Yes, yes of course."

Anyway, she was packed. And Rafe was only twenty minutes away, if he broke a few speed limits. And thirty-five, forty minutes to the hospital in Tucson. Hurry up and wait. That's probably what would happen.

It was just no good trying to read. It was nearly four-thirty. Why hadn't Rafe called? Some perfectly good reason, of course. Rafe had told her that the airport seemed to be in a constant state of emergency. Air freight increased suddenly with a railroad strike, or there was a rush of tourists, or there was some kind of breakdown in communications, and they acted as though Rafe were the only troubleshooter in the place. Everything that could go wrong always seemed to go wrong in the early-morning shift.

She flung the book onto the floor, making Maxie jump. "I'm sorry, boy. Go back to sleep." He nuzzled her hand with a cold nose and rolled his eyes in the direction of the foot of the bed and then back to her. Firmly, she said, "No." He gave up once more, sneezed, lay down, and licked a toenail.

She reached for a cigarette. It didn't taste very good and she put it out. "You're making me seasick, Bill. Be quiet, sh-h quiet." Tenderly, she patted and stroked the bulge above her hipbone. For a second she was dizzy and there was a wave of nausea, but it passed and she felt she could breathe better; there seemed to be more room.

"Who-o-o, that's better; thanks, Bill!" When she pulled her nightgown straight, the whole familiar contour had altered; for the first time she felt as though she could take a complete breath, and she relaxed.

She was having a nightmare when the phone rang. She was on a ski slope with Rafe, crouched almost double, ready for a jump; but her skis were stuck to the snow, she couldn't make it, she was too heavy, she was heading for a whole mountain of whiteness, she knew she would disappear, and they would never find her. But a bell kept ringing.

She staggered out of bed to the living room, and she felt the wetness on her legs. The back of her nightgown was damp, and her whole belly felt like a dead weight.

"Rafe—honey—" she panted, without bothering to say hello. "Rafe —call Titus—I'm losing water—I think the sac has ruptured. Get here, darling!"

"Mrs. March, Mrs. March!" The phone was chattering, and she struggled to give it her attention. "This is Carl Hergesheimer at the airport. Are you in trouble?"

"The baby's coming! Where's Rafe!"

"Mrs. March, I'm calling *for* Rafe. He just phoned in, said he'd been in some kind of an accident, that he'd be late, and to save time he wanted me to phone you that he's okay."

The nightmare, the fright, the water that shouldn't be coming, and the word accident, and Cora screamed, "What? *What?* What accident? Rafe! Oh, Christ!" But the phone wasn't in her hand, it was on the floor. She didn't hear the man say, "It's all right, Mrs. March, I'll get an ambulance out to you right away, and I'll tell Rafe as soon as he gets here. Mrs. March? Do you hear me?"

It was a series of judgments, estimates of volume, speed, space, and time. Faster than any man-made computer, the eye received, the mind decided. With more facts, decisions changed, action altered. Correct or incorrect, right or wrong, the result became the truth. "If only" was no longer a component. The sum, the solution, the answer—and then the consequence—became unalterable.

The clock read three-forty-five on the dashboard. The radio was playing softly; the car was pleasantly warm with the heater on low. The road was empty, and the night still stretched out in all directions. The paving rose and fell in gentle swells, and Rafe caught the moon in his side mirror each time he went over a rise.

About a mile ahead was a pair of red taillights that appeared and disappeared in the shallow troughs and rises. Beyond was a long, hardly perceptible curve that swung around and through a pass of low hills.

Rafe caught the moon in his mirror again. And then in his rearview mirror. Only it wasn't the moon. It wobbled. Rafe touched the mirror with his thumb, to center it. Car with one lamp out? Motorcycle? Cop. He checked his speed. Sixty-five on the nose. But just in case, he slowed up a little.

It was a section of the new highway that was still under construction some fifty yards to the left, and this old section was only two-way, sloping into the sand on either side.

The guy closed up and was tail-gating. "Well, *pass*, you stupe! Get off my tail!" In front of Rafe the red lights were still a safe distance ahead, moving slowly, and as he gained on the vehicle his own headlights picked out the shape. And empty gravel truck, flat, dark.

"There's lots of room, mister, but watch it." Rafe stabbed his brake in short, quick flashes as a signal that he wasn't the only car on the road. "Well, make up your mind, you sonofabitch. Go, *now!* No, *hold* it!" He had caught the glimmer of headlights coming from the opposite direction, and the thought ran briefly through his mind, why a guy had to wait until there were three cars in a cluster to get impatient about passing, when in a few seconds they would all be widely separated again.

The right moment was gone. The decision to wait or to pass had been made, and Rafe could see the whole thing as though it had already happened.

He heard the cycle roar and the light in his mirror shifted to the left as it went around him. Rafe swung the station wagon to the right, over the edge, slewing in the sand and gravel to give the motorcycle time to slow up behind the truck, which the cyclist obviously had not seen. Instead, the cycle turned sharply left again to pass the truck, and the lights of the car from the other direction came up fast.

The truck driver, through the rattle and rumble of his vehicle, heard a faint shattering of glass, and in his side mirror, silhouetted against the moonlight, he saw a man leaping in an arc as though he were bounced from a trampoline. He pulled up, set his brakes, and climbed down to investigate, but it was all over. He saw a station wagon stuck in the sand; he heard screams coming from a vintage Buick sedan. Over near the edge of the new highway there was a small but furious fire burning, licking at the feet of something lying on the ground.

He followed Rafe and a man from the sedan, who were running over toward the figure. Cursing, yelling, they pulled the cyclist away from the fire, and the truck driver peeled off his leather jacket and beat out the flames that had gathered and licked up the man's legs.

"He's dead, he's dead! Jeeze, look at his neck!"

"Damn fool kid! Prob'ly drunk!"

Rafe said, "You people okay? Anybody hurt in your car?" He looked over at the sedan.

The man said, "Naw! 'At's my wife yellin'. She ain't hurt. *Shut up*, Irene! That motor just bounced off us—broke our headlights is all. *Irene*, will ya f' Christ sake . . ."

The truck driver had pulled out a flashlight and trained it onto the cyclist's face. "Ain't no kid. But he's dead awright."

The Buick door opened, and a woman in a heavy sweater and slacks got out and started toward them. Her husband yelled, "Irene, you get back in there. You don't wanna see this!"

She paused, with her hand to her mouth. "Is he hurt? What can we do? Oh, *God!*"

"He's dead. Now *shut up!* Get back in the car!"

The truck driver said, "Looks like the guy didn't have either a helmet or goggles on. No sign of 'em. Pretty hard to see good with the wind blowin' in your eyes. What happened, didn't see me ahead of you, huh?" he said to Rafe.

"I don't think he saw anything but my car. I tried—I did my damnedest—to signal him, to give him room."

The Buick man said quickly, "I don't think it was anybody's fault. What the hell, he came out from behind you, like he'd been hidin' there. Never saw him until he smacked us. By the way, my name's Hoadley," he said and held out a hand.

Gravely the men gave their names and shook hands briefly. Johnson, the truck driver said his name was. He offered Rafe a pull out of the sand, said he had a good tow line.

Rafe said, "Thanks, but maybe we should stay put until we get the police. You're not involved, really," he said to Johnson. "Maybe you can phone the police from the gas station up ahead. It's about a mile from here, I think." He looked around to get his bearings. "Hey, somebody's comin' from that farmhouse. There's a light in it; maybe they put in a call already."

"Must have seen the fire," said Hoadley. "Maybe they heard the explosion. People are good about reporting stuff. Now, you take in the city . . ."

A jeep was bouncing like a jack rabbit toward them; it skidded to a stop, and a lean young man leaped out of the car before it came to a standstill. "Anybody hurt, anybody hurt?" Then, when he saw the dead cyclist, he groaned. "Oh, Jeez, what happened?"

The three men explained the accident, and the young man, who said he had been in the barn with his stock when he heard the noise, told them he had called the Highway Patrol Office in Tucson. The dispatcher told him there was a patrol car not too far away from them, and that he'd also send an ambulance.

After that there suddenly seemed nothing to say. They stood around, listening for a police siren. The young farmer said, "Hey, I got some bourbon up to the house. You want I should get it? You probably need——"

"Thanks, I think we should wait," Rafe said. "I don't think it would help much if we had booze on us when the boys get here."

They had all moved away from the figure lying on the ground. Someone had said they shouldn't touch him anymore till the police came. They would explain how they had to drag him away from the fire, and they all agreed that he must have been dead as soon as he hit the ground.

Hoadley had made a trip to his car and consoled his now quietly weeping wife, and as he rejoined the group on the edge of the highway he said, "She's okay now. Poor kid. She's had enough to upset her, lately."

The others stared at him.

"Well, I mean," Hoadley went on, hastily, "I know it's not so important. A guy's been killed. I know. But Irene's been worryin' her head off about her mother, who's been sick. That's where we're going. To her mother's in Albuquerque. We'd just got an early start. I sez to her yestiddy, 'What the hell, why don't we just drive up and see for ourselves,' and she sez——"

A faint wail in the distance snapped their heads up. The volume increased, and in moments they could see the headlights and the flashing, revolving red light of a State Patrol car. It braked to a fast stop, its siren quitting on a grunt, and two men came out of the car at a run.

It was all very expert and quick. Names, license numbers, details, were told; they were all asked if they knew the dead man, and they all said no. Until one of the officers joined them with the wallet and identification of the motorcyclist. He read it off to the group. "'David Durrell, Blue Sky Ranch, Kenyon Road, Sabado, Arizona.'"

Rafe blurted out, "For Christ *sake!*" and all the faces turned toward him.

"You knew him?" asked the officer.

"No, I didn't," Rafe said, truthfully. Easy now, easy, he thought. Think about it later. "I mean I know that he worked for Terry Ostander; I knew she had a trainer by that name at the ranch."

"Do you want to inform her of the death of this man, or would you prefer we do it?"

"No, I'll call her. I'll do it." It was the last thing he wanted to do, but he didn't see how he could explain why he didn't want to.

"She would know the next of kin, then?"

"I suppose so. I don't know anything about that."

As far as responsibility was concerned, the patrolmen agreed they were free to go; they might be contacted later by the coroner, if he decided on further investigation, and also by the insurance companies involved. The Hoadleys would have to stay put until daylight, which wasn't very far off, because of their non-functioning headlights. The young farmer invited them to wait up at the farmhouse and have a cup of coffee; he extended the invitation to Rafe and the truck driver, but they refused with thanks, and the Hoadleys went off in the jeep.

Quite without thinking, Rafe got himself off the hook about calling Terry. While they were getting his station wagon out of the sand he happened to mention that he wondered what Durrell was doing on one of the Ostander boys' bikes this time of the morning.

"You mean the motorcycle wasn't his?" one of the officers asked, and got out his notebook again. And when Rafe explained, the officer said, "You better let us handle it. We'll call her. Have to find out if he had it with her permission or what. Might have stolen it."

"What difference does it make?" Rafe asked, emotion beginning to gather in him. He wanted to get away from here. He had to call the airport. He was late. He had to call Cora. And what the hell was he going to tell her?

"Insurance," the man was saying. "Matter of responsibility. If it was stolen, it's one thing; if he had her permission, it's another."

"Yeah, I see, I see . . ." Rafe got into the station wagon and started the engine.

Switching on his headlights, he pulled away from the dramatic cluster of crisscrossing beams—from the patrol car, the ambulance, various spotlights, and emergency flares making the night seem black by contrast. In a hundred yards or so it became apparent that daylight was not far off; there was a grayness, the beginning of outlines, and in the distance the lights on the gas station looked weak as the strengthening dawn showed the form of a decrepit building.

Behind two spotless, shining gas tanks was a fly-blown lunch room, approached by a pair of wobbly steps and guarded by a wheezing ancient mongrel bitch who growled automatically as Rafe called out, "Hey, Brad, use your phone?"

"Sure. Say, what's going on down there? Heard sirens awhile back. Anybody hurt?"

"Uh—yeah. Tell you in a minute." Rafe was at the pay-phone on the wall, dialing his home. Just before he completed, before it could ring, he hung up quickly. What the hell was he going to say? In the few minutes it took to drive from the scene of the accident, he had begun to get the shakes. There was a mixture of emotions fizzing in him, beginning to smoke like incompatible chemicals. He'd said it so often: "I'd like to break his goddamn neck!" And there it was. For real. Durrell was dead. I'm late, Cora. I've been in an accident. I'm not hurt. I just killed Dave Durrell. *No!* I didn't! I actually tried to save his life. Well, not *his*, just a man on a motorcycle. Terry's going to be hysterical, think I killed him. No, the police will tell her that he struck a car driven by some people called Hoadley. Won't they? Ah, the hell with *her*. What about Cora? He started to dial once more, after fishing out his returned coin and dropping it again into the slot. He'd just keep it simple, say he had been delayed, go back to sleep, honey. . . . But she'd know, she'd listen to his voice and say, what's the matter? Darling, Durrell is dead, we're free of *that* nightmare, isn't it wonderful! I fixed the sonofabitch for keeps. . . . I had nothing to do with it. Never, never was I able to even get in one healthy swing at the goddamn bastard's face. All these months I've gone around with a knot in my gut, never even knowing what he looked like—until now. Not even knowing it was him, with what's his name's, Johnson's flashlight pointing at him, revealing an unmarked, serene face lying in the sand, twisted away all wrong from the body.

He had felt nothing but a twinge of compassionate horror, and by the time he learned his name, the ambulance boys had covered him up and were hoisting him into the back of their wagon. Even then, his first reaction was that it was a mistake. It was a mistake, because he, *he, Rafe March*, had a date with him, someday, sometime. He had always felt the time would come when they would be face to face, and all the poison would spill out of him in a wonderful, satisfying crunching of bone and gristle and blood all over the goddamn place. Instead, there he was, covered by a blanket, being slipped into the back of a meat wagon. A nothing. The innocent nothing.

"Brad—" He put the receiver back again before it could ring.

"Yah, Rafe?"

"Give me a shot of something, will you?"

"You know I don't sell liquor, Rafe."

"Who said anything about buying? Don't tell me you haven't got a bottle of something around?"

"Oh, sure, sure, Rafe. Gin is all. Okay?"

"Anything."

Rafe dialed the airport this time. Carl Hergesheimer answered, and before Rafe could say more than his name, Carl was raising hell at his being late. Julian, he said, was mad as the devil because he hadn't been able to leave. Finally, by shouting, Rafe got the man's attention and explained the situation. Carl's impatience was a good excuse for Rafe to say that it would save time if he, Carl, would call Cora. That way, she would get the bare facts, that he was okay and would call her later. Later, when he had sorted out his thinking and gotten hold of himself, he could tell her all about it.

It seemed like a plot, a conspiracy to make him feel guilty.

First Carl, at the airport: "What the hell took you so long? It's been twenty minutes since you called me."

"I—I had to have a drink. I was getting the shakes."

"The *shakes!* From a scratched fender? I thought you said you weren't hurt?"

"I wasn't—but——"

"Well, never mind. I've called Fred Hines to sub for you. You've got to get to the hospital."

"The hospital? I told you I wasn't hurt."

Carl shook his head. "Your wife. I called her and she told me. She must be on the way to the hospital by now."

"*What!* What happened to her?"

"Easy, Rafe. The baby's coming, is all."

At the hospital, the girl at the reception desk said coolly, "Oh, Mr. March, we've been trying to find you everywhere." Everywhere? There were only two places, home and the airport, to call. She sounded as though she'd tried all the bars and whorehouses in town. "Your wife's very worried. She heard you'd been in an accident." She said it with a lift of her eyebrows that indicated she was in the know, that it was a cover-up of some kind. We know men, we nurses. Fine time of the day to be on the town.

Rafe didn't feel like making explanations. He said, "Where do I go?"

"Up to maternity, fourth floor. Check with the nurse at the desk and she'll give you a gown."

"Give me a gown? Yeah, that's fine," he mumbled and turned to the elevator.

It was the same thing on the maternity floor. "Oh, *you're* Mr.

March. My, you *are* a difficult person to find! Dr. McCoy will take care of you."

Dr. McCoy was a young intern. At least he didn't say anything, just took him into a room where he had Rafe wash his hands and gave him a gown and a silly cap, and pointed vaguely at some swinging doors that said LABOR ROOMS.

Another nurse met him beyond the swinging doors. She gave him a quick "Who are you—you don't belong in here" look and said, "Yes?"

"I'm here to see my wife. Mrs. Rafael March."

"Oh, Mr. March. Your wife will be so relieved. We've had a time calming her down."

"How is she?"

"Oh, she's fine. Pretty slow. It's going to be quite a while, I'm afraid."

Cora's face was a little on the pale side, but she didn't look as though she'd needed calming down. She smiled cheerfully and put out her arms to receive him. From the weight of them and the way they slid limply down to the bed again, he realized she'd been given a shot of some kind, and when she spoke her tongue was thick.

"What'd he have to scare me for? You're all right, aren'tcha, honey?"

"I'm fine, darling."

"You really okay? Wha' happened?" Then she giggled and exaggerated the *t*. "Wha*t* happened?"

"I was just forced off the road and got the car stuck in some sand. Don't you want this shade raised? The sun's coming up."

"Huh-uh. No. It hurts my eyes."

The room was a small cubicle with one window, a straight chair, and a table. The metal shade of a lamp over the bed had been turned under the bulb, and the light was dim. The flat rays of the rising sun sparkled around the edges of the venetian blinds, asking to be allowed to enter.

"Mr. March," the nurse said at the door, "when you leave, please be sure and put up the guard rail again." He looked blank, and then the nurse walked over and illustrated. "It goes up this way— just like on a baby's crib."

"What's it for?"

The two women laughed at his ignorance.

"'At's in case I get a little rambunctious, honey," his wife said. And then her eyes filmed and she whispered, "Like this—" and she flung her arms out, grasping the rail till her knuckles whitened. Rafe's eyes widened in fright. The nurse was looking at her wrist watch. Then Cora relaxed.

"Good," said the nurse. "Ten seconds. Twenty-five minutes." She dropped the rail and said, "You take it easy, now. I'll be back in a while."

Rafe sat down on the edge of the bed again, took one of Cora's hands, and held it to his cheek, as much for his own comforting as for hers.

"You look pretty," he said.

"Oh, I'll just bet I do. No lipstick. And I've been shaved and enema'd and washed with stinky soap. Attractive. E-ugh! And don't you think this is a real boss number?" She fingered the hospital gown. "Very mod. Mini-skirt length, sleeves just above the elbow, and tied with a fetching bow at the neck. In back, yet."

"Where's all your stuff? Your suitcase and things. Or did you bring them?"

"Back in my room. I'm in a three-bed ward. Nobody else's in there, not yet."

Rafe shook his head. "I don't understand. I don't understand *anything*, it seems."

"That's because I can't talk very good."

"No, that's not what I mean."

"Oh. This is the labor room, darling. Delivery room is at the end of the hall—I think. I have the feeling I'm going to be in here for a long time."

"Not much fun, poor honey."

"Oh, just boring, darling. Dr. Wells said it would be. Something about not having the fluid to help dilate. He's very nice, Rafe. I like him." She closed her eyes. "You better go now, Rafe."

"Why? Why must I go? Don't you want me to stay with you?"

She shook her head. "No. I just want to be with people who won't mind if I start yelling or swearing or something."

"Oh, it won't be that bad. They'll knock you out, won't they?"

"Probably. Even so, honey, this is my party. You go back to work now. They'll call you. I want to—rest—a little while."

"Okay, whatever you say. I hate to leave."

He leaned over and kissed her, and she went "Mm," but her eyes were closed.

There was a coffee machine in one corner of the waiting room at the end of the hall. Rafe put in some coins and received a paper cup full of something that was at least hot. He lit a cigarette and wandered over to the window, which looked out over a parking lot and the rear entrances to several big stores. In the street beyond, morning traffic was in full swing, and the sounds came up harshly through the open window. The air still held a chill, and the wind blew in little gusts. Rafe slid the window closed.

He looked around at the room, with its standard plastic cushions and chrome chairs and sofa, a wobbly coffee table with some old magazines, and an ashtray full of cigarette butts. The leavings of the previous nervous father, Rafe decided, and decided that he would go nuts if he stayed in here very long, with nothing to do but look at a couple of "paint by numbers" school of oil paintings on the walls. One was the cliché of a red sunset behind a saguaro, and another of Mission San Xavier del Bac.

The smell of disinfectant, stale tobacco, and bad coffee began to work on his stomach, and he thought he would go for a walk and then come back.

The door swung open, and a young man in a white coat and a reflector stuck on his forehead came in and said,

"Mr. March?"

"Yes."

"I'm Dr. Wells. How do you do?" Rafe took the hand offered him.

"Anything wrong?" Rafe asked anxiously.

"Not a thing. Everything's fine. But slow. It's going to be a long while and I think, and Mrs. March agrees, that you'd be better off if you'd go on back to your work."

Rafe shook his head.

"They've already called in somebody else. For the day. I guess they thought I wouldn't be much use to them. For one thing, I was in an accident earlier this morning. I mean I was *there*. The guy passing me got killed."

Dr. Wells nodded. "I know. Your wife was really a handful until we checked and found out you were all right. We didn't tell her the details."

"That's good. I'd appreciate it if you could see to it that nobody tells her about the man that was killed. He was a man we knew. I think that can be saved until this is all over."

"Quite right. I'll tell the girls. Are you sure you're okay?"

"I wasn't even touched."

"Well, not physically perhaps. How are your nerves?" The doctor smiled. He seemed very young to Rafe. Very young and yet very sure. There was the intensity of posture and the stooped, drawing in of the shoulders that told of hours of books. There was the look around the eyes of not enough sleep for years.

Rafe said, "I think the baby coming kind of wiped out all the shock of the accident."

The doctor didn't speak for a moment. Then he said, "Maybe. You look as though you might be fairly resilient. You sure there's nothing we can do for you?"

"You mean, like a tranquillizer or something? No, thanks. Oh, if I stick around here"—he waved at the room—"I'm sure I'll go nuts. I'm not much good at just waiting."

Dr. Wells laughed. "I'm sorry I can't hurry things up for you."

"Oh, I mean, if I could be with Cora—if I could—hold her hand or something!"

"I know. You'd like to do something. I think it would be better for your wife if she didn't have to think about you being worried. Right now she's a little jazzed up from an injection and she's talking a streak."

"Oh? What about?" Rafe asked quickly.

"Taxes. She's got a whole theory about taxation. Very interesting."

They both laughed, and then the doctor said, "You've got nothing to worry about. It's going to be slow. It's a big baby, but it's in good position. I'd suggest you go home and try to relax, take it easy. I know that's easier said than done. Too bad you can't go back to work. Anyway, my guess is that you could check with us about—" he consulted his watch—"about five o'clock this evening. Of course, events can change, but the office has your number, and you can be here—in what?"

"About forty minutes."

"Fine. I'll see you later, then. And don't worry, okay?" He grinned and took Rafe's hand, and then Rafe felt that he was being hustled out. He was steered from the room and guided firmly, smilingly to the elevator.

Helplessly he said, "Tell Cora I—tell her——"

Dr. Wells said, "Don't worry, I'll tell her you love her—as often as she wants to hear it!"

Never had he felt so superfluous. It wasn't a question of not being needed. He was in the way; he not only couldn't help, he would be a hindrance.

Everything was functioning smoothly at the airport. His chair was filled; his console of knobs and switches and dials was attended by Fred Hines. No use hanging around there.

He passed the scene of the accident, and he wasn't quite sure of the exact spot, so efficiently had all signs been removed. Even the burnt-up motorcycle had been carted off. And Durrell? Lying in a drawer in the morgue, waiting for someone to come and look and say, that's Dave. Nothing he could do about that, either.

He drove into the carport and went into the kitchen, where Constanza looked like a big question mark.

Fearfully, and yet smiling, she clasped her hands tightly, saying, "The Senora? She has gone? To hospital?" And as he nodded, she whispered, "*Dios!* She is all right?"

"She's fine, Connie. Doctor says it'll be a long time. Tonight maybe." The language barrier kept him from going into further detail.

Turning from him, she sighed, crossed herself, shook her head, and went into some murmurings in her own language. Picking up a sponge, she absently wiped the immaculate sink, her gaze resting on nothing, musing (probably, Rafe thought, on the sweet, painful experience of birth).

"Anything I can do to help you? Constanza?"

"Senor?" She came back with a start.

She was right, Rafe thought. What *could* he do that would be helpful? Mop a floor? Wash a window? That was her department.

Somehow she understood. She looked at him and then smiled as though she knew what he was going through.

"*Paciencia, Senor.* You will have to—ah—" and she clasped her hands together and rotated her thumbs, and then burst into a peal of laughter and more Spanish.

Rafe nodded ruefully.

She said, "You no go to work?"

He shook his head. "No, they gave me the day off—so I could twiddle my thumbs."

He imitated her gesture, and she laughed some more. Then she held a finger in the air as though a brilliant idea had occurred to her.

"Senor, you maybe—clean the swimming pool?"

"Good idea. That'll use up a nice long half hour."

"I fix you lunch in a little while." It had a dismissive tone. Please, leave me to do my work; get out of the kitchen so I can get on with it.

He went out and crossed the hall into the nursery. Empty, waiting for its new occupant, clean, shining, sunny. What was it going to be like, he wondered, having a baby in here? No emotion accompanied the thought. It was—"a baby." Not *the* baby. *Our* baby. *Our* child. Somewhat surprised, he had no feeling of being deprived. He had beat it to death, that was what had happened. Deprivation, like rejection, was almost the most painful sensation one could experience. He had had enough of both. Somewhere along the line his mind had accepted the fact that there were certain areas that were intolerable and must be shut out, curtained off.

He went into the living room, but Constanza was busy waxing the TV set. The place smelled of lemon oil.

The bedroom looked done. The bed was made up, the venetians drawn, all signs of Cora's hectic departure eliminated.

He pulled the spread down, and removing his shoes and belt and tie, he stretched out, exhausted.

He examined his indifference again. It was not so much a suppression, he thought, but more like having heaved something overboard that was useless. He had had experience with suppression; whatever it was didn't stay suppressed, but wandered around in the body and the mind looking for a place to hurt. Like a lump of pain.

This was different. More comfortable. But lifeless. Mashed potatoes without salt. Tasteless. It didn't have the beauty contained in melancholy, nor the potential in depression: the surge back upward to excitement and interest.

This was as though he'd been scooped hollow. Like a . . . His mind searched for a simile. Cora was good at those. What would she suggest? A shell? Too ordinary. Not good anyway, a shell didn't have guts to begin with. Gutless. That was it. Not in the usual sense of lacking stamina, courage, grit. But just plain and simple eviscerated. The contents removed. The contents with which one experienced delight and love and wonder and curiosity and—caring. What could he do without them? What would the rest of his life be like if he couldn't coax them back into being again—about *anything?*

Cora. At the hospital. He hung on to that, because he wanted to feel *something.* Life without emotion was like an engine without fuel. He had felt from Dr. Wells's talk with him that to try to share her pain, to be helpful, would simply make it worse. If she had said, "Stick with me," they would have had to throw him out bodily. But instead, she wanted to go it alone, with the impersonal, uninvolved help of doctors and nurses.

In sudden remembrance he swung his feet off the bed and went to the phone in the living room. There was no reason why he shouldn't do the normal thing about the accident. He had been there. He could say he was sorry.

Paul Holloway answered the phone. Rafe asked to speak to Terry, but Paul told him that she was "pretty upset" and was lying down. His voice was so cold, he was so obviously anxious not to talk to him, that Rafe was led into defensiveness. "I hope she doesn't think it was my fault, Paul."

"Well, she does, Rafe. It's pretty unreasonable, I'll grant you— from what the police told us. She keeps saying that you knew, that you'd followed him, and what were you doing on the road that time of the morning."

"For Christ's sake, I was on my way to work! I never saw Durrell in my life. I didn't even know who it was until the cop read his identification from his wallet, so that's just ridiculous. Besides, I never touched him. He ran smack into the Buick that was coming the other way."

"I know, I know, Rafe. But—uh—well, she was—fond—of Durrell. She's not making much sense at the moment. She's been drinking, and I—uh—really have to go, Rafe. Thank you for calling."

"Okay, Paul. You bet. Just tell her I'm very sorry."

"I will. I will. Thank you."

Rafe hung up and went back into the bedroom. He thought, Christ what a pipsqueak Holloway's turned into. Why the hell does he stick around and take that kind of crap from Terry? Because he loves her? That kind of love was just plain suicidal. One-sided, slavish, the kind of guy who hops to a woman's whistle. Gutless.

Well?

Paul might say the same thing about him. If he knew. *If* he knew! Everybody in town knew. And everybody probably considered *him* gutless. On the whole, the attitude of the town had been mostly one of indifference. Fifty years ago, they would have made his and Cora's life intolerable. Whispers and heads tossed in righteousness, skirts pulled aside on the sidewalk, as though Cora and Rafe were diseased. Today, there was no pariah attitude. It was perhaps as disapproving, but it was subtler. It was more cynical. It traded truth for a more convenient explanation. He knew, he knew from some of the things the guys had said at the airport—while taking a coffee break—having a quick beer after work—from the brief encounter with Bennie Rousch. And that explanation was simply that it hadn't been a case of rape at all. Cora had had a quickie with some passing stranger, or friend, and had got caught and cried rape. And they didn't want to listen to people like Gus or Jim Wood, or even Doc Titus, who knew differently.

People! What the hell! Why should he give a damn? Like Brian Foley said, "Screw 'em!" And Cora, with her slightly raised chin and faint smile and eyes that twinkled with humor, had built an invisible, invulnerable fortress around herself. It wasn't an aura of "touch-me-not," it wasn't defensive or snooty; rather, it said, "Aren't you *nice!*" and people immediately became more dignified and *nice*, and embarrassed inside because they had ever for a minute thought

. . . Women like Jackie Kennedy had that look—and Grace Kelly, and Ingrid Bergman.

He wasn't so lucky; he just ducked his chin down into his collar and walked along, his hands curled into fists swinging beside him, and they called him Chief Thunder Cloud and didn't bother to hide what they felt.

Of course, their friends had been great. Not evading anything, they all in effect had said, "It's tough. It's your problem. But if you want help, you've got it." What more could a friend say? Then there were ever-widening circles of less intimacy. The people you worked with, the people to whom you said, "Hi, Johnnie," or "Good morning, Mr. Evans," or "Thank you, Miss Peterson." But they weren't important. Or they shouldn't be.

Anyway, it was almost all over now. Almost. At least it was going into a new phase. A new set of problems. Maybe the answer was to get away someplace for a while. Where? On *what*, for Christ's sake?

Cora's natural dignity, the sweetness with which she protected herself, fell apart when they were alone. She had told him she felt all chewed-up sometimes because people didn't react naturally. She said the most ordinary exchange was affected by a grim determination not to recognize her pregnancy. "Hi, Miz March, how are you?" And she'd say, "Fine, thank you," and then there would be an unhappy pause while they figured out what to say instead of "You're looking well," because it might open up a delicate subject. Cora said she knew how colored people felt when a white man shook hands with them. Of course, she didn't complain. She tried to make jokes about it; she said, "It's so tolerant it makes you sick. They really want to say, 'Some of my best friends are bastards'!"

And now—now it would be another problem. You couldn't avoid seeing a baby. They'd *have* to say, "How's the baby?" But they sure as hell would do everything to avoid the friendly "My, my, he looks just like his daddy, doesn't he?" But they would have to stop and think before they said, "He (or she) looks just like you, Cora!" because that might mean, "And isn't *that* lucky!" What a mess! The importance of the trivial. And it was worse for a woman. A fellow like Bennie Rousch could make a drunken crack and a man could pop him one, but a woman went to bed in tears because of something somebody *didn't* say! And someday the poor kid himself would come home from school asking what the word "bastard" meant.

He swung his feet off the bed and sat up. Put on his shoes and belt. Not much point in lying here and not resting, thinking in circles, thinking back to this morning, back to that brief moment that still played itself over and over in his mind. The sound of metal crashing and glass shattering, the smell of burnt rubber, and a woman's scream; and then he put his head into his hands because it sounded like Cora screaming. *Oh, darling, darling, does it hurt? You hate pain, physical pain, you're a scaredy-cat about pain. Remember how you nearly fainted when I had to take a cactus sticker out of your thumb?*

He got up and strode into the living room. Connie had the rugs rolled up and was on her knees waxing the tile. She looked up at him anxiously and said, pointing, "Is wet."

"Well, I can *see* that! Did it have to be done *today?* I don't want to be trapped in one room, for Christ's sake!"

Connie remained unmoving, relaxed on all fours, looking like Maxie when he was being scolded. "Si, Senor."

"Si, Senor, *what?*" Her face remained closed, expressionless. "Where the hell am I supposed to *go?* What should I *do?* Oh, hell, I'm sorry, Connie. *Lo siento*, okay?"

"Si, Senor." Her eyes twinkled.

"I'll be out in a minute. I just want to give the hospital a call."

"Si, Senor. I go get you a beer." She rose and padded in her bare feet to the kitchen as Rafe took the phone and began to dial.

"I don't want a beer," he muttered to himself, "and just stop saying 'Si, Senor.'"

The hospital said Mrs. March was doing fine. Coming along nicely. Did she want anything? Had she said anything about wanting him to bring something from the house—anything? Well, now, they didn't think so, but they'd let him know. And Dr. Wells would call him immediately if there was any change. And he wasn't to worry. She was doing fine.

Paciencia.

He went outside, and Maxie, making happy little sounds in his throat, dropped into stride with him.

He looked at the swimming pool, reached for the skimmer, and took a few desultory swipes with it. There were all kinds of little jobs he could do. There always were around a house. The weather was getting nice again. The daily quota of gusty winds was dropping, and the nights were not so bone-chilling; the foothills and the basin were showing a lot of color. Until the real heat began they would be spending most of their time out of doors.

He had an idea for a shelter, something made of split timber that would filter the sunlight at one end of the pool. Be a nice place to put some chairs and a table. And probably Cora would find it a good place for a playpen. For the baby. Be great for it. Him. Her. Would you have liked it, Dave Durrell? For your kid? And I'll teach him to swim and to ride. Would you have approved? A nice home, a nice mother? And a gutless sonofabitch to provide for it?

He tossed the skimmer aside, and Maxie thought he wanted to play and went after it with a couple of yips.

Rafe patted his pockets to see if he had his pipe. Hell, he'd have to go back into the house. Damned if he would. He went to the kitchen door and yelled, "Connie! Get my pipe—*la pipa*—and my tobacco, *por favor!*"

"Si, Senor!"

He groaned. "Si, Senor; Si, Senor!"

He walked at a good clip out into the desert basin. The sun was high, the air was thin and bright, visibility unlimited. Maxie began panting to keep up with him.

"You're gettin' old, fella! Short of breath, huh?"

A long time ago he had found Maxie lying beside the highway early one morning, the victim of a hit and run, and he had picked him up and taken him in to the vet's in Tucson, where he'd been treated for cuts and some bad bruises. There had been a rope around his neck that looked as though it had been chewed, as though he'd run away. Some of the bruises were old ones, and he was undernourished, so Rafe had never tried to find the owner, and no one had ever tried to find Maxie, and Maxie never wanted anyone but Rafe. It was a year or so before he had met Cora, when he was still living in the apartment in Tucson, and because of Maxie, Rafe had started driving out into the country where he could turn the dog loose and let him run. They kept coming to this particular spot just off the highway, and finally Rafe decided that he wanted to build a house, that he needed room, just like Maxie.

And then Cora came along and shared his feelings. She had been horizon-hungry, too. She had had her crowded home, oppressive with quarreling voices, and he had had nothing but dormitories and barracks and boarding houses and single-room apartments. They had both suffered from overinvolvement.

It was more important to him than to Cora, he knew. It was deeply satisfying to look around for miles without seeing another building or any evidence that there were other human beings on earth. A man could dream in all directions, and his dreams grew great and true for not having collided with people and their approval or disapproval, their criticism or indifference.

And yet all this space, this wonderful emptiness had not provided the moral remoteness, the inner stability to protect him. It had not protected him from being pulverized, ground down into panic for his identity.

Distant horizons, space, silence. Perhaps those for whom such conditions were prerequisite for comfort were the nonaggressive, the timid. And maybe all the talk, the muscle-flexing and breathing hard that went with taking on the difficulties of the weather, the heat, the sand, were nothing more than an alibi, a compensation. Maybe the desert was so empty for the very simple reason that nobody really wanted to live there. It was the ideal area for those who had a need to retire from the human race.

Brian Foley had talked to him about this very thing, but he hadn't really listened. Brian had said, "This was a good place to start, kid, but what's it been now? Four years? You're lost out here. Why don't you get with it? Get back to civilization. Get back where problems are more diverse, less limited, not so falsely enormous. Stuck in a secondary airport—in the middle of the desert! You're better than that! Hell, you ought to be in the Space Program. Maybe in communications, in tracking or something. They need guys like you."

Guys like me, he had thought. He had skittered away from the suggestion like one of the shy animals of the desert itself. It meant upheaval, learning new things—involvement. Moving to another place. Texas. Houston, wasn't it?

He stopped walking, knocked his pipe out on his heel, and then walked on, more slowly. Why not? It might be the answer to a lot of things.

He loved Cora. He admired her guts. And he'd done his best, his devoted, near-suicidal best. He hadn't been able to follow her down through all the layers of her thinking, but he'd consented to her right to have them. One layer of her belief, which he went along with, was that she had conceived a child and she could not kill that child. But there was another layer, which she didn't talk about— her desire for a child, a child that he had been unable to produce. And that uncovered, occasionally, other layers, not very nice ones. Small tyrannies, barely expressed contempt, blindness, selfishness, taking-for-granted. That couldn't go on, that had to be changed. Even if it took a different environment to change it.

He looked at his watch and then back at the house. Constanza would have sense enough to yell for him. There was still plenty of time, of course. Just in case, he started circling back.

Why should it take so long? Why wouldn't it help if I were with you? If I could just take on the pain for you. They say it's harder for women who haven't had children to have their first one after twenty-five. Bones are more rigid or something. Cora, Cora, Cora.

Damn it, there had to be some changes made. His role as head of the family looked bleak. He had no delusions that the pattering of tiny feet would transform him into a doting father, and he could already anticipate the times when he and Cora would blow up in a quarrel and he would yell something about "that kid of yours!"

If he couldn't ever again be proud of himself, if he was always going to feel like some kind of a cripple, maybe being part of something important would help. Work. Space. Not nothingness, not beautiful horizons to dream on but horizons unlimited, where success was important and not merely a status achievement. Working with people who looked beyond themselves and their petty problems, who had within them that mysterious pull of the unexplored: the river that hadn't been crossed, the mountain that hadn't been scaled. The expression "Because it's there" was the usual glib reason, but it wasn't the answer, it was only something to say. It carried with it the unexpressed "If you don't understand, buddy—if you don't dig it, forget it. It can't be taught, or talked about."

Space as a challenge. Capital S. Bigger than any goddamn desert. Working with those guys! Wouldn't *that* be something! He knew all the lingo. Sometimes, watching a mission on TV, he would strain to hear the often garbled conversations between space and earth and he'd unconsciously join in, "Say again?" He knew exactly what they were talking about, what the problem was. And often, from sheer nerves, he'd walk around the room, saying, "Why the hell don't they give him what he wants? He's asked for that figure three times now!" And Cora would say, "You tell 'em, Tiger." And he'd feel foolish and settle down and stew about it. But if he were *in* there, part of the team on the ground, he wouldn't feel foolish, and Cora wouldn't say things like "You tell 'em, Tiger!"

He remembered a tense scene at a tracking center during one mission. There was one guy in the foreground watching a monitoring screen, smoking a cigarette—*consuming* a cigarette. He'd put it between his lips, inhale, take it out and tap it hard into an ashtray, and put it back into his mouth before he was through exhaling. Over and over again, with the utmost concentration. Every one of the men, standing or sitting at consoles, were concentrated, deeply involved. Working together while a couple of guys in a shiny little capsule were arrogantly testing the reaches of space stretching out on all sides of them.

He stood still and closed his eyes. Maybe someday it would be his finger poised over a button while the countdown continued, while his own heartbeat double-counted the seconds ticking off . . .

And Cora was laughing and saying, "You and your rockets and missiles and things that go 'boom!'" And then she would remind him of something she'd once said about the phallic qualities of man's weaponry. Damn 'em all! Damn all bitchy females! So go ahead and *call* it an extension of sexuality. Tamper with that sexuality and what have you got? Zero—and no blast-off. Something that will leave you, my darling Cora, and all you females, leave you as barren as this goddamn desert. You can't cut off those vital parts and wear them around your neck like a trophy. Not with impunity.

He was walking faster, angrily, his eyes concentrated on the ground as though he were searching for a flicker of gold, a bright color, a talisman; something that would stop his anger, stop his day-dreaming, answer his need. The sun was hot on his back, and he was sweating. Maxie's tongue was hanging out of one side of his jaw and then suddenly he seemed to swallow it. He raised his head and gave a few short barks. Rafe followed his look and off in the distance he saw the fluttering of a white cloth. It was Constanza, waving a dish towel.

"My God! Cora!" He started to sprint, and Maxie burst ahead of him.

His ribs were heaving when he reached the back fence and Constanza said, "Your lunch—*almuerzo*—is ready, Senor. You eat som't'ing now."

The nurse he got on the phone when he called about two o'clock said she was Miss Farrington, and she was much more satisfying in her information than the usual "Doing fine—coming along nicely." She said, "It's slow, Mr. March. It's a slow, tiresome business. Your wife is a fine patient, though. She's a fine woman, Mr. March."

"I know. She's got guts."

Miss Farrington's voice was warm and she chuckled. "That she has!"

"What can I do? Is there anything——"

"You can come and wear out the linoleum in the waiting room if you like. There's not much point to it. I'm on until seven o'clock, Mr. March. I'm sure she'll deliver before that, and I will personally call you as soon as we take her to the delivery room. Now, does that help?"

"It certainly does. And I appreciate it, Miss Farrington. I'll be right here. Waiting."

Constanza left for the day.

He slept.

And came awake almost immediately with the kind of nightmare that is full of terror and no images.

He got up and carefully poured a small drink.

It would be a good excuse to get slightly drunk, but he had a feeling that it wasn't quite fair. When he finally saw her, Cora was going to be a very tired girl, and he felt it might be irritating to her to think he hadn't been able to endure the vigil without getting plastered. But a couple wouldn't hurt. In spite of Nurse Farrington, who had given no indication that Cora was anything but all right, his nerves were zinging. It had been, and still was, quite a day.

He thought of calling someone to come over and chew the fat with him. Charlie Eldridge, maybe. But he'd be working. Joe and Myra Deming would come like a shot, but they'd have to close up their place, lose customers; that wasn't right.

Besides, he really didn't want anybody. This wasn't the usual thing they made happy jokes about while taking care of the nervous father-to-be. Plying him with booze and telling hair-raising stories of what *they* did when the wife was expecting *their* first. Of how they'd spent the time with an interim girl friend, and how she cried because it was all over now and he was going back to his wife. And the usual waiting-room stories. Et cetera, et cetera.

He wasn't going to *be* a father. That was the difference. His wife, his girl, his love, his other heart—*she* was having a baby.

He poured out another drink. And then he took a small funnel that he found in a kitchen drawer and carefully poured the drink back into the bottle. It was too dangerous, that was the real reason he didn't want to drink. It stirred up things, it stirred up false emotions. Maybe later, after he was sure Cora was all right.

He watched the clock. He read. He fed Maxie. He turned on TV and sat for half an hour without seeing it. And about five o'clock— Dr. Wells had known what he was talking about—the phone rang.

"Miss Farrington calling, Mr. March. It won't be long now. She's doing fine—just went into delivery."

The waiting room still had the smell of nervousness, of stale cigars, and of a scented, ineffective room deodorant. He had had time only for a cigarette and a cup of the something that tasted a little like coffee when a nurse with the hottest red hair he had ever seen came in and said, "I'm Miss Farrington, Mr. March. You have a fine son."

He wore a silly smile of relief, and he supposed he looked like every other man in the world who has heard those words.

"How's my wife?" he said, and then, "Does that color come out of a bottle?"

Miss Farrington threw back her head and laughed. "With these freckles? No. And your wife is okay. She's had a long, hard time. There were some drugs she was sensitive to and we couldn't give her much help. But it's all over and she'll be down in her room pretty soon. In the meantime, wouldn't you like to come with me and see the young man?"

"Can't I see Cora first?"

"It'll be a few minutes yet. Come along."

There was nothing to see, of course. What was a man supposed to see? A line of squirming, diapered, red-faced little creatures waving their tendrils of arms and legs, mouths wide open like baby birds, featureless. Two of them, not so red, were asleep; one of them was quite swarthy, with a tuft of black hair, and it was this one that the nurse picked up and brought to the window for him and Miss Farrington to look at. Rafe said the first thing that came into his mind. "Looks like a Mexican baby. That's not the one, is it?"

"I imagine he's got his quota of Latin genes, Mr. March," said Miss Farrington softly.

Rafe leaned against the heavy glass, his palms and fingertips just touching. He felt that if he leaned too hard he would go right through the partition, and the glass wouldn't crack, it would be soft and yielding.

"I thought he'd be blond—like—like Cora."

Miss Farrington laughed. "Blond and beautiful? Well, he's not much to look at right now, but just you wait!"

On the other side of the glass the masked nurse displayed the infant, holding up one tightly curled fist and brushing down the wild black hair with the tip of her finger.

Realizing something was expected of him, feeling the concentrated, indulgent smiles of the nurses upon him, Rafe nodded with a smile of his own, somewhat vacant, and turned to walk away.

"No, it's this way, Mr. March," said Miss Farrington, taking his arm.

An orderly and a nurse were just wheeling some oxygen equipment from Cora's room. Cora opened her eyes, and there was a glimmer of recognition as Rafe leaned over to kiss her, and then the lids dropped again of their own weight.

Miss Farrington took Cora's wrist and nodded to Rafe. "She's conscious. She just doesn't want to wake up yet. I don't blame her. Everybody's been picking on her." Cora made a sound that indicated agreement, and the nurse said, "Okay, go back to sleep. Your husband can wait." To Rafe she said, "There'll be no other patients in here—tonight anyway. She'll have a good rest." She pulled an armchair closer to the bed and got out an ashtray from the drawer of the bed table. "You can smoke now. They're through with the oxygen. You want an evening paper?"

Rafe shook his head, then reconsidered. There might be something in it about the accident. "In the early hours of the morning death came . . ." No. He shook his head again.

"There's the button. Just call if you want something."

"Thanks." Rafe nodded.

"Oh, and—congratulations," she said softly, going out the door.

And Rafe said "Thanks" again, and grinned at her and shook his head in disbelief at the bonfire of red hair under the silly cap. And he meant thanks for being helpful and friendly, for not noticing that he felt sick and faint with shock outside the nursery, thanks for not expecting him to say anything that made sense, thanks for having freckles and red hair. He couldn't even think of her name.

He sat down, took Cora's hand, and leaned his head onto the edge of the high hospital bed. "I love you, honey, I love you," he whispered. For the first time he realized he was exhausted. He wanted to crawl in beside her, gather her into his arms, and sleep and sleep. And then, conscious that he shouldn't disturb her, he straightened up and lighted a cigarette. The smoke was fragrant and dispelled the unfamiliar odor, bitter, "mediciney," that hung over her, and he thought of all she had been through and wondered how bad the pain had been.

He watched her sleep. Purring softly through dry, puffy lips. Her forehead was damp.

When she wakes up, he thought, I've got to show how happy I am, how surprised and pleased, and I've got to say, "Of course, there's no doubt now, honey," and I've got to mean it. He'd have to listen and agree with all the words about how it looked like him, that it was the very *image!* The dark, peach-colored skin, the tiny brows that met in the middle, the thin upper lip, not the usual babyish cupid-bow.

For Cora's sake and for his own protection he must never express the slightest doubt. "What the hell does it take to convince you!" he could hear her say, angry, hurt.

Maybe it *was* his child, maybe it wasn't. He didn't know all that Mendelian Law stuff, how many ancestors contributed what, what the chances were, and all that stuff. One thing was certain, Cora was going to be so proud and so happy. She'd haul the child around the streets of Sabado. He could see her smug grin when people would say, "He looks just like Rafe!" That was good, that was wonderful.

He wondered why he couldn't accept it completely. Why wasn't he bursting with pride and handing out cigars? Well, you just couldn't do a flip-over, just like that. The months of self-doubt, self-hatred, had had a crippling, laming effect. The ego said, "Not so fast, buddy!"

He examined the thoughts he had had earlier, how good he had felt about trying to have something to do with the Space Program. About getting away from Sabado, that's all it had really been. But it *had* felt good. Maybe someday he could consider it again, apart from using it as something that would make him walk tall—a substitute, a crutch. That wasn't any good. What the hell, he could inquire about it anyway, send in his qualifications, see what happened. Someday. Cora had to get well first; he was going to get right to work on that lath shelter by the pool.

Cora was stirring, coming awake. She moved her shoulders, her eyes opening and closing heavily. "Hi, honey," she whispered. Then she gave a mighty yawn and fell deeply asleep again. It was such a funny "Plop! I'm asleep" change that it made Rafe laugh. He expected her to say in another second, "Boo! I'm awake!"

In the interval, the small second before he'd be putting his arms around her and kissing her and telling her he loved her, it wouldn't hurt to indulge himself in one thought that was sneaking around in his mind. Try saying it as though he believed it. Just try it out for size. "William Reedy March. My son, Bill." Not bad, he thought. Not bad at all.

Captain Brian Foley took a good look at the woman in Section 52, and he liked what he saw. He had just consulted the passenger list, and "Sabado, Arizona" had caught his eye. The name of the couple meant nothing to him, but Sabado was a small town, and he thought he might get some firsthand news of his friend Rafe March.

He had been watching the pantomime from where he stood at the closed door of the pilot's compartment. Apparently the lady wanted to stretch out, and her husband had gestured to an empty section on the opposite side of the plane and two seats to the rear. She had smiled her thanks, and he had fixed a pillow for her, and taking his newspaper with him, had moved to the unoccupied section.

Not young, but attractive, sexy, Foley summarized as he watched her stretching nyloned legs onto the seat. She propped the pillow into the corner against the window and looked out at the cloud formations touched by the setting sun.

Captain Foley moved down the aisle, smiling pleasantly at the passengers who looked up at him from both sides. They always had the look, even the seasoned travelers, that betrayed a certain anxiety, that said, "What are you doing back here? Why aren't you flying this thing?" Theoretically, everyone knew about automatic pilots and that he wasn't the only one "flying this thing," but his smile was carefully calculated to the proper degree of—not reassurance, for that would mean they needed to be reassured—but of controlled cordiality, like that of a visiting celebrity. By the time he reached the reclining lady he had turned on the smile full force, saying, "Excuse me, Mrs. Holloway?" and he liked it that she didn't jump or put her feet down; she merely turned her head from the view and said "Yes?"

But there were subtle changes in her face, in the tiny muscles around the mouth and eyes, that spoke for her, that told him what he knew anyway—that he was attractive. It was always nice to be told.

"You're our pilot, aren't you? How do you do? Why aren't you flying this damn thing?"

He laughed with her as though it were the first time he'd heard the joke. "I came back here to see you."

"Really? How nice."

"I happened to notice that you come from a place called Saturday."

"Saturday? Oh, Sabado. Of course, yes. Isn't it funny one never thinks—yes, we have a ranch there."

"Do you happen to know the Marches? Rafe is a very old friend of mine."

"Everybody knows the Marches," Terry Holloway said laughingly. Her laugh had an edge to it, but then, as if to qualify the implication of notoriety, she added, "Sabado's that kind of a place. Everybody knows everybody. They know everybody's business or *think* they do, which is just as bad." She moved as if to offer him the place beside her, but he shook his head.

"Have to go back in a second. Tell me, how is Rafe? I've sort of lost touch."

"Well, let's see, when did you see them last? Did you know they had a baby?"

"I was in Sabado to see Rafe about a year ago, and yes, I knew a baby was on the way."

Something about his manner, perhaps a shade of vagueness in his statement, conveyed to her that he knew more than was discreet to put into words on such short acquaintance, but Terry Holloway was happy to convey to him what he wanted to hear. She shook her head and smiled. "It's the image of Rafe. Looks like a small frowning Aztec warrior!"

"Rafe still working at the airport?"

"Oh, yes."

"Pity. He's better than that," Foley said, almost to himself. That disposed of Rafe. It had only been a conversational introduction, anyway. This was a very attractive woman, worth doing something about. The mild-looking husband looked typical—typical harassed businessman, glued to the stock market columns of his newspaper. He had looked up once when Foley leaned over the seat to speak to his wife, and then went back to his paper.

In a few minutes Foley had considerable information about them. They were on a combination business and wedding trip. They were going to Honolulu, where they would be staying with friends, and after a week Paul Holloway was going over to Hawaii on cattle business.

Captain Foley remembered he would be having some leave at about that time and maybe they could get together. Mrs. Holloway was sure they could.

To the rear, her husband watched them over the edge of the paper, right over the Standard and Poor's "500" Past Six Weeks' Activity Chart. The soft rush of the air conditioners muted their words, but he could catch the sound of a bell in her laughter, and he could see the direction of the pilot's glances, the way he leaned toward her, nodding, smiling.

"The stock market stumbled through another session Wednesday. Prices opened slightly higher, gyrated through most of the session and sank at the close." From behind the paper, Paul Holloway chewed delicately on a thumb nail.